MOTHER'S GENIUS

Essential Prose Series 170

**Canada Council
for the Arts**

**Conseil des Arts
du Canada**

ONTARIO ARTS COUNCIL
CONSEIL DES ARTS DE L'ONTARIO

an Ontario government agency
un organisme du gouvernement de l'Ontario

Canada

Guernica Editions Inc. acknowledges the support of the Canada Council
for the Arts and the Ontario Arts Council. The Ontario Arts Council
is an agency of the Government of Ontario.

We acknowledge the financial support of the Government of Canada.

MOTHER'S GENIUS

Kristin Andrychuk

GUERNICA
EDITIONS
TORONTO • BUFFALO • LANCASTER (U.K.)
2019

Michael Mirolla, general editor
Lindsay Brown, editor
David Moratto, interior and cover design
Guernica Editions Inc.
1569 Heritage Way, Oakville, (ON), Canada L6M 2Z7
2250 Military Road, Tonawanda, N.Y. 14150-6000 U.S.A.
www.guernicaeditions.com

Distributors:
University of Toronto Press Distribution,
5201 Dufferin Street, Toronto (ON), Canada M3H 5T8
Gazelle Book Services, White Cross Mills
High Town, Lancaster LA1 4XS U.K.

First edition.
Printed in Canada.

Legal Deposit—Third Quarter
Library of Congress Catalog Card Number: 2018968516
Library and Archives Canada Cataloguing in Publication
Title: Mother's genius / Kristin Andrychuk.
Names: Andrychuk, Kristin, author.
Series: Essential prose series ; 170.
Description: Series statement: Essential prose series ; 170 Identifiers:
Canadiana (print) 20190045841 | Canadiana (ebook) 20190045892 |
ISBN 9781771834247 (softcover) | ISBN 9781771834254 (EPUB) |
ISBN 9781771834261 (Kindle)
Classification: LCC PS8551.N395 M68 2019 | DDC C811/.54—dc23

For my husband Don and my children:
Paul, Patricia, Sylvia and Charles

WHEN WE WERE YOUNG

THE PORCH SWING grates "screech-squaaawk, screech-squaaawk" which to us sings "sum-*mer*, sum-*mer*." The swing belonged to my great-grandmother and spends winters in the barn. I like its squeaky voice. When I was little, I named it Screechy. Martin laughed at me. Said I was always naming and making pets of everything. The first day of the holidays and I've finished grade eight. If only summer could last forever.

I'm reading *Beautiful Joe*. The poor old dog's dying and I'm crying so much I can't see the print. Mother says to always finish a book no matter how sad it makes you. "Prepares one for life," she says.

Martin with Charlemagne, his yellow-striped tomcat, stretched out at his feet, is typing away at the Brailler. He can do thirty words a minute now. I'm glad he's home and never has to go back to that school. He hated it. He graduated grade twelve and is going to be a writer, already is. He plans to write a bestseller and go live in New York. I hope that doesn't happen right away. Mother says someday he'll be famous.

I pick up my book and read a little more.

"Gretchen, you're snuffling. Are you crying?" Martin asks.

"This book's too sad."

"What book?"

"*Beautiful Joe.*"

"That's a kid's book. Science fiction's better. You should read Arthur C. Clarke's new book, *Childhood's End*. Mother recorded it for me."

Though his cloudy eyes can't focus, he looks at me. The porch swing groans as I get up. "What are you writing?" I peer over his shoulder.

"About a fun band of aliens that accidently land on earth."

"You mean like our Juperians?"

"That was kid stuff. Your braille's slow, so I'll read you a bit. It's the prologue." He takes a breath.

*When the fiery meteor storms have abated to the chaos of a
fragmented moon, a band of drunken poets wake with
terrible hangovers. After much belching and farting they
collect themselves sufficiently to venture out and wander the
rubble-strewn, deserted streets.*

    *"Hey, what the fuck's goin' on?" says Elpin. "Did we
miss the war of the worlds or somethin'?*

I FEEL MYSELF blushing. "I liked our Juperians better. They tamed
groundhogs and lived in burrows."

"That was juvenile."

"You use dirty language, and all they do is drink."

"Time you grew up, little sister."

"I'm going riding."

The screen door bangs shut behind me and I stride off towards the
barn. Why does he bring dirty talk into everything? He never used to.

I won't spend this summer sitting around reading books. I'm fourteen and want a job. Old Cy Forbes hires kids to lead the ponies at the
amusement park. He and my great-grandmother were friends. I went
there a lot last summer before Dad bought me Misty, a dapple-grey
Welsh Cob. But I missed the pony track, and this summer I'm going
to do something about it.

THE NEXT DAY, riding Misty up Leaman Road, I can't believe how easy
it all was. Just told Mother I was going riding. She doesn't complain
when I take Misty on long hikes. She said that as a girl she loved hiking
through the fields when her mother wasn't doling out awful jobs like
gutting chickens. She wants me to enjoy my childhood.

I didn't come right out and ask Cy for a job. Just said I could lead
ponies and Misty would like to help too. I worked all afternoon. When
I told Cy I'd better be getting home for supper, he asked if we would
like a summer job — every day, noon to eight.

I can't wait to tell everybody. Cy's going to pay me fourteen dollars
a week. That's as much as kids make working at the popcorn and hot
dog stands. For the very first time, I'm glad to be a teenager. Little kids
don't have jobs.

I LIE IN bed grinning, thinking back on my afternoon leading Misty around the pony track. His ears prick forward listening to the music from the merry-go-round and the screams from the roller coaster. The other girls are leading Prince and Champ. The red-haired girl is Sharon. I don't know the other one's name, but I think she's Sharon's little sister. Ten cents a ride, three rounds for a quarter. I have a job! Dad said I was awfully young and should enjoy my freedom while I have it. Mother didn't say anything. Only Martin congratulated me.

"That's great, little sister. What are you going to buy with all your loot?"

I hadn't thought about that. Fourteen dollars a week—that would be one hundred and forty chocolate bars or ice cream cones. Of course, I'm not going to do that. I could get that porcelain horse in the china shop's window and I'll buy something for Martin. I wonder how much briefcases cost. One like Dad's.

Mother knocks lightly and enters. "Still awake?"

"Yes."

"Gretchen, we bought you a pony. There's no need for you to hang around the park. That's a rough crowd there."

"I'm old enough to work. I love the ponies and giving little kids rides. And Misty likes being with other ponies."

"Why do you persist in saying 'kids'? Kids are baby goats. Say 'children'."

"Everybody says 'kids'."

"Only ignorant people. You can tell a person's class the moment they open their mouth. 'Kids' sounds so common. I'd like you to be around home more. We'll hardly see you."

"I'll be home mornings."

"You're usually out at the barn. Your brother needs your companionship."

"He's either studying with you or on the Brailler."

"You could study with us. Philosophy's challenging, but interesting."

"I want to work at the pony track."

"Well, you're not working Sundays."

"I have to. Sundays are busy at the park."

"Your dad will have a talk with Cy Forbes. Goodnight, dear."

"Night, Mother."

She closes the door very quietly behind her. Does that when she's mad at me.

I sigh, stretch, can't get comfortable. Lots of people say 'kids'. Sounds so common, she says. Well, maybe I want to be like everybody else. Wish it was morning and I could get out of here. That makes me feel guilty.

As if I'd want to study with them. They're working their way through the Great Books. She says they'll have the equivalent of a university education. Martin won't go to her Great Books Club. Calls them the old biddies. Why would she think he'd go? Old Maid Wickham's a member. When we used to walk downtown, she'd wave and say, not to Martin, but to Mother: "How's the boy today?" I hate her as much as I hate those boys who called him Freak or Spook just because he walks funny and has cloudy eyes.

He'll show them. He's going to write a bestseller and be famous.

Through my open window I hear murmuring voices from the front porch, Mother and Martin discussing Plato. They've been studying him for a month now. Dad's no doubt in his study. I'm not surprised. When Mother and Martin are discussing something neither Dad nor I can get a word in edgewise. If I stay awake long enough, I'll hear Dad bringing them tea.

Philosophy's boring. Not like when we had school at home, before Martin went to the school in Brantford. He went away when he was ten. I was six. I hadn't gone to kindergarten — stayed home to have school with him. We didn't have books in braille or a Brailler. Mother read us lots of stories. They did math with Martin's abacus. I practiced writing the alphabet and numbers. Mother's a real teacher. Before she got married, she taught in Toronto.

The best part about our school was her stories about real people who lived around here when she was a child. Cars had been invented but farmers still used horses and wagons. The one about Harvey Leaman coming home from the beer parlour was scary:

> *In the horse and buggy days, drunk drivers didn't end up in the ditch. A horse always knows his way home. Harvey Leaman, the present Mr. Leaman's uncle, depended on his horse to get him home.*

Early one Sunday morning, when his brother Ben went out to do the chores, he cursed when he saw the horse and wagon by the barn doors. "Didn't even put the horse to bed!"

Ben came upon a gruesome sight. Harvey was slumped over the side of the wagon. Ben figured he must've bent over to vomit and passed out, and the steel wagon wheel ground against his head until there was no face left.

I GUESS SHE was warning us about the evils of drink. I preferred her stories about the O'Haras because I could use my imagination to make up different endings. Long before I was born the O'Hara farmhouse burned down. We used to hike around there with Mother. I remember her telling us:

The O'Hara children never wore socks. Bare feet in rubber boots in the winter, shoes with worn-down heels the rest of the year. Their ankles were chapped and red.

Bobby was older, but Colleen was my age. She wore dresses way too big for her. Maybe they'd belonged to her mother. The hem would be cut so the dress wouldn't drag on the ground. There were always holes in the elbows of their sweaters.

They were teased something awful. Bobby more than Colleen. He had cerebral palsy. Not a severe case but he had an uneven gait, and his speech was slurred. Children can be cruel. They called him Jigsy. "Into your pa's booze again, are ya?" I remember Henry Beam saying that.

Bobby always had the top mark in math. He should've finished high school. By the time he was 16, his dad had him out selling Watkins products door to door. From the ice cream shop we would see him go by after school. Mary and I always said hello to him. I think he was sweet on Mary. She'd always been nice to him at school.

Their mother was dead, and it was said their dad beat them. I'm pretty sure that's true. Once I saw welts on Colleen's legs, and Bobby came to school with a black eye on more than one occasion. It's possible, though, some of the rough boys had beaten him up.

IN MY OWN story the O'Hara children came to live with us and I looked after Colleen. She was my adopted little sister. I'd like a little sister more than an older brother. Martin and Bobby went away to a nice private school.

I LOVED OUR hikes to the O'Hara place at the back of Sherk's farm. That's where the Elgin Marsh starts. Where their house stood is just a clearing surrounded by cedars with some good elderberry picking in back. The house foundation and the well-curb are cracked and broken, overgrown with lilacs and goldenrod. Martin tripped over the rusted off hand-pump in the long grass.

Mother told stories while cooking hot dogs and corn. Once Martin and I made elderberry sandwiches. Boy, were they sour! Martin's blindness didn't affect us then, or his crippled legs. Now there aren't any hikes. He says his legs bother him too much. But I still ride Misty to the O'Hara place, alone.

There were so many changes, good and bad, the year Dad came home from the war. The good thing was Dad was home. I didn't exactly remember him. He went away when I was one. Dad bought a car and took us on Sunday afternoon drives, sometimes stopping for ice cream.

The worst thing that year was Martin going away to school. Mother didn't want him to. She and Dad argued about that.

I had to go to kindergarten even though I was a year older than everybody else. When I complained, Mother said: "Think how scared and lonely Martin must be. And he doesn't even get home for a weekend for a whole month." I felt ashamed of my complaining. I cried myself to sleep that night, thinking of my brother far away.

There were so many kids at public school. A few days after I started there, a big girl said: "Where's your retard brother?"

I asked Mother what "retard" meant. Knew it was something bad.

"It just means slow to learn," she said.

"Why would anyone call Martin that?"

"Ignorant, that's all, and afraid of what they don't understand."

I could see they were ignorant. They never talked about anything interesting. "Look at my new charm bracelet!" "Mine has more charms on it."

Who cares? I had a stone in my pocket and showed it to the girl sitting beside me. "That's granite," I told her. "The glacier dropped it."

"Looks like a dirty rock," she said and whispered something to the girl across the aisle. They both giggled.

Mother was right about ignorant, but wrong about them being afraid. They weren't afraid, I was. After a few months, I was moved into grade one. I hate school.

I'M RIDING MISTY home from the track. After working for nearly two weeks I've changed a lot. I'm making friends with the other pony leaders. But Donna's my best friend. She's new in town. She's pretty, shiny brown hair in a bouncy ponytail and isn't tall and skinny like me. I hate my limp hair. Everybody likes her, but she says I'm her best friend. She came to our barn one morning while I was riding in the paddock. I let her ride and told her my pony was named after one in a book, *Misty of Chincoteague*, by Marguerite Henry. Donna wanted to borrow the book and that's how she met Martin. She makes him act so goofy. And that's when the trouble started.

When we came into the porch Martin, his black curls falling over his eyes, was bent over a book.

"Sorry," I said. "Thought you and Mother were working in your office."

"We're done. Who's your friend?"

"I'm Donna Evans. You her brother?"

"Yes, I'm Martin and I'm eighteen."

"Same age as my brother. What are you reading?"

"We're studying Plato this summer."

"That's one of the planets, isn't it?"

Martin smiled. "No, you're thinking of Pluto. Plato's a Greek philosopher. We're reading *The Apology*, trying to answer the question: 'What is wisdom?'" He bent over the book and traced the words with his right hand. "He, O men, is the wisest, who, like Socrates, knows that his wisdom is in truth worth nothing."

Donna stared at him.

I scowled at her. She didn't need to stare but it would help if he stopped showing off.

"I'll get the book. Have a seat on the swing."

"Hey, I saw one of these swings in a movie. I like the red-flowered cushions."

Martin got up, leaned on his cane, and went outside.

Pushing with her foot, Donna got the swing moving. "Your brother's blind, eh?"

"He can see outlines."

"He's really smart. Good-looking too, in spite of his eyes. He walks funny. What happened?"

I ignored all her stupid questions. "I'll be right back." Just then, Martin opened the screen door. He held a single red rose.

"How well did art imitate nature?" he asked.

Donna looked at him with her mouth open.

"Is this more beautiful than those on the cushions?"

"Yeah, sure, I guess."

"For you," Martin said. He handed her the flower.

"For me?" Donna laughed, surprised. "Thanks."

That was their first meeting. She comes with me to the track sometimes and leads ponies. Most afternoons she has to babysit her little brothers because her mother sells real estate. Some mornings we ride Misty or hang out in the loft. Years back Dad built stairs to replace the ladder. He hung a swing with a board wide enough for two from the rafters. Martin and I had a lot of fun up there before he got too old to play. Donna and I pump that old swing so high our feet bump the roof boards.

Sometimes I get home from the track and find her on the porch, playing cards with my brother. Why's she hanging around him? She's my age, not his.

EACH EVENING I'm tired but I love the hot sun and the dusty track. I lead Misty around and around. Stop at the exit gate. Help one smiling tourist kid off and the next one on. Something about the ponies' placid walk calms even a fussy, loud kid.

I'd like to go barefoot like Sharon and Gloria, but Mother would have a fit. She's right about germs but there isn't any broken glass like she goes on about. We sweep the sandy track each morning.

I remove Misty's saddle and bridle and let him loose in his stall. I hold his head for a moment and kiss that spot on his forehead where his hair grows in a perfect swirl. "Goodnight, Misty. I can't wait to tell them."

Nearing the porch, I hear Mother and Martin talking. "I'm home! Martin, I brought you a treat." I hand him a Coke, a Jersey Milk and a bag of chips. "Hey, listen …"

"Loot, good. And she has news from the track? Who's going to win the daily double?"

"Martin, stop!" I'm laughing. "I want to tell you something."

Mother interrupts. "You're late. It's after nine."

"I was putting Misty to bed. Is Dad home yet?"

"No, he had a meeting in Toronto."

"Look." I dig in my pocket and pull out some bills. "I got paid!"

"That's great, little sister. Thanks for the Coke. Sure beats lemonade."

"Gretchen, come out to the kitchen, please," Mother says.

"What?"

"I'll fix you a snack. You must be hungry."

"Starving."

Mother fixes a roast beef sandwich. "I'm glad you're having a good time but don't go on about how much you're earning. How do you think that makes your brother feel? You know he isn't able to get a job."

I WAKE TO crashing thunder. The damp sheet is glued to my sweaty skin. Everyone must be in bed. The lightning flash makes me jump. "One one-thousand, two one-thousand." Thunder booms. The lightning's two miles away. Another flash. The thunder's immediate. I get up and open the window. Rain feels good on my face.

Tiptoeing down the stairs, I run my hand against the embossed wallpaper. In the living room I avoid the stack of books by Mother's chair and find the door to the porch. It's open. I pull the night cover off the swing and sit down. Lightning flashes. When the thunder rumbles, I laugh.

"Good storm."

I leap up. "Martin!"

"Scared you, did I?" He's in the rocking chair.

"The rain's coming through the screens."

"Feels good."

"Yep. That crash sounded closer."

"Maybe hit a tree in Leaman's bush," he says.

"Don't tell Mother I'm up."

"Of course not."

With my foot I shove the swing hard. Its squeal is drowned out by the storm. Lightning zig-zags across the sky, thunder roars and Martin's chair creaks. We don't talk.

The overhead light flashes on. "What are you two doing out here?" Mother's in her old green chenille bathrobe. "Both sopping wet. Get in here before you catch your deaths."

Martin grabs his cane and stomps in the house.

"Gretchen, help me cover up the furniture. Then to bed."

"It's such a hot night," I say. "The rain feels good."

"Sometimes I don't know what gets into you, or him."

I don't have an answer for that. "Good night, Mother."

"Dry your hair well. You'll have a cold for sure."

SUCH FUNNY THINGS happen at the pony track. Gloria and I are side by side leading Prince and Misty when a police car stops by the rail. The officer gets out. He's huge.

"He has a gun," Gloria whispers. She looks scared.

Is he here for Sharon and Gloria? They told me they sneak stuff from the souvenir stand.

We unload our riders. Other children are waiting in line. Cy's the one who collects the money but he's still talking to the policeman.

"Gretchen, go wake up Beauty, bring her out here," Cy says.

Old Beauty doesn't want to move, but I brush the flies from her eyes and push and pet her until she gets to her feet. She follows me from the centre ring.

They're laughing now. "Sorry," the officer says, "but when a tourist says you have a dead pony here, we have to investigate."

"I better not take a nap or some tourist will tell you there's a dead old man on the bench." Cy pats Beauty. "Us oldies better stick together."

We think that's pretty funny. Even the cop chuckles. Sharon laughs loudly and puts her arm around Gloria, who still looks scared.

In the late afternoon things quiet down. The tourists are at the beach. I groom the ponies for a while, then climb up on the fence rail with the other leaders. I like Sharon and Gloria, but they swear a lot. I don't mind "hot damn" and "Jesus Christ," but the rest of it, the dirty talk, I don't like. When I told Mother Sharon and Gloria Dutton were the other leaders, she called them a rough family, and asked: Did they use bad language? I told her they did sometimes. I'd noticed her new frown line a while back and now I could see how the furrow between her eyebrows had deepened even more.

Sharon's my favourite. Gloria just tags along. Sharon wears short-shorts and is always barefoot. She ties her blouse up high so her midriff's bare. Her clothes are old, but she looks snazzy anyway. She wears her red hair in a ponytail. Boys come to visit her and she flips her ponytail in their faces.

Once a boy said: "You got the same thing under your ponytail as that one there?" He pointed at Princess.

Sharon grinned, lifted her ponytail and wiggled her finger against her head. She pointed her still wiggling finger at the boy. "You better pay more attention in health class if that's where you think it is."

He blushed scarlet and so did I.

I don't tell Mother about that kind of talk, or about the shoplifting. I don't want to be like them but that night in bed, I make up a story about Sharon.

I imagine the owner of the drugstore catching Sharon shoplifting. He pulls down her underpants and gives her a spanking. Why do I make up stuff like that? I never used to.

SUNDAYS ARE FUN, except for church. Martin won't go anymore, says he's an atheist. Mother says: "Someday he'll realize he needs the church." She makes me go.

After church we're going to St. Thomas for dinner to celebrate Dad's new job; he's going to be designing a church there.

The restaurant's snazzy, another of my words on Mother's growing "unsuitable" list. I have a hamburger and fries, Mother, Dad and Martin have steak. Be nice if it weren't for the stupid waitress. She took my order, but instead of asking Martin what he'd like, said to Mother: "What will the boy have?" As soon as they see his eyes, they must think he can't speak. Or, they think he's retarded.

I hate too how those two old ladies stared. Martin sways from side to side when he walks. I heard the one whisper "that poor boy." I don't know which makes me madder, the pity of strangers or kids calling out: "Hey Frankenstein," when we used to go downtown together. When Mother was with us, all we got were the head-patting old ladies. Or maybe some little kid asking: "What's the matter with him?"

When we get home, Charlemagne is waiting by the door. His yellow fur is matted and the side of his face is all swollen.

"Not another infection!" Mother says. "We've got to get him fixed so he's not fighting all the time."

"He likes fighting," Martin says. "Eh, Charlemagne?" Charlemagne purrs loudly and rubs against his legs.

"I doubt he likes having a needle stuck in his cheek to drain the abscess," Mother says.

"The pain he endures for his freedom."

"If we get him fixed, he'll be content to stay home."

"Kill him and he won't wander either."

"Nobody's suggesting killing the cat, just a simple operation."

"Yeah, cut off his balls."

"Martin, how dare you talk like that? And in front of your sister!"

"Call a spade a spade, Mother."

"I won't put up with this." She turns to my father. "Brad, you talk to him."

"Martin, be civil to your mother."

My brother sniffs and bangs away to his room.

I pick up smelly Charlemagne and we sit on the porch swing.

"What's the matter with Martin?" Mother asks.

"Beth, I wouldn't make too much of it," Dad says. "He's growing up and he's frustrated."

"Shouldn't you be feeding your pony?" Mother says to me testily. Oh, oh. I leave them to it.

I WAKE UP in the middle of the night. When I go downstairs to get a glass of water, I hear music from Martin's room. He has this powerful radio that can get stations from all over the world. I knock. "You still up, Martin?"

"C'mon in," he calls out.

He's in his desk chair. I sit in Mother's chair. I like this room — big desk and a whole wall of books on shelves. A woman's singing about strange fruit. I don't know what it's about but it makes me want to cry. "What does 'strange fruit' mean?"

"Billie Holiday, a Negro, is singing about the lynchings in the southern United States. She's saying that in the South, it's as though the trees grow a strange kind of fruit, which are corpses of men hanging from the branches."

Suddenly, I could see it. It's night time under a full moon and in the silence the bodies sway gently in the breeze, like heavy fruit. I feel chilled. Not the kind you get after a hard ride with Misty on a cold morning. More like the sudden chill you get after seeing a body standing inside the bedroom door before you realize it's just your battered bathrobe hanging off a nail.

"Not fair how Negroes are treated."

"They're as handicapped as I am, just because of skin colour. They've turned their pain into music, the blues."

"Why don't you listen to happy music? Something like *How Much is that Doggie in the Window?*"

"That music makes me sad. I love this music. It takes me far away from here."

The next morning Donna comes over. Martin's in a good mood, and everybody seems to have forgotten about yesterday, even poor Charlemagne. He's stretched out beside me on the porch swing. He's on his back, legs up in the air. I'm stroking his belly. Mother lanced his abscess and sprinkled the vet's white powder on it. The swelling's gone down. Martin plucked all the burrs from his coat and wiped his fur with a warm, damp cloth. Charlemagne allowed this. He doesn't put up with baths.

"This is so neat." Donna's typing on the Brailler. "Like writing in code. If kids did this at school, the teachers wouldn't know what the notes said. 'Miss Green's not so clean. She scratches her bum, when she's glum.'"

I think, how stupid, but Martin laughs.

"She was my teacher in Hamilton. I got sent to the office for that one. Mr. Athol, the principal, did he ever yell. Said next time he'd give me the strap. Good thing he didn't know the one about him."

"Mr. Athol? Mr. Asshole. Naughty girl, Donna." Martin sniggers.

"That's disgusting," I say.

"Miss Green did scratch her bum. Haemorrhoids, probably."

Martin laughs so hard he spills his lemonade on his lap. "Oh, oh," he says, snorting. "Hope you don't think it's pee."

Donna titters and grabs a napkin. "I'll clean it up."

I tell them I'm going riding. They make me so mad. Why do they act so rude and silly? Martin's usually so serious, talking about philosophy and religion.

I'm saddling Misty when Donna climbs over the paddock fence. "What's the rush?" she says. "Why didn't you wait for me?" She picks up her bike.

"We only have an hour to ride. I have to be at the track by noon."

Donna's on our porch again when I get home from work. "When did you get here?"

"Around six."

"Why didn't you come out to the pony track?"

"Your mother invited me for peach pie. Martin's teaching me to play poker."

"Cy got a new pony."

"What's it like?"

"A white mare and almost as big as Misty. We were all riding her. There weren't many customers. Cy got her at the auction so didn't know what her old owners called her. I wanted to name her Merrylegs, like the pony in *Black Beauty*. They settled on Rosie. That was Sharon's idea." I don't say they all laughed at Merrylegs, and again when Sharon said: "How merry are her legs?"

"I'll try to get out of babysitting Monday."

"You'll like Rosie. She'd be a good one for you to get for the winter, or Prince."

"If only they'd let me. It's neat how your dad made holes in the poker chips so Martin could tell them apart. I counted mine with my eyes shut and didn't make a mistake."

"You didn't have many to count." My brother laughs.

"Yeah, big shot, you won most of them." She turns to me. "Your brother's a super poker player."

Mother brings out a pitcher of lemonade and more peach pie all around. It's nine-thirty when Donna leaves.

"You better get to sleep, Gretchen. Past your bedtime."

Not fair. Donna's my friend. I met her first. They're trying to take her away from me. And the only reason Mother let me stay up late was she didn't want Donna to leave.

The pagoda roof keeps us dry. Donna and I sit with the others on the fence rail. The track's so wet — every hoof print makes a puddle. "Too bad it's raining the one day you're here. You hardly got to ride."

"Yeah, rotten luck," Donna says. "Sharon, what grade will you be in?"

"Nine."

"Me too. Hope it's better than Hamilton."

"What's wrong with Hamilton?" Sharon's applying deep pink nail polish to her grimy fingernails. I wonder whether she stole it.

"This real prick of a principal — Mr. Athol. You can guess what we called him."

"Mr. Asshole," Gloria says.

"Yeah, he walked around like he had a poker up his."

"I hear Podger's not bad," Sharon says. "He's short and fat. Kids call him Pudge."

Donna makes friends with everybody. I can't figure it out. Sharon, Gloria and I are wearing faded shorts and tops. Mother always says: "Wear your clothes until there's no more wear in them." Donna's in another new outfit, all aqua this time. Sharon usually makes fun of girls who have new clothes. She says they're dressed like tourists. Yesterday, a new girl was leading ponies. She wore pink shorts and new white sneakers. "Careful now, wouldn't want to get those pretty shoes dirty." Sharon laughed. Even worse, she used a rag to pick up a fresh horse bun and rubbed it on the rail. The girl didn't notice and sat in it. Why isn't Sharon teasing Donna?

MOTHER SPEAKS TO Donna's mother at church and invites Donna for dinner. She told me after dinner we should play records on the phonograph Dad bought us. "That was very nice of him. One thing I have to say for your father is he's a good provider."

"But we like riding," I say. "We take turns on Misty and her bike."

"Not today. Do something that includes Martin."

We've played all three of our records. I love our porch on summer afternoons. At the back the lilacs have grown to the top of the windows. The insects hum busily against the screens.

Charlemagne's stretched out on the floor. Martin's stroking him with his bare foot.

Donna says: "Next time I'll bring my new Johnnie Ray—*Somebody Stole My Gal*. Let's practice writing on the Brailler."

She's really keen on learning braille. She comes over sometimes when I'm at the pony track. Says she likes riding, but leading ponies all afternoon's boring. How could she find it boring?

I type as quickly as I can. *Who's your favourite pony?*

She hands me one. *Misty. But I like Prince and Rosie too.*

My turn. *Which one would you like to keep for the winter?*

Either one.

Keep working on your dad.

Her turn. *I like your brother.*

Why is she always going on about him? "I'm going riding." I slam the screen door.

On Misty bareback, I ride through Leaman's fields. Goldenrod and grasshoppers bounce off my bare legs. We go back to the pond, now just dry, cracked mud. While Misty grazes, I sit on the dead willow the ice storm brought down. I think about my dad. Strange what Mother said: "One thing I have to say for your father is he's a good provider." Why does it feel she was saying: The only thing I have to say for your father is he's a good provider? Is she mad at Dad? Dad is kind and funny and good-looking—dark curly hair, just a bit of grey, and he's tall. The lines around his eyes turn up when he smiles. Mostly, these days, they turn down.

The sun's going down as I settle myself on the porch swing with my latest Zane Grey, *Wildfire*. I love the descriptions of canyons and the prairie smelling of sage grass. He spells canyon as *cañon*. It seems like it's all a long time ago. Wish I lived back then. Sometimes, riding Misty, I pretend we're on the prairie. We meet Lin Slone, the horse trainer, and Wildfire. I tame Wildfire and ride him in the big race.

Hopefully, Mother won't notice it's my bedtime. She's helping Dad pack for a convention in New York. While we were washing the supper dishes, Mother didn't say anything about me going riding when I was supposed to stay home. I'm catching on. It's Donna she wants here, as a friend for Martin, even though she's my age, not his.

Martin's at the Brailler. He must be in a good mood. Every few minutes he chuckles.

"What's so funny?"

"Here," he says pulling the page from the Brailler. "You might like this about a deballed, overweight cat."

I take it and sit back down on the porch swing. I like the part:

> *Why looking at you sleeping in your rolls of fat*
> *do I still wish for you another life as a fierce tom cat*
> *who caterwauls at night and fights 'til bloody ...*

"I DIDN'T KNOW you wrote poetry."

"Yeah, sometimes."

"You're right, no cat would want to be neutered." Tiger's so proud when she has a new litter. When she's nursing them, she purrs and purrs.

THERE'S TROUBLE AT our house. Mother's mad at Martin. Yesterday, she said to him: "What did you think you were doing?"

"Quit fussing over me." He went to his room and slammed the door. He was still in there when I left for the track.

First thing this morning she told me to darn my socks. "No more putting it off. There are holes in the heels of every pair you own." She sounded really cross. She's mad at Martin, why take it out on me?

So here I am on a beautiful summer morning, darning socks, the one job I hate the most. My mends are always lumpy, not neat little squares of weaving like hers. I get Screechy pumping and my yarn promptly tangles.

Martin's reading and I'm on my third sock when Mother comes out on the porch. "Gretchen, why don't you and Martin walk downtown? You could get sodas at the Quick Stop."

"I thought I was supposed to do my darning."

"You can do it tomorrow."

Talk about inconsistent. We haven't walked downtown in years. But I hate darning and would love a soda. "Do you want to, Martin?"

He glares. "I have work to do. I'm reading Aristophanes' *The Clouds*."

"Martin, you can do your reading this afternoon," Mother says cheerfully. Not her usual voice at all.

She's gone back in the kitchen. Five minutes later she's motioning to me to join her. She's rolling out pastry. Says she wants my help. This is odd, as she usually wants us to keep out of her way.

"You two used to go downtown a lot."

"Mother, that was years ago."

"Well, you should start again. Martin needs to get out more."

"He doesn't like to go for walks, because of his legs." As she well knows.

"They can't bother him that much. He walked downtown in the middle of the night. Why would he do a thing like that? He could've been hit by a car."

"I don't know." I do know why we stopped going downtown. We had to pass Waddells to get to the Quick Stop. The Waddell boys would mimic Martin's walk. Call him names.

"Your brother's a brilliant boy but his handicaps will make life difficult for him. He needs companionship. That's why it's so nice Donna comes to see him."

"Wouldn't somebody his own age be better?"

"Donna is, of course, intellectually his inferior, but she's socially advanced. Martin suffers from his isolation."

"Why didn't he make friends at his school?"

"I hoped he would. Some other students, jealous of his intelligence, bullied him. And there was an emphasis on sports. Martin couldn't take part. But mainly, Gretchen, he resented being lumped together with other handicapped children. Martin should've been grouped with other brilliant students."

"I don't think he would've liked Grenville Public."

"Of course not. We should've found a private school that recognized his superiority. Finish your darning now."

"Do I have to?"

"Yes and talk to Martin. Suggest an outing."

I go back to my pile of socks. "Martin, why'd you go downtown in the middle of the night?"

"So she's complaining to you now?"

"She's scared you'll get hit by a car."

"I can hear a car coming."

"But what if you met up with the Waddell boys?"

"The whole town was asleep."

"But what if?"

"Shall I let you in on a little secret?"

"What?"

"You won't say anything to Mother?"

"Of course not."

He takes from his pocket a leather sheath and pulls out a thin, sharp knife. He smiles. "I can take care of myself."

"Where'd you get that?"

"Dad gave it to me a long time ago."

"Why?"

"To try my hand at carving balsawood. I wasn't any good at that." He chuckles.

"You stab somebody, you'll go to jail."

"Shh, she's coming." He puts it back in his pocket.

SHARON AND I are grooming the ponies. The track doesn't open for another hour.

"Gotta go feed the baby," she says. "You wanna come with me?"

We cross the field back of the pony track to Cherry Street, a gravel road lined with old cottages. All the streets here have fruit names. It's known as The Orchard. Sharon's house, at the end of Plum, is tall and narrow and has several attached sheds. Honeysuckle bushes grow right over the first-floor windows. On the ragged lawn a fridge with no door is tipped on its side. A little boy crawls out and says: "Hey, where youse goin'?"

"That's Joey and his fort," Sharon tells me.

Inside the house I wouldn't have seen the woman sleeping on the couch, but a rip in one blind lets the sun light up her head. She has red hair, but an old face. The house smells funny, old wood like our barn, but something else too. Sour milk? Maybe pee.

"Mom's resting. She just got home from the hospital yesterday."

Upstairs a baby, wearing just a diaper, jumps up and down in her crib. She has one pink and one blue barrette holding her blonde hair back from her eyes. She's surrounded by stuffed toys—bears, a blue dog and a grey rabbit missing an ear. There's another bear on the floor on top of a pile of laundry. "Is she the baby?"

"No, silly, that's Judy. She's over a year old."

In a rusty white buggy is the tiniest baby I've ever seen. Fine black hair swirls across his head, which is no bigger than an orange. He looks right at me with bright eyes, like a little animal.

"I'll get his bottle," Sharon says. I follow her back downstairs. The sink and counter are stacked with dirty dishes and on the drainboard a yellow cat's licking an unwashed frying pan. Sharon takes a filled bottle from the fridge, runs it under the hot water tap for a moment. "That's ready. I better bring one for Judy too."

"Baba," Judy yells, flops down her back and guzzles the milk.

Sharon tickles her belly. "You stink. Somebody better change you, but it ain't gonna be me. You wanna feed the baby?" she says turning to me.

"Okay." I'm scared to pick him up.

"Just keep one hand under his neck." She places him in my trembling arms.

I hold the bottle to his lips and he sucks. He's not much heavier than a half-grown cat. I sniff his head. His hair smells like newborn kittens. "He's wonderful."

"Just another baby. Youse got any babies in your family?"

"No. How many brothers and sisters do you have?"

"Too many." She laughs. "Joey, and this is Charlie, and four sisters. Gloria, the brat, you know her. And this one here. Phew!" She unpins Judy's soaking diaper and drops it on the laundry pile. It just misses the teddy bear. "Hand me a diaper, would ya? They're over there."

I look where she's pointing, at a basket of unfolded laundry. I'm trying to stand up without dropping the baby, but Sharon has already got a diaper and is folding it. She grabs Judy, who's hopping up and down naked. "I know you like wearin' nothing but we'd have one big shitty mess, wouldn't we?" She holds her down and expertly pins on the clean one. "I have two more sisters, Debbie and Emily—they're around someplace."

Leaving the house, we're greeted by two grimy little girls each carrying a kitten.

"Does Pixie know youse guys got her kittens?"

"We'll give 'em back," the bigger girl, with curly red hair like Sharon's, says. "Got any money?"

"What youse want money for?"

"Popsicles."

Sharon digs three nickels out of her pocket. "Okay, but take Joey with you."

RIDING MISTY HOME from the park that evening, I pretend I have little sisters who like to play with our barn kittens. I would comb their hair and wash their faces, buy them Popsicles and ice cream too.

Four sisters and two brothers. How come with nobody looking after them they're all okay?

I TELL MOTHER about the new baby and that the Duttons have seven children.

"And Mrs. Dutton was sleeping?" my mother says.

"She just got home from the hospital yesterday."

"And your friend gave the new baby his bottle?"

"No, I did."

"Did you wash your hands first?"

"No."

"That baby could get sick. And who was looking after the other little one? You said there was an older baby too."

"At first I thought Judy was the new baby. Sharon laughed at me. I've never seen a newborn baby before."

"Such careless people," Mother says. "They breed like rabbits."

LATER, LYING IN bed, I worry about the baby getting sick. But Sharon didn't wash her hands either. Maybe Dutton children are extra-healthy. Sharon goes barefoot at the pony track. Laughs at me when I won't take my shoes off. Sharon had never heard of lockjaw.

Mother called them careless. We're the careful people, always on the lookout for germs, but my brother is blind and can hardly walk. I flip my pillow, pull the quilt over my head.

I dream I'm in the barn. Misty's stall is full of loose hay, and rabbits are everywhere. I take my clothes off and lie down. It seems the right thing to do. The rabbits hop on me. Their furry paws tickle. A mother rabbit gives birth. The blood-smeared babies flow right out of her. There are dozens. I kiss and pet them, and they crawl all over me. My belly and thighs are bloody. I must have my period. Somehow that's all right. I'm not at all embarrassed. Okay too that I'm naked in the hay. The newborn rabbits turn into human babies, no bigger than baby rabbits.

I wake up in the dark. This is the most beautiful dream I've ever had. The birth smell like when the kittens were born. Blood, hay, and something else — a musky smell. I want to lie naked in the hay and have a baby just like Sharon's little brother. I want it so much I'm crying.

THE NEXT DAY, at the track, I ask Sharon if the baby's okay. I tell her I'm sorry I forgot to wash my hands. She laughs. "He's fine," she says.

When I wash my hands under the tap before eating my lunch, she says: "Watch out! Lockjaw germs sneaking up on yah!"

That's pretty silly. You can't see germs. I don't say that though. I want her to like me.

ON THE FIRST day of high school Donna comes to my house, and we walk to school together. I'm wearing a white blouse, a green plaid skirt and brown Oxfords, all ordered from Eaton's catalogue. The shoes are stiff and uncomfortable.

Donna says she'll ask her mother to drive us tomorrow. "A mile's too far to walk," she says.

Not far enough for me. I wouldn't care if we never got there. And I've just realized I'm not dressed right. Donna's wearing penny loafers, a sleeveless blouse and a straight skirt with covered buttons down the front. She went shopping in St. Thomas.

I'm in Nine A, and both Donna and Sharon are in Nine B. I can't bear it. Not that I don't know anybody in my class. Janet Day sits right behind me and beside her is Doreen Jacobs. I call them the Sweater Twins and sure enough they're both in angora today. Last year I heard Janet say she gets all her clothes dry-cleaned, that way they stay perfect. Her father owns Days' Drycleaners. Doreen's father is Dr. Jacobs. All Doreen and Janet talk about is clothes.

They've never really done anything to me. Unless you count Janet pretending to faint when I handed her the toad I brought for show and tell in grade two. They told me only boys liked toads and frogs. "Do you want to be a boy?" Doreen said. Janet said, "Maybe she is. Who's to say?" They snickered as I walked away. I don't want to be a boy and I don't see why being a girl means you're supposed to be a sissy. Mother's not scared of anything. When we get bats in the house, she's the one who catches them and puts them outside. Dad's afraid of bats—says they're creepy, and he's not going near them. Mother laughs, calls him city boy. I like it when they joke like that.

In this class there are a lot of people I don't know. The kids from the rural schools and Orchard Public go to Grenville High too. Sharon would've gone to Orchard. I wish she was in my class. We're not divided according to marks either. Brian Shaw and Ed Green are in Nine A, and they both failed grade seven.

DONNA STOPS IN at my place on our way home. Mother brings out lemonade and leaves us. We sit on the porch with Martin.

"How was first day?" he asks.

"Fun," Donna says.

Not a word I would've used.

"Lots of cute boys," Donna tells him. "I passed Sharon a note asking about the dark-haired hunk that sits in front of her in homeroom. Mr. Adams, the poker up his you-know-what type, snatched it and gave us a lecture and about what will and won't be tolerated in his class. We'll have fun loosening him up."

Martin laughs so hard he chokes on his lemonade.

DONNA AND I are best friends. Dad even divided Misty's stall in two —still plenty big. We took Prince for the winter so Donna and I could ride every day after school. We did at first.

Now, she wants to stay for the stupid Friday night sock-hop. I hate dances. The boys are lined up on one side of the gym and the girls the other. Some smirking boy asks you to dance. And you're supposed to be grateful. Nobody asks me, and I don't care.

Mostly, when Donna does walk home from school with me, we hardly have time to ride. Mother always wants us to play cards or Scrabble with Martin.

DONNA NOW HAS a boyfriend, Ian Talbot, a pimple-faced jerk. He thinks he's a big shot because he's in grade eleven and on the football team. Donna's changed. She smokes. She got me to try it but the taste was horrible. Of course, Ian smokes. She only comes riding with me a couple of times a week. It's always "Ian and I are going to the Quick Stop." Or it's the sock-hop. Or the movies. She doesn't even hang out with me at noon. She's always with that bunch in the auditorium listening to records and dancing.

Sharon's there too. She only speaks to me if I'm with Donna. Her boyfriend's Billy Sider. He's in grade ten. He's 16 and had to repeat grade eight.

Donna thinks I'm jealous. She tried to set me up with a couple of
boys, both idiots. I don't want a boyfriend. I want to go riding. Why
can't I have school at home?

Not true I don't want a boyfriend. I want somebody like Lin Slone
in *Wildfire*. "A magnificent horseman, whose gentleness showed his love
for horses, whose roughness showed his power … a strange, intense,
lonely man."

Tonight Donna and I walk home together. Ian has football practice.

"Do you want to go riding?"

"If I had my jeans with me, I would. If I go home for them, I'll get
stuck babysitting."

"I could lend you some. You'll have to roll up the legs."

"Okay, let's ride to the swamp."

Martin's on the porch. Mother invites Donna to join us for hot
chocolate and cookies.

"We're going riding," I tell her.

"There's plenty of time."

"Hey Martin, did you hear about the big scandal at Port Erie
High?" Donna says.

"What's that bunch of dummies been up to?"

"You know their school and ours have the same board and my dad's
on it. Well, at the meeting our principal, Podger, said their principal
should resign. Mr. Snider's daughter, who's in grade ten, is pregnant.
Mr. Podger said if Mr. Snider can't control his own daughter, he shouldn't
be principal of a high school."

"Pregnant in grade ten! She's a hot chick," Martin says, laughing.

I cringe when Martin uses slang. Coming from him, it sounds so
phony. "Did he resign?" I ask Donna.

"No, the board wouldn't let him. Know what my mom said?"

"What?"

"She said, if she were Michael Podger, she'd be a little more careful
about making such statements. His daughters aren't through high school
yet."

"Are they wild?" Martin asks.

"I don't know them all that well. Pity them though, with that creep
for a dad. One's in your class, isn't she, Gretchen?"

"Nancy, she hangs out with the Sweater Twins."

We don't get to go riding because Donna's mother phones and she has to go right home. If my mother hadn't delayed us, like she's always doing, we'd have been long gone.

At dawn I ride Misty out to the beach. Warm for November. Unless it's pouring, I ride every morning before school. Misty and I don't mind a light rain. After all, his ancestors lived outdoors in Wales year-round.

Close to the water, where the sand is wet and firm, Misty breaks into a gallop. The lake spray hits my face and wets my jeans. Riding in the near-dark is fun. The whole world is ours.

The sky's getting light over Blackstone Point. When I was little I wanted to look for the black stone. Mother said it was the name of the family who farmed there for generations. I like how every farm has its story. Mother said Mr. Blackstone was so cruel to his horses that none of the other farmers would sell him one. Now Blackstone Point has a summer dancehall and an ice cream stand. Mean old Mr. Blackstone is long dead.

Five minutes from home, I see my brother up ahead. "Hey, Martin, wait up." I trot Misty alongside him and jump off. "Where'd you go?"

"Downtown." He reaches over and rubs Misty's neck.

"Oh, Martin! Do you still have that knife?"

"I do."

"You could go to jail."

"Quit worrying, little sister. It'd be self defense, which is legal."

"I suppose. If you came out to the lake, there wouldn't be any danger of running into some jerk. We had the beach all to ourselves."

"My cane gets stuck in the sand. Slows me down."

"Martin, why don't you carry a white cane? People could watch out for you better."

"I don't need any damn advertisement."

"Mother doesn't like you going out at night."

"I'm a man. I'll go where I like."

A car blasts its horn as it passes. Misty shies, but I hold tight to the reins. "Why do they honk?"

"Assholes, that's why."

"Martin, that's dirty talk."

"Better walking at three a.m. — by myself."

"The sky's pink now," I say. "It's beautiful."

"Even prettier though, if it were the New York skyline we were looking at, not the trees in Leaman's bush."

"Martin, can you see the trees?"

"They're a blurred mass, and I can see the sky is lighter, but not the pink. I remember colours though, from before."

"I guess New York would be so bright, you could see it."

"Feel it anyway."

As we turn in by the barn Charlemagne comes to greet us. He rubs against Martin's legs. "Had a good night, Charlemagne?" my brother says.

"Oh Martin, his ear's bleeding."

"Brawling again, were you? Bet the other guy's worse off."

I CLOMP DOWN the stairs. Saturday afternoon and I can't go riding. I hate the weather in February.

Dad's reading in the living room. Strange, but nice to have him home all the time. He was in the hospital for a couple of days. Nobody told me why. Mother says he just needs a rest.

"Ah, Gretchen, you up to making me a cup of tea?"

"Sure, where's Mother?"

"Your mother and Martin are in his room. His office I should say. Discussing Aristotle, I believe."

I make the tea, a cup for myself too. Having tea with my dad was a treat.

"I've been thinking, Gretchen. While I have this time off, I could teach you to drive. At fourteen, you can get your learner's permit. Your mother doesn't think the government should allow learners' permits at fourteen, but you're a sensible girl, so why not?"

"Dad, I'd love that."

"We'll wait till the ice goes, of course."

APRIL BEFORE DAD makes good on his promise. He's back at work but not away as much. Mother says he has to cut back. My first time driving, I'm afraid I'll go in the ditch. Driving a car is scarier than riding a pony. A car doesn't have a brain. If I give it too much gas, I could run into the car ahead of me. A pony would slow down on his own. But I don't go in the ditch or hit another car and after a while the car stops making that big growl when I let up on the clutch.

Donna's so jealous — her dad said she won't be driving until she's twenty-one. They're having enough trouble over her brother, Ted. He smashed up his car. His girlfriend broke her arm, but he wasn't hurt.

I can't get my license until I'm sixteen, but I can drive as long as an adult's with me. On Friday Dad took me with him to London, where he's designing an office building. I got to miss school. I drove until we got to the city outskirts and he left me at the library while he was at his meeting. I did my geometry homework and the following two pages of problems. That's more than the teacher would assign for the weekend. Then I finished reading *Merchant of Venice*. In class we're still in Act I.

FRIDAYS AFTER SCHOOL Donna and I have confirmation classes. I don't want to get confirmed. I asked our minister if animals went to heaven. He said people are made in God's likeness, and animals were put on earth for our use. That's why it's all right to kill an animal and eat it but wrong to kill a person. People have souls—that's what separates them from animals. It's our souls that are immortal. But just like animals, our bodies die and decay.

I don't want any part of a heaven that doesn't have room for animals.

I told Dad what the minister said and that I didn't want to go to confirmation classes. He said that's just theology, nobody really knows, and if I think animals have souls, maybe they do, and maybe they go to heaven. The church, Dad said, should be a place of spiritual searching—a lifelong search. Then he said: "Your mother will be terribly disappointed if you don't get confirmed. She's had enough disappointments in her life."

Lilacs scent the air when Donna and I leave the church. What a waste to spend the day, first shut up in school, then at church. "Why don't you have supper at our place? If we eat quickly, there'll be time to ride."

"I'll tell my mom we have to study together."

We have supper on the porch, first time this year. Mother scrubbed it today and got the screens up. Dad usually helps with the screens as they have to be hauled from the barn but he's away and Mother said the weather's too lovely to wait any longer.

Mother's in the kitchen when Donna asks Martin why he doesn't go to church?

He's sarcastic. "I believe in God the Father Almighty, Maker of heaven and earth. And in Jesus Christ, his only Son … and so on and so forth. You believe all that?"

"I dunno."

"Do you know how babies are made?"

"Of course." She rolls her eyes and titters.

"It says in the Bible the Holy Ghost entered Mary's ear and made her pregnant. You believe that?"

"Ummm ..."

"The creed says Mary was a virgin when Jesus was born. Can you have a baby if you've never done it?"

"No."

"Then how come you recite that crap at church?"

"The virgin birth's a miracle. God can do anything."

"Crap. Karl Marx said: 'Religion is the opiate of the people.' Do you know what that means?"

"No idea."

Why does Martin have to take over my time with Donna? "There's not much time left to go riding," I say.

"Gretchen, don't interrupt. It means the rich and powerful feed us all that crap so we'll believe we're poor miserable sinners and do as we're told."

"I don't know what you're talking about. Yeah, Gretchen, let's get going."

"About time," I say.

First of June, a gorgeous day and less than a month till summer holidays. Dandelions frizz along Leaman Road. A perfect day to ride to the O'Hara place but Mother was at the dentist having a root canal and told me to put supper on. Turn on the oven to three-fifty. Set the table, use the blue-flowered cloth. Bring in lettuce, onions, and radishes from the garden for a salad. At five put the stew in. When I grow up I'm going to live on my own and never cook—eat hunks of cheese, bread and raw carrots. Sit outside on a tree stump to have my supper.

I come in the back way.

I don't believe this! In the dim living room Martin and Donna are standing very close together. His hands are all over her. They're whispering. Now they're kissing. She has her hands on his behind.

I run outside, slamming the door behind me. Cuddle with the cats in the barn. What's the matter with her? Ian's her boyfriend.

THE NEXT NIGHT after school I'm saddling Misty when Donna shows up.

"Can I go riding with you?"

"If you want. Prince needs some exercise."

"Do you want to go to the O'Hara place?"

"Okay."

We don't talk much on the way there. But when the ponies are grazing and we're sitting on the foundation blocks, I ask her. "Is Ian still your boyfriend?"

"Yeah."

We're quiet. Then she says: "You saw Martin and me necking, didn't you?"

I couldn't look at her.

"Ian doesn't own me. Martin and me were just fooling around. Doesn't mean anything."

I don't understand her. I understand Martin. He really likes her, it means something to him. Can't trust her. She can't belong to the popular kids and us too.

ONCE SCHOOL'S OUT, I don't see much of Donna. She got a job at the souvenir shop. Sharon's not at the track either — she's working at Siders Restaurant. But Gloria's there and some new kids, all younger than me.

When Donna isn't working, she's out with Ian. Once in a while she plays cards with Martin.

Can't believe I'm bored at the pony track. I love leading ponies but hate being stuck with the little kids while Donna and Sharon have moved on. Sharon's different. I thought she was like me and didn't care about clothes. The last time I saw her she was in new red pedal-pushers and a flowered halter.

There are no more business trips with Dad. I can't skip work like I can school.

Martin's seldom up before ten. Sometimes at night I'll hear him typing away on the Brailler. The only other sound is that sad music he likes, "the blues." His radio gets stations from all over the United States. I know he still goes walking at night.

Aunt Maggie's visit is the one thing I have to look forward to. She's my dad's sister and comes each summer, except last year when she went to Europe. She owns a dress shop in Toronto. Mother calls it a dress shop. Aunt Maggie calls it Chez Paris. She has a cottage on Lake Huron where she spends the rest of her summer holidays. Sauble Beach — I've never been there. We're often invited but Mother says that her garden would suffer. Two summers ago we went to the Mayo Clinic, though that was no holiday.

Mother doesn't like Aunt Maggie, who she says drinks and is extravagant and foolish. There's another reason — she's divorced. She's the only divorced person I know. Mother says she was married to a really nice man, a lawyer, and the divorce was all Aunt Maggie's fault.

Aunt Maggie lives in an apartment in Toronto. I was there once with Dad. The living room is all in white, shaggy carpet, soft velvety couches and drapes. The tables are chrome and glass. When I told Mother about the living room, she said: "There's a song, *Ain't We Got Fun*, that was popular when Maggie and I were young. Sums Maggie up. But life isn't just about having fun."

I can't wait to see her.

DAD AND MAGGIE are on the porch when I get home Wednesday. I hear her raucous laugh before I see them.

She and Dad are having rye and ginger ale like they always do when she visits.

Aunt Maggie jumps up and hugs me, the ice in her glass tinkling. "Go wash up and I'll fix you a Shirley Temple."

I scrub my hands and face and change into clean shorts and blouse. Mother isn't in the kitchen but I look out the window and sure enough, she's working in the garden. She gardens a lot when Aunt Maggie visits.

When I come downstairs, I hear my aunt in the kitchen. On the counter are the usual two bottles of Canadian Club along with jars of nuts, olives, maraschino cherries and boxes of fancy crackers. I see smoked salmon too—Mom says it tastes too fishy—well, yeah, it's fish —but it's one of Dad's favourite treats.

She fixes my drink—ginger ale, ice, cherry juice and lots of cherries. She always remembers how I like it.

"Is the kitchen always this hot? Your mother must be doing a roast." She opens a wooden box that I expect is more salmon, but it's a variety of wrapped cheeses.

"We'll take a tray out to the porch." She loads up the goodies. "Call your brother."

Martin says he's busy. He'll join us shortly.

We're munching on a feast by the time he appears.

"I think Martin's old enough for a light one, don't you, Peewee?"

My aunt's the only one who calls my dad Peewee, his childhood nickname. She's a year older.

"Sure, a light one," Dad says. "Rye and ginger makes me remember the football parties at Western, eh, Mags?"

"Yeah, I was going with Bob Barnes, the captain of the team."

"We sure had some fun."

"That championship game against Queen's," my aunt says.

"My first year on the team."

"Your dad got the winning touchdown," she tells us.

"Dad, I didn't know you played football," I say.

"He was a star all through high school and university. Martin, you look so much like your dad. If it hadn't been for your accident, I bet you would've been good at football."

"Football's for dummies," my brother says.

"You're ruining your appetite for dinner." Mother stands in the doorway. "We're having roast beef with Yorkshire pudding."

"You shouldn't go to so much bother on a hot day," Aunt Maggie says. "Sandwiches would be plenty."

"Beth, let me fix you a drink," my dad says.

"I'd better get the dinner on. What's Martin drinking?"

"Just a light one," says Maggie.

"He's not twenty-one."

"Beth, it won't hurt him," my dad says.

She gives him the look and heads for the kitchen.

Dad sighs. "Gretchen, please help your mother with dinner."

Just before dessert, Aunt Maggie hands out her gifts. She starts with a two-pound box of Laura Secord chocolates. You can't buy them in Grenville. She's brought me red pedal pushers just like Sharon's and a sleeveless white blouse with red embroidery. Martin and Dad get sport shirts and wallets. Mother, a pink nylon nightgown from Chez Paris and a travel magazine. The magazine will arrive every month.

"It's time you two started to live a little. See the world."

"Thank you," Mother says. "Brad does so much travelling with his work, he's happy to be able to stay home on his time off."

Dad stares at the floor and nobody speaks for a moment.

Mother brings in the dessert — peach pie with ice cream. "I made your favourite," she says to my aunt.

"Looks delicious, but can I have it later? I've eaten so much."

My mother only buys ice cream for special occasions.

Each evening of her three-day visit, my aunt, Dad and I go for a drive. Mother and Martin won't come. One night we go to St. Thomas.

We drive past the house they lived in as children and their grandparents' house. They talk about their father, who was a colonel in the First World War.

"A shame Mother died so young," Maggie says.

"And how she suffered. Cancer's a cruel killer." My dad sighs. "And to think Father had his first heart attack the next year."

"When we were kids, we had so much family—Gran and Gramps right down the street."

"Yes," my dad says. "And by the time I got home from the war, they were all gone."

"Just you and me now." Aunt Maggie echoes Dad's sigh.

"Let's take Gretchen to the Star Grill for ice cream."

"Let's! Gretchen, that's where all the teenagers hung out when we were in high school."

THE DAY BEFORE she leaves she invites me to go with her to Sauble Beach.

"I'd love to, but I have to work."

"I'll talk to Cy," Dad says. "You need a little holiday."

He talks to Cy, and I'm going. Mother, Dad and Martin will come on Saturday, stay overnight and bring me home. Five whole days. I'm so excited I hardly sleep.

AUNT MAGGIE DRIVES with one arm on the wheel and the other hanging out the window. I'm a little nervous. Mother said Aunt Maggie's a terrible driver. I think she wanted me to say that I didn't want to go. Aunt Maggie's telling me how much fun she has buying clothes for Chez Paris. I like the way she treats me, like I'm an adult.

The cottage is near the beach and in bed at night I hear the waves. There's a little village with stores selling tourist stuff, and a few ice cream stands and a fragrant chip truck.

Just us at the cottage. "Hope you won't be bored," she says. "We'll have lots of people over."

After Aunt Maggie wakes at noon, we go for a swim. Then we walk a couple of miles down the beach. We have lunch at the cottage but more often, it's fries and hot dogs from one of the stands on what Maggie calls "the strip," a sandy road leading down to the beach. We eat supper at home twice and both times it's hamburgers.

The very first day she buys me a red Jantzen bathing suit. Says it shows off my cute figure and complements my dark hair. "Your daisy one looks like a kid's suit."

I feel self-conscious in the red one and only wear it when I'm swimming with her. In the afternoons and evenings she and her friends play cards, either at her cottage or theirs. My mother would have a fit about all the drinking.

There doesn't seem to be much housework to do. We do dishes when they pile up. We don't cook much. I have fruit and corn flakes for breakfast and anything I want out of the fridge when I'm hungry. I'd be in big trouble at home if I took stuff out of the fridge without asking.

I worry about the drinking. We were at her neighbour's cottage last night. Everyone drank beer. A little boy, still in diapers, picked up somebody's beer and drank some. Everybody laughed. I feel sorry for him. He'll grow up to be an alcoholic.

Mornings are my favourite time. I get up with the sun and pull on my "kid's" bathing suit. I bought it last year with my pony-track money. I dog paddle, head well out of the water. Funny thing is, I think Martin can swim. We used to walk out to the beach by ourselves. Martin would lie on the sand while I played in the water. One time when I was nine he went in the lake with me. He took a deep breath, put his face in the water and kicked his arms and legs. He was swimming. I was amazed. The Waddell boys sneered. "Hey Frankenstein swims like he walks." That was the last time Martin went to the beach.

This beach is much larger than the one at home. A type of shrub I've never seen before grows where the sand meets the trees. Sparse, with shiny leaves, they smell like green, if a colour could have a smell. After swimming, I walk through the town. The second day I go barefoot. The roadsides are sandy and there are lots of barefooted people. Here, I don't worry about lockjaw. I'm immune. I swim and walk and lie on the sand. Forget all about Grenville. And feel guilty when I realize I haven't even thought about my family for days. But on Saturday when they arrive, I'm really glad to see them.

The night before, Maggie's son Peter, the basketball star, had visited. He's tall and has slicked back blonde hair. He jokes around with his mother and me and then goes off with his friends and we don't see him again until after my folks arrive.

Mother looks nice. She's wearing a pale-green shirtwaist dress. Must be new. She has wavy dark hair and big brown eyes. And she's slim. Until this week I'd forgotten that, but my aunt and her friends are always talking about losing weight. My aunt isn't fat exactly but not slim like my mother. Her bleached hair looks brittle. Mother told me if hair is bleached often enough, it'll fall out. My aunt has lots of hair, but she's not as pretty as my mother. I'm amazed that my mother's pretty.

My aunt and Dad go shopping and then we barbeque steaks and eat cherry cheesecake for dessert. A woman in the village makes cakes. I've never had cheesecake before and it's delicious. How many other amazing foods are out there and will I ever taste them?

Pete and his friends are here for the barbeque, four girls and three boys. One girl talks a lot with Martin. I hear him telling her about his writing and his plan to move to New York City.

After supper we set up the card tables on the porch and play poker, even my mother.

Pete and his friends drink beer and the girl Martin was talking to opens one for him. I'm surprised my mother doesn't object. Not one of them is twenty-one. To my surprise Mother allows Dad to fix her a "very light" gin and tonic.

I have root beer and potato chips. We're enjoying ourselves until Pete says they better get going. There's a party at somebody's house.

"Martin, have fun and don't do anything I wouldn't do," Pete says.

We hear them laughing as they walk off toward the beach.

We try to keep on playing cards. Mother says: "We can't quit now." Her laugh is high-pitched. "We can't let Martin win all the chips." She laughs again. I try to make my face expressionless.

Martin says he has reading to do and goes inside.

Mother says she's going to bed and I should too. Dad stays up with Aunt Maggie. Mother doesn't say a word while we're getting ready for bed. She has that look, like her lips are glued together. I have trouble falling asleep.

We leave early the next morning. Mother and Martin are pretty quiet. Dad's chatty. Asks me about my vacation and I tell him about the swimming and walks and the new bathing suit. He says he knows a good restaurant and wants to stop for lunch but Mother says we can have lunch at home. Dad lets me drive the rest of the way.

That night I offer to help with the dishes. I feel guilty, but don't know why. What did I do wrong? Or for that matter what did Aunt Maggie do?

"Did you have a good time?" Mother asks.

"Yes, Aunt Maggie's a lot of fun. We went swimming, and she was always buying me stuff. She's very generous."

"Generous with your dad's money. The one time we go to that cottage and, of course, she has to take your dad shopping. She needs a few things. And guess who pays for the steaks and the liquor and that blessed cheesecake?"

"She bought us all lots of gifts."

"Oh yes, a regular Lady Bountiful. And why didn't she make Peter stay and visit with Martin?"

"I don't know."

"She didn't care whether Martin had fun."

After that, we don't talk about Aunt Maggie. I feel guilty about having such a good time but why should I? Mother didn't care whether or not I had fun. For her everything's about Martin.

THE PONY TRACK closes up on Labour Day. I don't take Prince for the winter. Donna so seldom came over to ride. I felt bad when Misty and I went out for a ride and left Prince behind.

Donna and I are in the same homeroom. She chooses the desk right across from mine. She flirts with all the boys. They all wear ducktails and she messed up one guy's hair, saying: "Your duck just took off." And she walks around with her chest sticking out. So much so that the boys joke: "Which part of Donna comes through the door first?" You'd think she'd be ashamed. She laps it up.

She knows all the gossip. She tells us Nancy Podger married John Robinson in August. Most of our class already knew that. But only Donna knew what went on at school board meetings. She said her dad told them at supper last night and they almost fell off their chairs laughing. Mr. Podger had offered to resign. Nancy's the same age as the Port Erie principal's daughter who "had" to get married.

But they turned down his resignation.

At supper I tell Mother and Martin about what Donna said.

"So the joke's on Pudge," Martin says chuckling.

"It's no laughing matter," Mother says. "And don't call him that. And you" — she turns to me — "shouldn't listen to gossip."

DONNA ARRANGES A date for me with Barry Jones. He got 97 on the algebra test. I got 89. And he's about my height — five foot six. Donna's five foot two. We're all going to the Halloween dance.

Mother's helping me make a gypsy costume from one of Aunt Maggie's hand-me-downs, a red taffeta evening gown. "That's all it's good for," she said.

I make a kerchief, a shawl and a full skirt out of the taffeta and trim them all with black lace.

Mother rolled up the living-room rug. Donna's teaching me to dance. I tell her we should practice in the loft.

"There's no wall plug out there for your record player and anyway what's the matter with the living room?" Donna brought over her new record, Bill Haley and His Comets.

"*Shake, Rattle and Roll* would sound pretty strange on the old Victrola," Martin says.

What's wrong with the living room is Martin. He's always butting in. Balancing on his cane he's trying to swing Donna around with his free arm.

She should tell him to leave her alone but she carries on like she's enjoying it.

Mother must see what's going on. Why doesn't she tell him to go read a book? Donna's supposed to be teaching me to dance.

"Mrs. Thorton, could you help fix my costume?" Donna asks. "The girl who lent it to me is bigger."

"Certainly dear, try it on. You can change in the bathroom."

Donna returns in a pink ballerina outfit.

"See, it gapes," she says, pulling at the neckline so you can see right down her front. "My bust isn't very well developed."

"I'd say it's developed just right," Martin says grinning.

Donna laughs.

Mother makes me so mad—standing there smiling. "Let me see now," she says. "If I just take it in a bit in the shoulders. There. How's that?"

"I want to know what your costume looks like," Martin says. "May I touch it?"

"Why not?"

Because, I want to yell.

He smoothes his hands down Donna's sides to the ruffly skirt. "Stiff, stands straight out. What do you call this material?"

"Tulle. The skirt's called a tutu."

Martin slips his hands under the skirt.

Donna wiggles and feigns embarrassment.

I look around to see what my mother thinks of this performance but she's halfway to the kitchen, mumbling something about tea.

I follow her. "Why don't you tell him to leave her alone?"

"Gretchen, they're friends."

"She's teasing him. Ian's her boyfriend."

"Why don't you put some of those butterscotch squares on a plate? After all that dancing, you children must be hungry."

Donna's making him look like a fool. If she really liked him, she would invite him to the dance. Fat chance of that. At school Donna picks the football hunks like Ian.

WEARING HEELS, I'M taller than Barry. His hands are sticky and he backed into the couple behind us. I step on his foot and almost trip him.

"Let's sit this one out," he says.

"Okay."

"You want a drink?"

"Yes, thanks."

I watch Donna and Ian dance. He twirls her around and she kicks her leg up, giving us a full view of her flowered panties. They show right through her pink tights. She's not embarrassed. Now they're doing the jive. Not fair Martin can't get up and dance like that. If he hadn't been injured, he'd be better looking than Ian and his lank blonde hair, not thick black curls like my brother. If Martin wasn't blind, she would like him best.

THERE'S A FULL moon and the cold air feels good after the stuffy gym. Barry takes my hand. His hands are still sticky. Donna, with a pink sweater draped over her shoulders, is walking ahead with Ian.

They stop to kiss. Barry and I stand there like a couple of dummies.

When we reach my place, Donna and Ian wave goodnight and walk on. Barry puts his arm around me and pulls me to him. He clamps his mouth over mine and I can't breathe. Then he touches my breast.

I pull away. "Sorry, I have to go in. My mother'll be out in a second, yelling. I had a really good time. Good night." I leap up the porch steps.

"Hey, wait a minute. How about the show next Friday?"

"Okay, goodnight." I slip inside.

"Good time?" Martin's in Mother's rocking chair.

"Okay."

"Want a snack? I just made tea."

"Kinda tired."

"Sit down a minute and tell me about the dance."

I sit on the edge of the chesterfield. "Everybody wore costumes and there were prizes."

"Did Donna win one?"

"No, the prizes went to this girl dressed as Cleopatra and her boy-friend in a Julius Caesar outfit."

"What music did they play?"

"*Shake, Rattle and Roll.*"

"Bill Haley and His Comets. Did they play any Frankie Laine?"

"I don't know. Has Mother gone to bed?"

"An hour ago. I've got Coke and chips ready. Thought you'd bring Donna. Did you invite her?"

"No. Ian was walking her home."

"I said to ask them all in. I wanted to see Donna."

"Martin, Ian's her boyfriend."

"He's just a kid she hangs out with."

"I'm going to bed. Goodnight."

With my shoes in my hand, I run upstairs. I pull off my costume and throw it on the floor. Yank my flannelette nightgown over my head and crawl into bed, pulling the quilt over me. Then throw it off. Can't get comfortable and I'm not at all sleepy.

I didn't like it when Barry kissed me. I'm supposed to like it. Maybe it's something you have to get used to.

IAN HAS HIS father's car tonight. The movie's funny, *Seven Brides for Seven Brothers.* Not that Donna and Ian are paying any attention.

After the show we go to the Quick Stop. Thank goodness Donna talks so much, since I don't know what to say.

"Guess who I saw last Friday going into the pine grove?" Donna says, smirking.

"Who?" Ian asks.

"Rob Mallory and Marilyn Ellerbeck."

"Isn't he supposed to be going with Karen Green?" Barry asks.

"Karen's visiting her grandma in Toronto and when the cat's away ..." Donna says.

"The mouse goes after the cow." Barry says, sniggering.

"That's not nice." But Donna laughs.

"Accurate though. You seen the tits on that one?" Ian says.

Donna pokes him in the ribs. "Watch your mouth and you better not have noticed them."

I'm relieved when it's time to go home. But we don't go home; we drive up to Blackstone Point. Donna and Ian are fooling around in the front seat. Barry's sweaty hand finds mine. His fingers work their way up my arm. His other arm's around my shoulders. He leans in and kisses me. I close my eyes and feel his hand on my breast. I push him away. His glasses fall off. Oh, I didn't mean to do that.

"What the heck?" Barry mutters. "What's the matter with you?"

I stare out the window. Oh God, I'm blushing. *Domus, domus, domui, domum, domus, domu*—as if Latin could get me out of here. "Donna, let's go home."

"What?" Donna mumbles from the front seat.

When Ian parks in front of my house, Barry doesn't get out of the car. "Goodnight," I say. Wish I could disappear down the nearest groundhog hole.

Quietly, I open the front door. Oh no, Martin's waiting for me.

"How was the show?"

"Okay."

"What did you see?"

"*Seven Brides for Seven Brothers.*"

"A comedy?"

"Yeah."

"Did Donna like it?"

"I dunno. I'm going to bed."

"You're home early. Is everything okay?"

"Fine. Goodnight." I'm up those stairs like a rabbit.

It was horrible when Barry felt my breast.

Too hot. I throw all the covers off and dig my fingernails into my ugly arms, all freckled and hairy. Not any uglier than the rest of me. I smell funny. A bath would be good but I'd wake Mother and Dad.

I open the window, lean out. The cold air feels good. Maybe I could go out to the barn and sleep in the hay.

But Martin's downstairs, or has he gone out? Always asking about Donna. And when she's here, finding excuses to touch her. I hated their canoodling while we were getting ready for the Halloween dance. Made me think about how Martin and I used to play.

Everything would've stayed good if Martin hadn't gone away to school. Our hikes with Mother, the camp fires. And the stories Martin and I made up about the Juperians, tiny half-animal, half-people who came from Jupiter and lived in groundhog holes.

When Martin came home for the summer after his first year away, he was different. Didn't smile much. Sometimes we'd play in the loft on the big swing or fool with the Victrola. The music sounded funny as it wound down. I danced, Martin did his imitations. Or we sat on the couch and made up stories. Martin changed the Juperians into fierce creatures who didn't just ride around on their groundhogs, gathering food from our garden. They'd met their enemies, the ape people. These huge creatures had apelike heads on human bodies. Armed with sling-shots and clubs, they wanted to beat us up. We constantly outwitted them. They were clumsy and stupid.

Rarely that summer did Martin even want to tell stories. Dad had bought him the Brailler. He would sit for hours on the porch typing on the Brailler or reading books in braille. Mother called him "my genius." She wasn't joking. She believes he's a genius. Maybe he is.

The next summer, when he was twelve and I was eight, the other stuff started. In the loft we played "Let me guess what you're wearing."

The trunk was full of dress-up clothes we used for plays. Dad gave us his army uniform. We even had our grandfather's First World War uniforms. Martin was always dressing up in these. I liked Aunt Maggie's flapper dresses. Mother's flapper dresses are preserved in the attic.

Martin said I should wear a blindfold — that would make it fair. It was fun. Blindfolded, it was hard to tell if Martin was wearing the khaki or the red one. The red one, our grandfather's dress uniform, was softer wool, and the buttons were different.

I don't remember when the game turned into something else. I remember giggling a lot as Martin felt me all over trying to figure out which dress I had on.

Martin was thirteen by the time Mother caught us. My underpants were down and Martin was touching my crotch.

Everything changed after that frozen moment. She sent us to our rooms, visited us separately. She spanked me with the leather slipper. The things she said were far worse than the spanking. "How could you engage in such dirty behaviour? I hope you're ashamed of yourself." There was worse to come. "It's your fault," she said.

"He started it."

"Doesn't matter. All you had to do is walk away. Your brother is blind. Boys that age can't help themselves. It's up to the girl to put a stop to it."

We never played the game again. For the rest of that summer we hardly spoke to each other. Martin didn't play in the loft anymore. Said the stairs bothered his legs.

Worst of all is that I liked it. And what sense does that make? When Barry touches me, I want to run away. When I see kids necking behind the school, I'm disgusted. There's something wrong with me. They're not disgusting, I am. They're normal. Me and Martin are the freaks.

I'm glad when Barry doesn't ask me out again.

APRIL NOW, AND most days go on so long I can't stand it. More than ever I want to have school at home. Mother says I should be thankful I can go. And of course she tells me again about how hard she had to work on the chicken farm. How she had to battle her parents to be allowed to go to high school. How her mother would say: "Why do you need more schooling? You're just going to get married."

Dad doesn't say anything about whether or not I should like school. He lets me skip and go on business trips with him.

Those trips have kept me alive all winter. He used to invite Martin to come along but he always says he has work to do. Doesn't have time to be traipsing around the countryside. "Traipsing around the country-side" sounds like something Mother would say. I don't like it when he uses her expressions.

Dad says he's more rested for his meetings if he has some help with the driving. I'm surprised Mother doesn't object more to my missing school. Of course, she knows I'll be ahead in every subject when I get back. I pride myself on that.

I hate school so much that sometimes on my early morning rides I'm tempted to keep on going, ride all day. But every day I come back home and get ready for school. I'm not the rebel I'd like to be.

Today I've been freed. Dad and I are going to Rochester in New York State. I remember going to the Mayo Clinic in Rochester, Minnesota when I was twelve. Nobody told me what the doctors said about Martin.

We leave in the middle of the night and, as we step into the cold fresh air, even the birds are quiet.

By dawn I'm driving on the Thruway. I've never been on a highway like this. A long white truck hurtles past. Our Ford trembles, but I'm not scared. I can't even see the oncoming traffic. The median is treed and as wide as a field, and we have two lanes. A silver transport with two trailers pulls abreast. I speed up and keep ahead of him. We're climbing a long hill. That'll slow him down. Our Ford's V8's a match for any truck.

I'm flying along this grey strip that goes on forever. The sun's just coming up. I'd like to drive to the Florida Keys that Martin's always talking about. That's where Hemingway lives. Martin's reading one of his books. He's supposed to be reading Herodotus, one of the Great Books. Hemingway has adventures. I haven't read anything by him, but driving the New York Thruway at dawn, I'm ready for an adventure.

Dad and I are going to meet for lunch at the Howard Johnson Hotel. Before his meeting he took me into the hotel and showed me where the dining room is. When I come in, I'm just to give my name and the waiter will take me to a table. If Dad's a little late, I should just order a Hires and wait for him.

The hotel's on a main street, Erie Boulevard. I take the first side street but don't make any more turns. Too afraid of getting lost. I walk for a long time. At first it's just dull businesses — a hardware store, a radio repair place, a dry cleaners. Soon, grand houses line the streets, with their gingerbread trim, second-storey balconies. But most of them need painting. The lawns are littered with old bicycles, toys, even a rusty fridge. They make me think of Sharon's place. The first person I see is an old Negro man sitting on a front porch. At another house an old lady is rocking on the porch, and two toddlers are playing by the steps. They're Negroes too. There aren't any Negroes in Grenville. I know it's not fair how they're treated. I'd like to sit on that porch and talk with the grandmother. Ask her if "the blues" is her favourite music. I won't, of course. She'd think I was nosy. I'd better go back. I'll do some French vocabulary in the lobby before lunch.

Dad shows me sketches of the church he's designing, very modern looking, all wood and glass. All the buildings he's shown me are modern, even the houses.

"Dad, you must like modern-looking houses."

"Yes, I do."

"But we live in an old one."

"You know it was your great-grandmother's place."

"Do we live there because Mother wants to?"

"Her grandmother died while I was away in the army. Your mother inherited the house. She wanted to be near her family. Do you remember your grandparents?"

"Granddad had a lot of unfriendly chickens. He died when I was four, right?"

"You would remember your grandmother better."

"I didn't like her much."

"Neither did I."

"Oh!" I didn't know that. He was always nice to her. Unlike me who deliberately messed up the doilies on the arms and backs of her chairs. She was always crocheting.

"She said your brother's accident wouldn't have happened if your mother had stayed in Grenville. She also said to your mother: 'You thought yourself so smart going off to Toronto.' There are some people, Gretchen, who can't stand anyone, not even their own children, doing anything they didn't do."

"Martin fell from a fourth-floor balcony, didn't he?" Will he talk about the accident?

"Yes, but accidents can happen anywhere. Actually, the majority of childhood accidents occur on farms. Children fall out of haylofts or get hurt on machinery."

"Billy Knapp was killed falling under their mower. We said prayers for him at church. You were away that Sunday."

"I heard about the Knapp boy. Your grandmother made your mother feel so guilty."

"How did Martin fall? Mother won't talk about it."

"All I know is he unlocked the balcony door and fell over the railing."

"That's awful."

"Yes, it is. But nobody's fault. When I was six, I fell off the porch roof. Fortunately, I only broke my leg."

"Did Martin break his legs?"

"Yes, but the head injuries were more serious."

"Why can't he walk properly?"

"There was brain and spinal damage, with his pelvis and both legs badly broken."

"Mother never talks about it."

"And best you don't ask her questions. She feels so guilty even though she shouldn't. Parents can't watch children every second of the day, and accidents do happen. If my head had hit the sidewalk instead of my leg, I could be in Martin's condition. Do you understand what I'm saying, Gretchen?"

"Accidents aren't anybody's fault. That's why they're called accidents."

"That's right. Now, what would you like for dessert? They have fifty-five different flavours of ice cream."

We're on our way home now. Dad had an unexpected meeting in the afternoon. He took me to the library. I did next week's French chapter, three pages of algebra and studied for my history test.

The low sun and red sky make the fields look silky. Even the high-way looks soft like one of those French paintings Dad showed me at the gallery in St. Thomas. It seems the road goes on forever. Doesn't, of course, ends in Buffalo. "I'm always sad at dusk and want to get home," I tell Dad.

"I could take over the driving. You must be getting tired."

"I like driving. And going places. But then I start feeling lonely for Misty and Mother and Martin. I don't want to grow up and leave home. Donna says she can't wait to."

"Later on you'll want to see new places. Grenville's a small old town."

"I like old things."

"So do I, but new things too. I admire old churches and old hous-es but I like to design new ones. And you'll have new experiences—some good and some not so good. 'Yet all experience is an arch where through gleams the untravelled world.' Do you know who wrote that?"

"No."

"Tennyson. A good line to remember."

He gets me to repeat it after him, memorize it. "Yet all experience is an ..."

"Arch."

"Where through gleams the untravelled world."

THIS SUMMER I'VE got a job at Haun's Tourist Camp, across the road from the lake and two miles from our house. Widowed Mrs. Haun is really nice. Each morning I clean the cabins. She does the bathrooms. The bathrooms are separate, one building for men and one for women. She says that's not a nice job for a young girl. I'm usually finished by one or two in the afternoon. She pays me $20 a week.

The clubhouse has a kitchen and a big comfy room with couches and tables, where the tourists cook and hang out. There are outside picnic tables for good weather. I start at seven-thirty and the first thing I do, while the tourists are still sleeping, is clean the clubhouse. There's a bookshelf with stacks of magazines and books the tourists have left behind. I found a Zane Grey, and Mrs. Haun said to borrow any I wanted.

I should be cleaning. Instead, I'm searching the shelves for another Zane Grey. When I can't find one, I browse through the magazines. *Look* and *The Saturday Evening Post* we have at home. *True Romance* and *True Confessions* I haven't seen before. In *True Confessions*, I read a story about this girl running away from home because her father beats her. I forget all about cleaning until Mrs. Haun comes in. I stick the magazine back on the shelf and apologize.

"Take any you want home with you," she says.

Tonight, I ride my bike straight home after work and take the magazine up to the loft. The girl, Tammy, uses her babysitting money to get to New York. When she's out of money and hungry, she meets a tall dark-haired man who takes her to a fancy restaurant. She falls in love with him. I think this is going to be the happy ending. But it isn't, because later on he beats her up and makes her be a prostitute. She runs away and hitchhikes back home. I think her father will be pleased to see her and sorry he hit her. She walks in the door and says: "Hello Pa." He yells: "You slut" and knocks her down. I can't believe this is the end of the story. I'm crying, but I want to read the next one.

It's about a brother and sister who fall in love without knowing they're siblings. They think they're cousins, which is bad, but not as bad as brother and sister. They run away together. The police catch them. The policeman calls them ignorant Okies who don't even know incest is a crime. The boy goes to jail, but she's sent back to her parents, I guess because she's only fourteen. She takes a razor and slashes her wrists in the bathtub.

I don't cry after this story. I go for a long walk. Don't even take Misty with me. I think about the game Martin and I used to play. Now I have a name for it, incest. For a long time I've thought something was wrong with me. Now I know. I'm definitely a freak.

TODAY, AUGUST 21ST, 1956, I got my driver's license. Donna's so jealous.

Dad let me borrow the car and I picked Donna up after work. We drove around for a while. We stopped for ice cream at the restaurant at Blackstone Point. She's been to the dancehall there.

I'm in big trouble and it's not fair because when I borrowed the car Mother and Martin were in his room working on St. Thomas Aquinas —third year of the Great Books. I'm not supposed to interrupt when they're working.

Martin didn't say anything to me afterwards but Mother came into my room as I was getting ready for bed.

"Why didn't you take your brother with you?"

"You and Martin were busy. Dad said I could go for a drive."

"Martin would've enjoyed it. And with Donna along it would've meant a lot to him."

I'M BEGINNING TO regret getting my driver's license. Martin wants to go to the drive-in. How could he watch a movie? Of course, I didn't ask him that. He said: "Why don't you invite Donna to come with us?" I should've known that's what he had in mind.

He won't let it rest. He asks me practically every day that Dad's home with the car. Fortunately, Dad's away this week. He's speaking at a convention in Rochester and attending the dedication of that church he designed.

Come Monday, Martin's right back at me. "Ask Donna to go to the drive-in."

Mother says: "Ask her for Friday or Saturday. Either night you could have the car."

"Why can't Martin phone her?"

Mother frowns. "All three of you are friends. Why shouldn't you call her?"

"Why shouldn't he?"

"We don't know how her family would react. Her brother's a rough type."

EVEN THOUGH DONNA agreed to Saturday, I think I'm saved. Dad wants Mother to go to a concert in St. Thomas.

"Martin needs the car tonight."

"Martin?" he says.

"Gretchen's driving him and Donna to the drive-in."

I see she understands as well as I do my role as the chauffeur.

"Doesn't sound like much fun for Gretchen." He understands too.

"Nonsense," Mother says, "she likes the drive-in."

MARTIN INSISTS ALL three of us crowd into the front seat. He's in the middle with Donna squished against the door. When we get there, he tells me to get in the back. He slides over into the driver's seat.

I wish I could go to sleep.

Martin has his arm around Donna. He kisses her.

She kisses him back before pushing him away. "The movie's starting," she says.

"They're all written from the same formula," my know-it-all brother says.

"I like westerns," she says.

"I'll tell you the plot." He nuzzles her ear.

"No thanks."

"Indians are attacking the settlement."

"Martin, shut up!" She punches his arm.

"Oh my, female screams. The Indians must be kidnapping the blonde maiden."

"Martin!" She laughs and clamps a hand over his mouth.

He kisses her hand, and even more disgusting, licks it.

"Bad boy," she says, giggling.

What a flirt.

"I'm the rescuing cowboy. Bang, bang, Indians fall down dead. Cowboy has an arrow in his arm, but he yanks it out himself, greatly impressing the fair maiden."

"Martin, shut up and keep your hands to yourself. Ian wouldn't like me fooling around."

"That kid? Forget him."

I try not to listen.

O
N A LATE September day when the maples lining Main Street form a brilliant arch, I take the long route home — out Main to the Garrison Road. School and my lack of a boyfriend seem far away compared to the golden leaves and the roadsides abloom with purple asters and goldenrod. Royal colours.

When I open the screen door Martin says: "You're late. Dad had a heart attack. Mr. Leaman drove Mother to the St. Thomas hospital. You're to make supper. Call Donna and invite her over."

"What?"

"Call Donna."

"When did it happen?"

"I think he'd just set out."

"Is he really sick?"

"I doubt it, because he drove himself to the hospital. Mother said she might not be back till late so call Donna."

"I'm going riding."

"What about supper?" he says.

"It's only five. Maybe Mother'll be home soon."

I ride Misty out to the lake. I don't bother with the saddle.

People can die from heart attacks. Mother's friend, Miss Hunt, did. She was old. Dad's only forty-eight.

He was sick last winter. Had to rest a lot. Mother said he'd been working too hard. He does work hard — all that driving.

He should've let me go today. I wanted to. Mother said: "You're in grade eleven now. You miss too much school."

I work on my own and am ahead in every subject. She knows this.

When he and I drove to Windsor last week we stayed overnight at Miss Talbot's apartment. She's a reporter for the Windsor newspaper. Mother and she taught at the same school in Toronto. She has a balcony garden with plants in black pots from Oaxaca in Mexico. She gave me two black pottery cats, one for me and one for Mother. Miss Talbot spends her holidays in Mexico. She's writing a novel. But she doesn't have a husband or children. She must be very lonely.

I could've driven Dad to the hospital. And if she'd let me go with him to Toronto yesterday he wouldn't have been tired and had a heart attack.

We didn't know there was anything wrong with his heart. Why was he home sick that winter? Couldn't have been anything serious or they would've told me.

I urge Misty into a canter. Maybe Mother's back.

I'm almost there when I see Mr. Leaman's car pulling out of our driveway. Mother must be home. I let Misty into his stall and run to the house.

She and Martin are in the living room, drinking Dad's sherry. That's strange. They don't notice me. Mother's eyes are all puffy. She's been crying. My mother doesn't cry.

"Hi, I'm home."

Mother looks up. "Oh Gretchen ..."

I'm scared. She has such a strange look in her eyes.

"Your dad ... he had a heart attack." She chokes and pushes her clenched fist against her mouth. She gets up and comes to me. "He died at two-forty-five this afternoon."

"No. He wasn't even sick."

She sets her glass down. The sherry sloshes. She hugs me and I feel her shaking. "Sit down, dear. I know it's a shock." She leads me to the chesterfield and sits down beside me. Clenches my hand. She sobs. "He's had a bad heart for a long time."

"Why didn't I know that?"

"We didn't want to worry you," Martin says. We?

"I better get some supper on." She lets go my hand, stands up. Looks around as if she can't remember where she is.

"I told Gretchen to start supper," my brother says.

"You were riding, dear?" She speaks in a whisper.

"I'll help now."

"Thank you, Gretchen. We'll just have sandwiches and tea."

I get out the bread and start buttering.

"There's ham and cheese," Mother says. "Not much of a supper."

"Doesn't matter."

"Where are those jam tarts? Martin likes those."

She's looking in the fridge. She doesn't put tarts in there. I get them out of the cupboard.

Just as we're sitting down to eat, Martin says: "Gretchen, call Donna. She's one of the family. Somebody should tell her."

I ignore him.

"Then I'll call her," he says.

"Do that, dear," Mother says, stirring and stirring her tea.

The phone's in the hall. I hear him giving Donna's number to the operator. The sandwiches are dry, the ham smells. I drink my tea. When can I go to bed?

I'm helping Mother with the dishes when the Hylands arrive, Lois and her mother. Lois has taught grade four for at least twenty years. They've brought tins of cookies. Mother makes more tea. She seems calmer now. The phone's going to ring. It'll be the hospital. They'll say it was all a mistake.

"We'll have our tea in the living room. Gretchen, put some of the cookies on a plate. No, not that old white one. Get one of the cake plates from the china cabinet."

Why does the plate matter now? They're all perched on the living-room chairs.

Old Mrs. Hyland's talking about my parents' wedding. How my dad was so handsome. She's holding my mother's hand.

Shut up, you old bat. He still is handsome.

Mother withdraws her hand. "More tea?"

Donna arrives and hugs me, erupting in tears. I know I should be crying, but I can't.

Donna hugs Martin. He clings, his hands moving all over her. I squirm. He should be ashamed. Has he forgotten our dad is dead? Mother tells me to get a cup for Donna.

Everybody's drinking tea and eating cookies, just like a party. "I have to do my homework."

They all stare at me but Mother says: "That's a good idea, dear."

I go to my room. The air's stuffy. I open the window and pull the screen off. Mother nails the screen on each spring and every summer I remove the nails. It's raining. I stick my head out. The icy rain feels good. I'm so hot. I stick my arms out too.

Dad will never again feel rain. I throw myself on my bed and weep.

When Mother comes in I pretend to be asleep. She tucks the quilt around me and leaves.

THE VISITATION'S HORRIBLE. Mother and Martin and I are lined up on a row of chairs. Dad's in his casket at the far end of the room.

People keep coming. I don't know most of them. We have to stand up each time a new person comes over. Some people just pat my shoulder. Others hug me. Total strangers. A few even kiss me.

Some of the people are from the church but the others, Mother says, worked with Dad to design buildings. She sits very straight, her hands clasped together. She did a strange thing before we left. She ate a raw onion sandwich. "Need to fortify myself," she said.

They all tell me what a wonderful person my father was. I know that.

Most people shake Martin's hand. Except the old church ladies who pat his arm. Nobody hugs and kisses Martin. He wears a big scowl. I scowl too, but they still hug me.

I want to go home. Want to go to bed.

The women from the church are the worst. "Doesn't he look nice," one says.

And another: "Such a handsome man."

He looks awful. I can't bear to look. He looks like a wax doll. Like this doll has stolen his hair and clothes. My dad has thick, curly grey-black hair. Now only his hair looks real.

Donna comes in and hugs me and I hug back. I want to say: "Let's get out of here. Ride double on Misty out to the beach." I don't speak.

Martin pulls over a chair for Donna and she sits between us. He holds her hand. She looks uncomfortable.

Aunt Maggie comes in. I stand up to greet her. She envelops me and I'm terrified I'm going to cry. She tries to hug my mother but Mother turns away. Aunt Maggie talks to everyone, telling them all about her brother.

She comes home with us.

"Shall I make tea?" I ask Mother.

"Yes, make a cup for your aunt. Then go to bed. I'm going to lie down."

Martin comes into the kitchen and gets Dad's bottle of whiskey from the cupboard. "What are you doing?" I ask him.

"Maggie needs a drink and so do I."

"Mother won't like it."

"I'm in charge now."

For a moment I truly hate him. Dad has to come back. I want Mother to get up and make Martin behave. I pour the tea and bring it in. My aunt says I should have a little drink — it would make me feel better. I say no thank you and go to bed.

The church was full. Aunt Maggie wore a red dress. Said she didn't believe in wearing black for funerals. "We should celebrate his life," she said.

Mother wore her beige suit and said nothing.

Everybody came back to the house. We used the good Wedgwood dishes and Mother's best damask cloth. The women from the church were doing it all. Mother sat in her rocking chair. Martin walked around holding Donna's hand. He spoke to everyone.

Aunt Maggie left right after the graveyard. Evening now and everybody has gone home. We're here without Dad. Shouldn't feel so strange. After all, he was often away days at a time.

Mother sits hunched over in her rocking chair. My mother who said so often: "Sit up straight or when you're an old lady you'll have a hump on your back."

Mother looks like an old lady. I hadn't noticed the grey in her dark hair. Stranger still, she seems smaller. I want her to tell me it's past my bedtime. I want her to notice I'm squirming with itchiness. I've broken out in hives. She just sits there like she's gone away.

I want my bossy mother back. I want her to tell me what's wrong with the neighbours, the town, what's wrong with me. I want her to fix things.

Martin brings her sherry. Where's all this sherry coming from? Mother always drinks tea.

Martin, strangely, seems bigger. He keeps saying: "Don't worry, Mother. I'll look after everything."

In the past when people visited, he either read a book or went to his room. Now, he greets visitors at the door and ushers them out when they leave. Tells Mother to stay seated. Just rest. He'll look after everything.

I heard him tell Donna that he'll take charge of business matters. Mother has always looked after bill paying. Dad was away so much. How could Martin pay the bills? Has he forgotten he's blind?

He also told Donna that Dad left an insurance policy worth $200,000. Just the interest on that will give us a generous income, he tells her. It almost sounds like he's boasting.

FALL WAS ALWAYS so beautiful but now September will mean one thing, my dad's death. I go to school in a daze and come home the same way. Misty and I wander the back roads.

Martin never used to want to go anywhere. Now he wants to go all the time. "Call Donna up. Let's go for a drive." I ignore him.

Friday, when I come in from school, Martin hands me the car keys. "We're picking Donna up at five," he says. "We're having supper at the Quick Stop."

"I didn't phone her." He'd been nagging me about it ever since the funeral.

"No, I did," he says.

When we enter the Quick Stop, I'm relieved to see there are only a few kids from the high school and nobody I know. Martin chooses a booth by the jukebox and orders hamburgers, fries, Cokes and butterscotch sundaes for all of us.

He flashes a twenty-dollar bill. "Do you think this two-bit place can change this?"

Mrs. Taylor's face is expressionless as she brings our food, takes his money and brings him his change. We'll eat, and this will be over.

The worst isn't over. Martin bends over the jukebox, his face almost touching the buttons. He waves his ten-dollar bill and in a loud voice demands nickels.

Donna jumps up, takes the bill and gets change, a whole roll of nickels, from Mrs. Taylor.

Donna reads off the songs: *Rock around the Clock, Love and Marriage, Ain't That a Shame, Yellow Rose of Texas.*

He inserts nickel after nickel. Oh no. We'll never get home.

Martin complains about the sound quality. His Philco radio produces a better sound. He pulls a silver flask from his pocket. I read the initials on it — BJT. "Is that Dad's?"

"Dad's rye too, little sister. He doesn't need it." Martin pours rye in our Cokes.

"I don't want any and it's not yours."

"Mine now. Drink up."

"Shh," Donna says. "You're going to get us kicked out."

I hope we are kicked out. That Mrs. Taylor just stands there by the cash register looking away means she feels sorry for us.

Some kids from the high school come in. They wave and call to Donna. Martin glowers at them. Donna blushes. At least Ian's not with them.

"Sorry Martin, but we're going to have to leave. I start work at the drugstore at seven," Donna says.

A likely story. Whose shift starts at seven? The drugstore closes at eight. But, thank God, we can go home.

I'm so mad at Martin. I feel like telling Mother about the flask. I don't though.

SATURDAY NIGHT MARTIN and I are on the porch. It's dark but Mother's still out in the garden walloping away at the weeds. Martin made tea for us. Out of the blue he asks me: "What does Mrs. Taylor look like?"

"Plump, grey-haired."

"I figured her as a bleached blond. Does she smoke?"

"I can't remember. Yeah, maybe."

"I'm sure she does. Hard to be certain. The restaurant was so smoky. A cigarette always in the corner of her mouth would suit her."

"Oh, Martin!"

"And a tight, red dress, or gold slinky fabric."

"She wears flowered blouses and navy slacks."

"Tight I bet, showing her bum."

"Martin! Mrs. Taylor's slacks are baggy. She's not some character in those Mickey Spillane books you read. She's just a dumpy woman who runs a crummy restaurant."

RAIN POUNDS THE windows. Even in bed I'm cold. Mother won't turn the furnace on until Thanksgiving. The woodstove in the living room keeps the downstairs warm but it's so clammy up here. Might as well get up.

The living room's cold too. Before Dad died Mother was usually up by six. I fix the cats some bread and milk, grab my raincoat and step into my barn boots. Outside, I stand, letting the rain wet my face. I watch the wind whip the last leaves from the maple. I want my dad. Not fair I'll never see him again. Not fair he's dead, and we're still alive. I don't feel so sorry for Martin anymore. I used to think Dad had everything that Martin could never have. He was a handsome architect who'd been a football hero and a soldier. It was only Martin that God cheated. He cheats everybody. We all have to die.

Dad, I need you. I never even got to say goodbye. I yank up my hood and head for the barn.

There's a corrugated cardboard box next to the door. The wind must've blown it here. I pick it up and hear a faint mewling. A baby blanket covers a soaking-wet kitten. It's shivering but starts purring the moment I pick it up. I tuck it inside my raincoat and open the door. Misty whinnies. Tiger and Muggins run to the food dish. Her new kittens totter along behind.

I set the wet stray down next to the dish. Tiger hisses. Her paw darts out, and she rips the kitten right across his face. The kitten streaks toward the hay bales and I grab Tiger before she can go after him. I feed and water Misty. "Too wet to ride this morning," I tell him and groom him while he's eating.

Tiger's at the stray again. When I pick him up, he purrs desperately. There's blood on his nose. He's about three months old, looks well fed. Not the first time somebody's dropped off a kitten. I'll have to take him up to the house. Mother'll call the Humane Society. No way Tiger'll let him stay.

I tuck the kitten under my raincoat and head out. There's something on the road. I go and look. A dead tabby kitten — must've been hit by a car. I put it in the long grass by the barn. I'll bury it later.

Mother's up now and has the fire going. I fix some bread and milk for the kitten. Mother helps me find a box and an old sweater to line it. The kitten curls up and goes to sleep. We sit down by the stove with our tea. She strokes the kitten with her stockinged foot. It purrs and chews at her toes. "It's a tough life, eh little cat?" Mother says.

"Mother, don't you just hate how people drop off kittens? They don't care what happens to them."

"One time at the church supper I mentioned the trouble we were having finding homes for the kittens. Ray Green says: 'Knock 'em on the head and bury 'em.' I told him that was cruel. 'No it ain't. They don't know what's comin'. I was digging the hole and they were playin' around, jumping in and out.'" Mother sighs. "I've always thought if Hitler came to Grenville he could find people to do his handiwork. Hitler wanted to dispose of all crippled children."

THE WEATHER HAS become summery with less than a week till Thanksgiving. The little stray, now called Caesar, didn't go the Humane Society. Martin wanted him. Said he's a spunky little devil.

I was hoping the new kitten would get Martin's mind off Donna. No such luck. He's determined we all go to the dance hall at Blackstone Point. "But Martin, you can't dance," I said.

"We'll listen to the music. Soak up the atmosphere."

"I hate dances."

"You don't have to dance. Take a book and wait in the car if you want."

"Martin, Ian's Donna's boyfriend."

"For the moment."

"Oh Martin."

"I need to get out, Gretchen. We have the car. Why not? The dance hall closes up after Thanksgiving, so this Friday or Saturday are the only times we can go."

I phone Donna, praying she'll claim she's busy. She agrees to Saturday night.

MARTIN ADDS RYE to their Cokes. They're giggling like a couple of idiots.

"Want some, Gretchen?" Donna asks.

"No!" The sight of Martin with Dad's flask is enough to make me feel like throwing something.

"One, two, three o'clock, four o'clock rock." His foot pounds the floor in time to the music. "We're gonna rock tonight. C'mon chick, let's dance."

"Put your flask away. You're going to get us arrested," Donna says, tittering.

He's so keen on her, why doesn't he listen to her?

"Have a little drinkie and forget the cops. Those dumb buggers are too busy eying the chicks."

AFTER THE FIASCO at the dance hall, there's big trouble at school for Donna. I heard one of Ian's friends, another football player, say to her in the hall: "Where's your weirdo boyfriend, that Martin guy?"

"He's not my boyfriend."

"That's not what I heard. Why would you choose a retard over a swell guy like Ian?"

"He's not my boyfriend and he's smarter than you are."

DONNA AND I walk home from school together. I can tell she's really down in the dumps.

"Did you and Ian break up?"

"Yeah."

"I'm sorry about the way Martin acted."

"Not your fault, or his. I would've broken up with Ian anyway. You know Martin could wear dark glasses and his eyes would look more normal."

"My brother looks fine!"

"I know. I'm just saying ..."

"He can see outlines and light and dark. He couldn't with sunglasses."

"Don't get mad. I was only trying to help."

"Sorry. Too bad you and Ian broke up. I know you liked him."

"Sharon saw him flirting with that slut Judy Baird. I'm just mad I don't have a date for the Halloween dance."

"You'll get one. You're really pretty."

"At the moment I don't feel pretty."

"When we get home, do you want to ride Misty in the paddock?

She shakes her head and walks faster. "Got a lot of homework."

"I could help you with it."

"I better go straight home or Mom'll yell."

We part at my house. I don't go in. Once she's out of sight, I go to the barn and sit in the hay with the cats. She doesn't fool me. Homework? Donna doesn't do homework.

THE TRIPS WITH Dad made school endurable. Sometimes when I wake up, I forget he's dead. Feels like he's just off on a trip. Sometimes, I deliberately fool myself into thinking that. I pretend today's the day he's coming home. When I stop pretending, I feel worse.

SOMETHING GOOD HAS happened. I guess Mother knew how bored I was. I'm combining grades eleven and twelve, doing some courses by correspondence. I wanted to do it all at home, but this was the compromise.

At least I'm not bored. I have to struggle to keep up. I like the correspondence courses. I do them at night. Since Dad died, I've had trouble sleeping. Now I do schoolwork far into the night until I'm so tired I fall asleep with the light on and my books spread out on my bed.

I haven't won. Wanted to quit school. But I'll be out of there a year sooner. I'm still in homeroom with Donna. In both grades, the kids leave me alone. This suits me fine. I just want out.

HOME GETS ODDER every day. I guess I should be thankful Mother's getting up early like she always used to. But by mid-November she still wasn't using the furnace. When Mother finally turns the furnace on she keeps the thermostat at fifty-five. I told her my room was cold and she spread another blanket on my bed. She lets Martin use a plug-in electric heater, even though his room isn't far from the living room.

"Why don't we turn up the furnace?"

"Oil costs money. There's lots of good firewood just outside."

That's another thing. Now the garden's finished, she's down in the bush getting wood. Every fall, for as far back as I can remember, we bought a cord of wood.

Sounds like we're poor. Was Martin wrong when he told Donna Dad left us so much money? But Mother told me there's a separate ten thousand he set aside for my education.

I'm freezing. I jump out of bed and pull on my clothes. Quickly use the bathroom and head downstairs. I stop by the roaring fire to rub my hands back to life. When I open the back door, a now familiar scene greets me. A branch, must be ten inches thick and as many feet long, is slung over the saw horse. For years that saw horse was stored in the barn. Now, here's Mother, Swedish saw in hand, working away. A cold morning, but her face is dripping sweat.

"Mother, please, turn up the furnace."

"Gretchen, what's the matter?" Mother stops sawing and wipes the sweat from her face with her coat sleeve. "Those trees the ice storms brought down should've been looked after years ago."

"Are we poor now?"

"No dear, your dad left us well provided for. I don't want the wood to go to waste."

"You could use some of the money he left for my education."

"We have plenty of money. But it's important I manage the money so your brother will be looked after."

"Isn't he going to make money as a writer?"

"That's an uncertain future. After I'm gone, he'll need a house-keeper and an income."

"I would rather I had the place and Martin the money. He wants to go to New York."

"Gretchen, you'll grow up, leave this small mean town, get an education, get married and have a new home. Not going to be so easy for Martin. Your dad and I agreed that after I'm gone this place would be Martin's. It wasn't necessary to give you the money for your education because I would've seen to that. Always been my dream. But your dad wanted to do it this way, directly—from him to you. You better get along now and do your chores."

All the time I'm doing chores, I keep thinking there's something peculiar. Why was my education mentioned in the will? Dad would've been fifty when I went to university. Did he know he was going to die? I had a right to know.

Did she love him? She must, she mourns him so. Last night, when I was doing my homework next to the wood stove and she was reading, out of the blue she said: "If after the war we'd moved back to Toronto, he wouldn't have been away so much. I squandered the years we had together."

"He still would've travelled. That one project was in Rochester."

"When I took the job teaching in Toronto, Ma said: 'You think yourself so smart.' I did, you know. Thought I could walk away from the chicken farm and have this wonderful life. Teaching public school was just a stepping-stone to university. How naïve I was."

"Do you wish you hadn't got married?"

"Of course not. I loved your father and I'd always wanted children. We had such plans. We were going to live and work in England, but times were tough during the Depression. Your dad always had work but sometimes had to work as a draughtsman. The war changed everything. Five years is too long to be apart."

I didn't know what to say. I turned to my Latin translation. *Cum Caesar in Galliam venit ...*

I give Misty his oats and curry him until his coat shines. This place will be Martin's — the barn, Misty's stable, the woodlot, everything. He already refers to "his" house. Supposed to belong to all of us — our home. He'll sell it and it'll be gone. He told me so. I would never sell our great-grandmother's house.

Not until I'm walking to school do I realize Mother's never intended that Martin go to New York.

A couple of days later, Martin thumps off to his room and we're alone after supper. They must've been arguing before I got home. I come right out with it. "Don't you want him to go to New York?"

"Not a matter of wanting. It's facing reality. He couldn't possibly look after himself."

"He can get a meal when he wants to, make tea."

"New York's a rough place. There are muggers on the streets. What chance would Martin have? Gretchen, I haven't told you this but the Mayo Clinic doctors told us he'll most likely be in a wheelchair by the time he's forty. The arthritis had already started in his spine and hips. Don't say anything to Martin about this. I don't want him worrying."

"He walks pretty well, same as always."

"You don't understand what medical expenses there'll be. The Shislers were well off, retired farmers, nice little house in Grenville and a tidy sum in the bank. Then John got cancer. He was in and out of hospital. By the time he died they'd used up all their savings. She had to go into Sunset Haven. That's not going to happen to Martin."

WITH THE WOODSTOVE blazing, it should feel cozy here. Snow pings against the window, only ten days till Christmas. I won't think about Christmas, but about Caesar's wars. Latin's not my best subject. Having to concentrate so hard is good. Yet another battle. Caesar and the Gauls have nothing to do with me. I like that.

Nine o'clock. A year ago Mother would've been telling me to get to bed. She's in her rocking chair on the other side of the stove, reading Galileo. She's doing the fifth-year readings now. Her Great Books club disbanded in its second year. One of the older ladies died and another moved into Sunset Haven. Some of the others wanted to branch out in their reading. One even suggested an Agatha Christie. "How could she think that was educational?" Mother said. "The retired schoolteachers are the backbone of the club."

Sad music's coming from Martin's room. This evening, like most others, he's working in his room. At ten Mother'll make tea. With luck, he'll join us. He's in his third year of readings, doing *Paradise Lost* with Mother. Most often, he reads modern books and works at his own writing. He's written several stories about the Silorians but published nothing yet. Mother says he should take out all the vulgar language and do something more realistic. She told me he's writing a children's story that she quite likes.

She's made the tea now and, thank goodness, when she asks him to join us, he does. He's actually smiling.

He hands me a stack of typed pages, not braille. "'The Invisible Kitten' is a kids' story. Let me know what you think. Mother's already read it."

"It's good," she says. "The realism in it reminds me of Ernest Thomson Seton's stories. The fairy tale element is of course another genre."

"Damn it, Mother, just let Gretchen read it."

I hate the hurt look on her face but she's smiling now. "Anyone for an oatmeal cookie with their tea?"

I wait until I'm in bed to read, glad it's not in braille. Mother must've retyped it to send it to a publisher.

In the story the father tells his children the kittens will get good homes if they drop them off at a farmer's barn. The children believe his lies.

Cold and hungry, the kittens wander down the road. A truck driver going too fast runs over a kitten named Tiger. Fluffy and an invisible kitten sit down by Tiger and wash her with their tongues. But she's dead and they're cold and wet, so they go on, looking for shelter. There isn't any.

I'm crying long before I get to the end. Mother says to always finish a story — doesn't matter how sad it makes you. And she's right. People should know how cruel it is to drop off kittens. I think back to the dead kitten I buried. Dug the hole, made him a hay bed and shovelled in the dirt.

I go quietly down the dark stairs. The light's still on in Martin's room. I knock.

"Who is it?"

"Gretchen."

"Come in."

"Your story's wonderful. It made me cry."

"I'm going to send it to an American children's magazine."

"I'm sure you'll get this one published."

"Let's hope so."

"I like it a lot more than that science fiction stuff."

"An entirely different genre. I write a lot of science fiction. Good market for it in the States."

THE NEXT NIGHT Donna comes by and the three of us play poker. Mother brings us some of her light Christmas cake. My favourite — lots of whole almonds and candied cherries.

"Delicious," Donna says. "Sure tastes better than the store-bought cake my mom gets."

"It's supposed to season for six weeks. I'm late with it this year." She always fusses over Donna. She's already apologized twice for there being only ginger ale. It's embarrassing.

She didn't tell us she was coming and it's been two weeks since she's visited. Needless to say, Martin's been making a fool of himself from the moment she arrived — laughing too loud and making dumb jokes at which Donna giggles with phony enthusiasm.

We play poker until ten. Mother brings us tea and tells us she's off to bed.

"Going to bed soon, Gretchen?" Martin asks.

That's his third hint but she's my friend too. "Yeah, I'm tired. You going soon, Donna?"

Martin scowls.

"We'll just have a nightcap," she says. "You want some, Gretchen?"

"No thanks." As I head upstairs, I see her open her bag and pull out a bottle of beer. She's sixteen. She's not supposed to have beer. If Mother knew, she wouldn't be so delighted every time Donna shows up.

She only comes to our place when she has nothing better to do, or because she feels sorry for us.

MONDAY, WHEN I get home from school, there's a sorry-looking Christmas tree leaning against the living room wall. "Will you give me a hand, Gretchen?" Mother says.

I hold the tree steady while she hammers it to the base made from a couple of pieces of two-by-four. The same base we've used for years. Now it's falling apart like everything else around here. "At Donna's they have a metal one you just set the tree in."

"An unnecessary extravagance." She hammers a couple of small pieces at an angle to the trunk. "There. Let go now."

I do. The tree falls over and we both leap to catch it. She hammers on another support. "That should do it," she says.

I let go. The tree's a small straggly pine she cut from our woodlot. Our trees used to touch the ceiling. Dad always brought home the tree and put it up.

"Call your brother. You children can decorate it while I get supper."

Children—I'm sixteen, he's twenty—he won't help. But he surprises me. Without speaking we untangle the lights and get them up. We work quickly—on with the tinsel and glass balls. I fasten on a glass bird Dad bought in Toronto.

"Enough?" Martin says.

"Yeah." There are lots more decorations. I push the salt-dough Santa I made in grade two to the bottom of the box.

He sits down with a book. Caesar, who's about twice the size he was when he arrived, jumps on his lap. Martin strokes him and the cat curls up and purrs. I want to go to sleep. I pick up Mother's Galileo and try to read. Can't make head nor tail of it.

Mother frowns. "Why didn't you plug in the lights?"

"Guess we forgot," I say.

She plugs them in. Rummages in the box and pulls out the star. "You forgot the treetop star too. It was my grandmother's," she says, and fastens it to the top branch. "There, that's better. Come to supper now."

ON CHRISTMAS MORNING, Mother and I walk to church. Since Dad died I haven't objected to going. Usually we drive but today she wants to walk. There's fresh snow and every house has Christmas lights turned on. I feel like smashing them. What does she feel? I don't know.

Normally, I like the Christmas service. We sing lots of carols. Today I just want it to be over. She must too, because she hurries me out without talking to anyone. We stride through the snow without speaking.

Mother puts the turkey platter at her end of the table. She asks Martin to sit in Dad's place at the head of the table. Why don't they leave Dad's chair empty in honour of him? After a mostly silent dinner (Mother did go on about the beauty of the fresh snow) we sit around the tree to open our presents. Mother hands them out. That was Dad's job.

Aunt Maggie sent a great pile of gifts: two shirts for Martin, a blue-velvet bathrobe for my Mother, a pearl necklace and a mauve angora sweater for me and her trademark two-pound box of Laura Secord chocolates.

"She always overdoes it," Mother says.

I feel like saying: She's generous and she's not spending Dad's money, so why are you complaining? But what's the point of saying anything?

Mother gives me a flannelette nightgown and an illustrated boxed set of *Jane Eyre* and *Wuthering Heights*.

After the gifts, Mother plays hymns on our piano, which is usually silent. As a child she took piano lessons, but all she learned were hymns.

"Martin, do you remember how you could pick out a tune when you were only six?" Mother says.

"No, I don't."

"Such a shame you wouldn't take lessons. You would've done so well."

He says: "Isn't it enough that one of us produces bad music?"

He never cares how much he hurts her feelings. Not that I like her hymn-playing any better than he does.

"I'd better get at the dishes," she says.

"I'll help," I say.

"No dear, why don't you read your new books?"

Martin's off to his room.

Just me, my books and the tree now. I sniff the cover, that lovely new book smell. Our little Christmas tree makes me think of the war years. She would've brought in a tree from the bush then too. I remember lining up my new crayons like Martin's tin soldiers. Stretched out on my stomach beside the tree, I printed my name in big letters on the inside cover of my colouring book. Mother was reading in her chair by the stove. New crayons and pine scented the room. I didn't miss Dad because I hadn't yet got to know him.

FRIDAY IS MARTIN'S birthday and I was amazed when Donna agreed to come to for supper. She was absent most of the winter—just once in a while to play cards with him. Even when we were young our birthday parties were always just with our little family—mother said no child needs all those presents.

When Donna shows up Friday night, she's her old bubbly self. Ever since her breakup with Ian she's been quieter. More than once I heard kids say something about her and Martin. Now she knows what it feels like to be teased.

Tonight though, she's laughing and fooling around from the moment she comes in the door. She gives Martin a birthday kiss, right on the lips.

Mother has made a roast beef dinner and, strangely enough, has put the wine glasses on the table. She pours Martin a full glass and just a bit in mine and Donna's and even less in her own.

Mother says: "Martin, congratulations on your twenty-first birthday. May the coming year bring you much success in your writing."

We drink to Martin. I don't much like wine. The last time I had a taste was a year ago Christmas, when Dad gave me a little. On that occasion Mother disapproved. Tonight she drinks her wine, but she has that awful sad look. Is she remembering him too?

Martin opens my present first. I got him a box of Black Magic, his favourite chocolates, and Mother got him Shakespeare's plays printed in braille. He thanks us but a big grin spreads over his face when Donna hands him hers—something sounds like glasses clanking. He chuckles and puts his arm around her.

"Help me open it," he says, not letting go of her. He runs his fingers down her arm. "Silky blouse, nice."

She wriggles and together they tear the paper.

I don't believe this! Several bottles of beer! I expect to hear Mother gasp but she's smiling. Why is it Donna can do nothing wrong?

"You're legal now," Donna says, giving him another kiss. He's sitting, and she's standing. Her arm's around his shoulders and his are around her waist. Her thick ponytail rests against his dark curly head. I know he loves her. Is it possible she loves him too?

"We'll save this for later," he says.

"We better have one now. I can't stay too late. Some kids are picking me up."

No, as usual, she's just flirting.

"I've got an opener right here." She pulls one out of her purse.

"Do you think you should, on top of the wine?" Mother says.

"It's his twenty-first birthday. Let him celebrate."

Mother gets two glasses from the sideboard and places them in front of Martin.

"What about Gretchen?" Donna says.

"She's too young," Mother says. Has she forgotten that Donna and I are the same age?

"I don't like beer, anyway."

Donna and Martin, sitting close together, are having the beer. Mother pours a cup of tea for herself and one for me.

A car honks loudly, repeatedly.

"Oh, that's my ride," Donna says.

"Don't go," Martin says.

"I'll be over on Sunday. Save me some beer." A quick peck on the cheek this time and she's at the door. "Thanks for dinner, Mrs. Thorton."

"You're welcome, dear."

I peek out the window. It's a convertible, but too dark to see who's driving.

AFTER SCHOOL ON Monday the mystery's solved. As I'm going out the side door, my arms weighed down with books and binders, I'm just in time to see Donna climb into a red convertible. I can't believe it. The driver with his slicked-back, blonde ducktail is none other than Rick Waddell. How could she?

He's Martin's age and was out of high school by the time Donna and I started. I think he works at his dad's car lot.

Two weeks later I'm just leaving the schoolyard when Donna yells: "Wait up!"

Reluctantly, I wait for her.

"Haven't seen you in a while," she says.

"I guess you've been busy."

"Yeah, a little," she says, grinning.

"Are you going with Rick Waddell?"

"Yeah, did you see his red convertible?"

"He and Jimmy were the guys who bullied me and Martin."

"Huh? What are you talking about?"

"I've told you how they called Martin names."

"Yeah, you said that. But that's years ago."

"So? They still did it." I kick a paper cup off the sidewalk.

"They were kids then. They're all grown up now." She laughs.

"They're not nice people. I thought you were our friend."

"I am your friend and Martin's too. Rick's a nice guy. All little boys act like that. Girls do it too. In Hamilton we all called this girl Rabbit. She had a harelip. And the boy with a limp was nicknamed Gimpy. He didn't mind. The smallest boy in our class was Shorty. That's just kid stuff. I'll introduce you to Rick and you'll like him."

"No, thank you." I turn in at the barn.

"I'll just go in and say hi to Martin," she says.

I ignore her.

When I go in, she's gone, but I hear Martin telling Mother that Donna's coming over tomorrow night to play poker. He wants Mother to get some beer.

"I can't do that, son. You may be twenty-one, but she isn't."

"Donna's been drinking since she was fourteen."

"Oh, dear." Mother actually wrings her hands. "I can't encourage a minor to drink."

"You're such a stick in the mud, Mother."

"Donna likes tea or I'll get some pop. She likes Cream Soda or Coke. Which shall I get?"

Martin's already slamming his door.

She sighs and turns to me. "Oh Gretchen, everything's so hard for him."

"Donna's dating Rick Waddell."

"Oh? She always has lots of boyfriends."

Mother doesn't know who Rick is. Of course, we never told.

I intend to tell Martin but he's in a surprisingly good mood at supper. Right afterward I head upstairs and go over Latin declensions. *Domus, domus, domi, domui, domo, domum, domo, domu.* Like chanting. I can do it for hours.

When I get home from school the next night, Mother's sawing wood. Whenever she and Martin have a fight, she goes out to the woodpile.

While we're doing dishes, she tells me Martin went to the beer store. Even though he showed the clerk his birth certificate, he was turned away.

Mother went down there and told the clerk off. "At least it won't happen again," she says. "Why do people think the handicapped must be mentally defective?" She sighs. "I never thought the day would come I'd be seen in Grenville with beer."

"Nobody noticed. Lots of people drink beer."

"They notice. And only some people drink beer. So low class."

"Then why did you get it for Martin?"

"Martin is a man now. He has a right to choose what he drinks. He and Donna think they're big shots, having beer. They'll grow out of that stage."

"Donna's not twenty-one."

"I know, dear, but she told me her parents let her have beer at home. And we know she drinks when she's with her other friends."

"So that makes it all right?"

"Of course not, but they're that type of people. They're not like us."

Yeah, they're normal.

Donna arrives around eight. She and Martin both ask me to play cards. I play for a while, but then I tell them I have a lot of overdue assignments.

Neither of them urges me to stay. When I get up later to go to the bathroom, I see a light on in Mother's room. She deliberately leaves them alone. What does she hope will happen? Does she hope they'll get married? Has she forgotten I told her Donna's going with Rick? She sure wouldn't want me to get married at sixteen. Anyway, Martin can't get married. He's not earning any money yet. All that's going on down there is Donna's endless flirting.

I'll go down and make a sandwich. Then do more Latin until I get sleepy. Mother would notice if I took some of that chicken we had for supper, so I just take a slice of bread.

I'm buttering the bread when I hear Donna say: "You naughty boy. Let's get on with the game." He must've tried to make a pass. I'm not intentionally eavesdropping. Why doesn't he catch on she's teasing him? He's such a fool. Now she's telling him about drinking beer in Enrights' abandoned barn.

"The guys wanted to play strip poker."

"Now there's an idea," Martin says.

"Forget it," she says laughing. "I wouldn't with Rick and I won't with you."

At the mention of Rick, I hold my breath. But Martin doesn't catch on. He doesn't know what Rick she's talking about. Should I tell him?

MY MOTHER, WHO keeps the thermostat at fifty-five, has become extravagant. The old chicken house in the orchard is being turned into a writing studio for Martin.

She hires a carpenter who tears off the roof and walls, leaving only the framing and cement floor. He lays a new floor over the cement—pine boards.

The outside and the roof are now cedar shingle. The whole place has that lovely new wood smell. There's a big window at the back that looks out on the pear tree, and smaller windows on each side. Martin wouldn't let the carpenter cut down any of the shrubs growing against the walls even though he complained about not having room to work.

Honeysuckle and lilacs grow right up to the roof. Oh, I wish the place was mine!

Mother buys a couch and two chairs. The carpenter builds in a desk, counter and shelves. Martin has a hotplate so he can make tea whenever he wants. Electricity runs from our house to his studio.

Martin's out there a lot. While I'm oohing and aahing over it, he says: "Not New York, but step one in leaving home."

When Mother and I are alone she says: "He should be more content now that he has his own little place. Stop this foolishness of thinking he has to go to New York in order to be a writer. Don't you be jealous. Chances are this is as close to New York as he'll get."

ALL THE GOSSIP at school these days is about The List. Donna's brother Ted married Laurie Brown in a private ceremony in Rev. Everet's office. Laurie's fifteen. Her family owns Brown's Electric. The scandal isn't she's pregnant—lots of girls at our school have to get married. And they have big church weddings and white dresses. The talk is that nobody's too certain who the father is. She had several boyfriends. Her father made her give him a list. Nobody knows who all's on the list.

Stevie Blake is. Donna said he's been bragging about it at school. He's fifteen. The others, I hear, weren't much older, except for Ted. The families had a meeting and decided Ted should marry her. He's twenty-one, out of school and has a job at the White Rose gas station. Donna said: "He doesn't make much money pumping gas, and he shouldn't have to marry that little slut. On the other hand, it serves him right."

I asked Donna if Ted's in love with Laurie. She laughed and said: What do you think? If I knew, I wouldn't have asked. Then she told me he said: "Marrying jail bait's better than sitting in the slammer."

I'M BACK WORKING at the tourist camp. My grade twelve marks were okay, my average was 81 per cent. One more year and I'll be at university. I know a good education is important but I'd like to have a farm and raise Welsh Cob ponies. I'd have a pony riding school where I wouldn't only teach little kids to ride, but love and care for animals too. But, as Mother's told me many times, these aren't realistic ambitions for a seventeen-year-old girl.

Though I'm not particularly anxious to get to university, I do want to get out of here. Which I don't understand. I love Misty and my family. I don't want to leave but can't stand watching Mother and Martin. She has no life of her own. Dad told me she blamed herself for Martin's accident. And she blames herself for Dad's death.

Sometimes, when I crawl into bed at night, I cry and cry. I'm too old for all this crying.

I wonder if Old Mrs. Haun spends her nights crying too. She's gone deaf. One day she woke up with a roaring in her ears and now can't hear anything. I have to write notes to her.

I stay till six o'clock every night. By then most of the cabins are rented. Even if they're not, we put up the "no vacancy" sign.

She still won't let me clean the washrooms. I clean cabins all morning. She has a really loud whistle and if she needs me, she'll blow it. She could ask the tourists to write down what they want, but I think she's too embarrassed.

I thought this summer I might get a job in one of the stores or in a restaurant. Sharon works at Jerry's, the new restaurant by the beach, open from June till October. Sharon's become a flashy dresser. Nobody would know her family's poor. I would've liked to be Sharon's friend. I wonder what Baby Charlie looks like now. Donna told me there's another new baby, two if you count Gloria's baby. Gloria had a baby when she was fourteen.

I don't mind working at the tourist camp. Every day, when I come back to the house for lunch, Mrs. Haun has cooked me a big dinner. Chicken, roast beef, things like that, and the most wonderful desserts —pecan pie or strawberry glaze, heaped with whipped cream. When Mrs. Haun goes grocery shopping she buys whatever she wants, without looking at the price. "Such a luxury," she said. When she was young, she and her husband were poor, but they saved their money and bought this land—one acre. They built the first cabin, rented it out all summer and lived in a tent. Then they built another and another. There are ten cabins. In the 1920s they built their house. "Those were the good years," she said. They rented the upstairs rooms and she cooked for the tourists. During the Depression her husband lost his job. He'd worked for a carpenter but then nobody was building houses. And there were a lot fewer tourists. But they had savings and didn't owe anybody.

She told me they waited too long to have children. Then she said the nicest thing: "I wish I'd had a daughter just like you."

I asked Mother how married people could wait to have children. She said back then women douched themselves to prevent pregnancy.

"What does 'douched' mean?"

"Rinsing out the body with chemicals. Too much of this made a woman sterile."

Mother'll answer any questions about women's bodies, though I rarely know what she's talking about.

When I was little and asked questions about sex, she'd tell me to watch the cats. When I was older I asked her how men and women do it. She told me I didn't need to know. "When you fall in love and get married it all happens naturally."

Mrs. Haun is sixty-four and has nobody. Her husband died fifteen years ago. "What I regret," she told me, "is he never got to know we would be rich. I would love for him to have been able to go in a grocery store and buy whatever he wanted."

I think she's feeding me the dinners she wasn't able to cook for him.

I'm happier at the tourist camp than at home. As I ride my bike up

Leaman Road, I wonder will Mother and Martin be in one of their battles or will they be discussing St. Thomas Aquinas' *Summa Theologica*? I never know what to expect.

Leaning my bike up against the porch, I hear Martin holding forth about the church and Mother's determined interruptions. This is what they enjoy. Accusing each other of filibustering as they try to make their points. "Define your terms," Martin demands as I enter.

"Oh, hello, dear. I was just about to bring out supper when we got talking. We're having new potatoes and fresh corn, and for dessert I made raspberry pie."

"Mrs. Haun puts whipped cream on pie," I tell her. "It's good. We should get some."

"Why does she waste her money on that?"

"She goes to the grocery store and buys whatever she wants without looking at the price."

"She'd be better off saving her money for her old age," Mother says. "What if she needed to go into hospital?"

"Donna was supposed to come this afternoon," Martin says. "I have a piece I want to show her. Did you see her?"

"I don't see anybody at work."

"Don't you go swimming, afternoons? Maybe she went to the beach."

"Martin, I've told you. This summer I'm working full days."

"Call her and see if she's home."

"Martin, why don't you call her?"

"It'll raise suspicions. That boyfriend of hers is jealous."

Martin knows all about Rick now. He found out in May. All he said was: "Donna needs to zip around in fast cars. I can't give her that yet. What Donna and I have is special. She said so."

Silently, I cursed the little tease. "Martin, I don't want to call her."

"Look, just invite her for pie. She loves Mother's raspberry pie."

"I'm taking a bath. I'm hot and sticky from working all day." I head for the stairs.

Mother waylays me in the hall. "It's the least you can do for your brother," she whispers.

I shrug and go to the phone. By the third ring, I'm praying nobody's home. On the forth Brenda answers.

"Hi, it's Gretchen, Donna there?"

I'm relieved she isn't. "She's not in, Martin."

"Who answered?"

"Brenda."

"Good, it wasn't their mother. She's trying to break us up."

Break up? They're not together. "What's the piece you're working on that you wanted to show her?"

"A new science fiction story."

"I'd like to read it."

"Too racy for you, little sister."

"Well, in that case I'm off for my bath."

How do I tell my brother that Donna's in love with Rick, who she thinks is a hunk?

Donna's always smiling and all she wants to talk about is Rick. "We went to the dance hall at Blackstone Point. He's the dreamiest dancer."

All summer I've hardly seen her. Just occasionally when I get home from work, she's on the porch with Martin and Mother and once in a while she comes over for an evening of poker with him. We never do anything together. Martin's taken everything; my friend, my home, my mother's attention.

ON A THURSDAY afternoon I'm sitting on Mrs. Haun's sun porch that doubles as the office. The cabins are cleaned and she's sleeping.

I'm reading an historical novel about Marie Antoinette and all the carryings-on at the French court. I had to stop reading to take one family to their cabin. We're not likely to be full on a Thursday. Too many tourists go to the new motel.

"People have got so fussy," Mrs. Haun said. "They all want their private bathrooms."

I'll put up the "no vacancy" sign at six so nobody will bother Mrs. Haun in the evening.

Been a lazy summer. Tonight, I'll take Misty for a long ride on the back roads. I'll dream of meeting someone. I don't read Zane Grey books now, but Lin Slone, the hero in *Wildfire*, has become my man. My modern Lin Slone would be a stranger who's come to Grenville. I fantasize he's inherited Leaman's farm, fixed up the old barn and will be raising horses. He's a retired rodeo rider and Mr. Leaman's nephew. I have no trouble killing off Mr. Leaman because he really has sold the strip of land next to our place. The framing is already up for a new house.

When Lin Slone takes up residence on the Leaman farm, he buys the lots and bulldozes the new house. He wants the land back the way it was, he tells me.

I've forgotten all about Marie Antoinette and the French court and am daydreaming about Lin Slone when Donna arrives.

I'm surprised she would walk all the way here.

"Can I talk to you?" She looks really hot and tired.

"Sure, sit down. I'll get you a Tropicana. Mrs. Haun buys fresh orange juice, trucked up from Florida."

"Just water, please. My stomach's a little yucky."

I get her a glass of water and a Tropicana for me.

"I wanted to tell you my big news," she says.

"What is it?"

"I'm getting married."

"What!" I say, gasping. "You're not really going to marry Rick?"

"He's a nice guy, Gretchen. When you finally meet him, you'll see."

"Are you ... you know ...?"

"Yeah, I am. Will you be my maid of honour?" And she bursts into tears.

"Oh Donna, I'm sorry."

"I do love him." She sniffles.

"Then why are you crying?"

"I don't know," she says. "Wasn't supposed to happen. I can't go back to school." She sighs. "Anyway, will you be my maid of honour? You're my best friend."

And what can I say but yes?

She hugs me and I hug her back.

She phones her mother. "She wasn't home when I needed a ride out here."

Her mother's home now and shows up in a few minutes. "Thanks," Donna says and hugs me again. "Mom's in a hurry. I better run."

Maid of honour. What have I got myself into? Oh, poor Martin. Has she told him? Should I?

I DON'T TELL Mother. I don't tell Martin. I can't. When I got home they were happily discussing St. Thomas Aquinas.

The next morning Martin's not up when I leave. Mother is. I should tell her. I don't. I go to work.

The moment I get home it takes one look at Mother's face and I know they know. "Donna assumed you'd told us," she says.

"I should've."

"Why didn't you?"

"I don't know. I don't want to be her maid of honour."

"We feel sorry for her. She's far too young to know what love is. At that age they're just in love with love. Anything in trousers would do."

"How's Martin?"

"He'll survive. We all have disappointments in our lives."

Martin doesn't appear at suppertime. Mother calls him three times. Finally he roars: "God damn it, Mother, leave me alone."

Mother frowns and bites her lip. "Your supper's on a tray on the dining room table," she calls through the closed door. There's no response.

Our meal is silent. As soon as I finish, I ride all the way to the O'Hara place. I haven't been there in ages.

I don't see Martin until the next night. He seems okay though he taps his foot on the floor all through supper. This normally infuriates our mother. Tonight she doesn't comment.

When Mother's in the kitchen, doing the dishes, he says: "Busy at the camp these days?"

"We're full tonight. Usually are on the weekends. Martin, I'm sorry I didn't tell you right after she told me."

"Doesn't matter. Better I heard it from her. That bugger should be strung up." He pounds his fist on the table. Then his face sort of crumples and I'm afraid he's going to cry. "Poor Donna, this shouldn't be happening to her. And this damn town has determined she has to get married." He sighs. "Oh Gretchen, we live in a crazy place. I told her I'd look after her."

"What?"

"She'd come live here. Mother wouldn't object."

I don't know what to say. I should tell him she loves Rick. But she didn't seem exactly thrilled about the whole business. But that's because of the baby. As far as I can see, that's the only good thing she's getting from Rick. Why would Martin think she would want to come live with us?

"This is a bad time for her to get through, but she knows I'll be here for her when it falls apart."

"What are you talking about?"

"It won't last."

"Martin, she's having his baby."

"So what? I'll look after her and the baby. She loves me, Gretchen. Someday she'll know I'm the one she should be with."

I go for another long ride. He'll think I'm a traitor when he finds out I'm going to be her maid of honour.

When I get back, Martin's gone to his studio but Mother's on the porch. "Maybe I could tell Donna I can't be her maid of honour because it would hurt Martin's feelings."

"Nonsense. She's your best friend."

At least she didn't say my only friend, which is the truth.

"Martin has to understand our disappointments are learning experiences. She's invited us all to the wedding, and we should all go."

THE NEXT NIGHT I walk down to Donna's house. She phoned me. There's a meeting to discuss wedding plans.

I expect a sober atmosphere. When I arrive, Mrs. Evans, Brenda and Sharon are oohing and aahing over swaths of taffeta. Brenda and Sharon must be the other bridesmaids. One likes the mauve, the other the fuchsia.

"What do you think, Gretchen?" Mrs. Evans asks.

"They're all nice."

"Myself," she says, "I like the baby blue."

Sharon, Brenda and Donna all snigger.

"Well, maybe not," Mrs. Evans says, laughing. "What about the lime green?"

"Let Donna decide," Sharon says. "It's her big day."

"Fuchsia's my favourite," Donna says.

Next there's a discussion on hats. Then gloves—short or long? Flowers are next. Donna's going to carry white roses and we'll carry pale pink.

Donna's mother takes our measurements. A dressmaker's doing all the dresses. Donna's dress is white taffeta with Belgian lace on the bodice and train. They'll be done in three weeks which is good as the wedding is set for September seventh.

We have pop and chips—like a party. Sharon says we should get together to plan the shower. "We better have it at your place," she says.

"Okay, I guess. I'll ask my mother." I can't suggest we have it at her place. I know they're poor and their house was an awful mess the time I went to see their new baby. I liked it though.

"Do that. I'll phone you tomorrow."

As I'm walking home all I can think about is, again, what have I got myself into? I've heard girls at school talking about showers but I've never been to one and have no idea how to plan one. And we're going to have a party at our house? How will that make Martin feel?

When I tell Mother, she says: "Of course, we'll have it here. You could hardly have it at Duttons."

"Do we have to have one?"

"The bridesmaids always put on the shower."

Sharon calls and I invite her to come over the next night after supper. She brings Brenda with her. Martin's in his studio again.

Mother says: "We'll have the party in the living room."

"Lots of space in here," Sharon says.

I realize it's the first time she's been in our house. Why didn't I ever invite her over when we worked at the pony track? She had so many friends. I didn't think she'd want to come.

Mother has a book from the library about planning showers but Sharon already knows about what games to play and how we should decorate. Mother says the day of the shower we should spend the afternoon together doing the food and decorations. We'll have a light supper, and the guests will arrive at seven. "How will that be?"

"Fine," chorus Brenda and Sharon.

"I can book the day off from the restaurant," Sharon says.

"I have to work. Mrs. Haun can't manage."

Mother says: "I'm sure she could get a neighbour to come in and help for one afternoon."

THE WEDDING'S A week away and Martin's refusing to go. But not because he's mad at Donna. He can't enter a church. Against his principles. "James Joyce refused to take Easter communion, even though his mother was dying. He refused her last request because he had to stand up against the lies of the church."

"Son, listen to me. James Joyce didn't live in Grenville. Here, people will think you're getting peculiar. You have to guard against that."

"You think I care what they think?"

"You should. We have to live here."

"Actually, we don't. We could sell this place. Move to California."

"This is my home, the home your father and I made."

"Ha, ha. The home you made. Dad would've preferred Toronto."

"What do you know of what he would've preferred? He loved this place. Called it a refuge from the hectic world of business."

"If he loved it, why was he so seldom here?"

"You know he had to travel for his work."

"Mother, would you like me to make a pot of tea?" I can't stand any more of their quarrelling. Martin can be so mean.

I'm filling the pot when she joins me in the kitchen. "Martin shouldn't talk to you like that," I tell her.

"It's all right, dear. He's just so disappointed. He should go out more. We don't want people to think he's getting odd. The handicapped do have to guard against that. Such a shame he can't accept that religion could be a source of comfort for him. And if he went to church he'd meet other girls. There are lots of Donnas in the world."

WE'RE LINED UP at the back of the church. I'm balanced precariously in satin pumps dyed fuchsia to match our gaudy dresses. Rick and his best man Jimmy are standing beside Rev. Everet. Jimmy pokes Rick and grins. Their ridiculous white tuxedos look like Halloween costumes. I expect any moment for Rick to slick back his hair. And then he does, elbowing Jimmy and sniggering. Rev. Everet frowns at them. If Zane Grey's Lin Slone were standing here, he wouldn't be acting like some school kid.

A magnificent horseman, whose gentleness showed his love for horses, whose roughness showed his power ... an intense, lonely man. Not much chance of meeting a man like that.

I did have to go to the rehearsal party at the Waddell's house last night. Elvis was blasting from the record player. Rick said hello. I mumbled a reply. Rick and his friends were all a little drunk. Everybody was drinking beer. There was a lot of joking about the stag party the night before. About a certain little gift for Rick. "And wasn't she cute?" one of the guys said.

"He won't be getting any more of that." Jimmy said, laughing.

"I bet they had a stripper at the party," Sharon whispered.

Sharon told me that, after she graduates, she's going to get a job in an office in St. Thomas, maybe even Toronto. Her one definite plan, she told me, is to get out of this hick town. "And one thing you can be certain of," she said, "I'll have a ring on my finger before I have a bun in the oven."

It took me a moment to catch on. "Good idea." I said. It's funny because I'd thought if anybody had to get married it would be her. She's had lots of boyfriends. "Doesn't matter though," I said. "Donna says she loves him."

"Maybe for her it doesn't. Her dad has lots of money. Buys a new Ford each year from Waddells. Neither father would've let Rick weasel out of it. Our Gloria had it a little different."

"Didn't her boyfriend love her?"

"He was more: 'Why buy the cow when the milk's free?'"

I wished she'd stop talking in riddles. Gloria was awfully young to have a baby. "I saw her at the post office with Tamara. Her baby's so cute and I like the name she chose."

"All babies are cute. What's that got to do with anything?"

I didn't know what to say to that but was saved by Jimmy coming over and asking Sharon to dance.

Sharon's red curly hair was escaping its ponytail. She was wearing a pale blue sheath dress. When Jimmy put his hand on her behind, she smiled sweetly up at him, picked up his hand and placed it on her waist. Why couldn't I learn to flirt?

A few minutes later she was back beside me. "Do you like him?" I asked.

"He thinks he's a real hunk, only because he's at college."

I'm pleased I'm not the only one who dislikes the Waddells.

I FOLLOW THE other bridesmaids down the aisle. We stand opposite the guys. I watch Donna walk down the aisle on her father's arm. She's downright elegant with her hair done up in a French roll. But she's pale and isn't smiling. She told me she was terrified she'd throw up during the ceremony. How awful to have to think about that instead of your wedding vows. Still be lovely to have a baby. Donna and Sharon don't think so.

THE RECEPTION'S OKAY, lots to eat, but the speeches are stupid. First Mr. Waddell goes on about welcoming Donna into their family.

Then Jimmy stands up with a big smirk on his face. "I'd like to say a few words about my brother. He was a great football player from the time he was ten. Back then he was making touchdowns in the living room. Mom needed a new lamp anyway, eh Rick? Too bad about the garage window. I'm sure Mom and Dad forgave and forgot when in 1951 he ran right through, or more accurately, over Port Erie's defensemen, thirty yards to get that final touchdown."

The guests cheer.

"A little too much celebrating that night, eh Rick? Sorry about your car, Mom. Rick threw up all over the backseat and a not-to-be-mentioned girl. We were good boys, though. Clean up your messes, Mom always said. How were we to know bleach would wreck the upholstery? Of course, as Rick totalled the car a month later, the upholstery didn't matter. Walked away without a scratch. Rick's a lucky guy. Rick's a lucky guy today too — marrying the cutest girl in Grenville High."

Everybody cheers.

Once the dancing's starts, Mother whispers to me: "I'm worried about Martin. Do you mind if we leave now?"

"Fine with me." I can't bear to think Donna belongs to the Waddells. There won't be any more poker games. She won't ever go riding with me again, though it's been ages since we've ridden together. But even this summer, she'd sometimes stop in at the barn, pet Misty and play with the cats. She's Donna Waddell now. I'll really miss her. Though not half as much as Martin will.

When we get home Martin's not there. Mother clenches her hands together and digs her fingernails into her knuckles. I get so angry when she does that.

"Oh no, he's out walking." She's almost wailing.

"I'll make us tea." If we didn't have tea, what would we do instead?

Though the night's turned cool, I bring our tea out to the porch. Mother has changed out of her beige suit into her old chenille housecoat. "Look, Mother, a harvest moon! It's so bright, let's leave the light off."

She turns the light on. "I like to think of our yellow porch light as a beacon leading him home."

"We should go to bed," I say.

"You go, dear."

"Good night, Mother." I have no idea how to comfort her.

"Good night, Gretchen."

THE NEXT FEW weeks I don't see much of Martin. He spends a lot of time in his studio. I'm busy getting into my courses. Grade thirteen's going to be a lot of work, plus I have to do grade twelve physics and algebra.

Sharon joins me sometimes in the cafeteria. We only have math together as she's in grade twelve.

"I hope to get the Commercial Prize," she says. "In grade eleven I had the top marks in typing and shorthand."

"You should be able to get a job wherever you want."

"My English marks aren't too good."

"I could maybe help you with English."

"Gee, thanks. It's mainly grammar that pulls my mark down. I haven't heard from Donna. Have you?"

"No. I guess she's busy with the Waddells."

"Too hoity-toity now for us high school kids."

I DO GET a call from Donna, and I'm surprised she sounds so down in the dumps.

"Will you come to my apartment tomorrow after school?" she asks.

"Sure." I know they're living over Brown's Electric.

"There's an outside staircase in back of the store," she says.

Donna greets me at the door. Some dance show is blasting from the television.

"*American Bandstand*, really good. Rick bought me the television. Just a small one with rabbit ears. You guys should get one. There's all sorts of good shows."

"My mother and Martin don't like television. You okay?" Her face is puffy.

"I've stopped throwing up but now I'm getting fat."

"You're going to have a baby. That'll be great." I wonder if I'll ever have a baby.

"I'd rather be thin and in school." She looks like she hasn't washed her hair in a while. So unlike Donna.

"School's boring."

"Soon they'll be getting ready for the Halloween dance." She sighs. "Remember the giant pumpkin I made out of crepe paper stuffed with newspapers?"

"It looked great hanging over the stage."

"Danny Chambers, drunk out of his skull, knocked it down." She laughs. "I was so mad. Oh, I miss them all." Now she's crying.

"Donna, what's wrong?"

"For starters I got a letter from your brother."

Oh, no.

"I want you to read it."

"I don't know if he'd like that."

"Just read it!"

The letter's in braille. I haven't read anything in braille for a while so it's slow going.

> August 28, 1956
> *Dear Donna,*
>
> *You must understand why I couldn't attend your wedding. As a non-believer how could I enter a church? Mother said you looked lovely. Your loveliness I do believe in. Even my sightless eyes know how beautiful you are.*
>
> *I wanted Mother to take you our roses. She said it wouldn't be proper to arrive at church with an armload of flowers. Mother worries a good deal about what is proper. If I'd been there, I would've piled all the roses from our garden at your feet. They're blooming more ardently than ever as if they know it's their final hurrah before frost.*
>
> *Do come and see the roses. Their sweet perfume reminds me of you. I am waiting, not patiently. I'm not known for humble patience.*
>
> *I turn to my typewriter. The work proceeds. Let me tell you where I am with my science fiction story.*
>
> The Silorian Elders preach the virtue of patience: "Wait and we will be saved."

Parg is tired of waiting and has been sneaking into the observatory and exploring the telescopes. He figures it's safer than sneaking into Tercheran tunnels where his father caught him exploring a young Tercheran girl. The result was the expected whipping. Parg, watching the night sky, sees the pale globes of her breasts floating there.

In an attempt to keep his mind off pale Tercheran flesh, he has searched for and found twenty moons of Polumbia (the planet earthlings call Jupiter.) He hasn't found the twenty-first, Siloria.

Having read the old books written by the first Silorians on Earth, he wants to see Siloria, his ancestors' home.

They write of how bland Earth is with its single moon. Siloria faced Mother Polumbia with her undulating bands of light and dark clouds and her great red eye always guarding. Siloria was surrounded by her twenty sister and brother moons, more varied than anything seen from Earth. Crusts of sulphur volcanoes, of ice, of cratered rock. Moons that glowed in myriad colours. Siloria herself was bathed in such intense blue light that returning flying saucers could spot home from thousands of miles away. Parg sees the sister and brother moons, but not a hint of Siloria's blue light.

Something happened. If that's true, there's no more waiting, no more preparations. This is it, these dark tunnels and this dangerous Earth. Learn to make do, Parg figures.

Unlike Parg, I'm still waiting. Come soon, Donna, my darling, so beautiful in your white dress.
Martin

"HE TOLD ME he was writing science fiction." I don't know what else to say.

"How is he?" She frowns and takes the letter from me.

"Did I ever tell you that, when we were little kids, Martin and I made up stories about creatures called Juperians?"

"He doesn't sound mad at me." She folds and unfolds the letter.

"No. He wouldn't be."

"The stuff he's writing is sad."

"Isn't everything he writes? Even in his kids' story, the two kittens die."

"Gretchen, is Martin unhappy?"

"I guess."

"He's always joking around when I'm there."

"Well, you're not there."

"Do you think I should go see him?" She seems unsure of herself. Again, unlike the Donna I knew.

"You're married. Would Rick like it?"

"Half of my life's been ripped away." She sighs.

"Huh?"

"I loved all my visits to your place—my poker games with Martin."

Why didn't she think of that before dating Rick? "I better get going. I have oodles of homework."

"How's your mother?"

"Fine."

"I miss her."

She has her own mother.

"Has she made the tomato conserve yet?"

"I don't think so. That and the green tomato mincemeat are always last."

"I love her tomato conserve with the lemon slices. You wouldn't think tomatoes could be made into jam."

"Grade thirteen's a lot of work and I have a French test tomorrow."

"Come again real soon. You're my best friend."

"Okay."

I walk home slowly. Why does she go on about me being her best friend? She always has so many friends. Martin shouldn't have written her a letter. Called her "darling." What if Rick saw the letter? What am I worrying about? Rick can't read braille. Martin makes such a fool of himself. Why can't he see that? Should I say anything to him?

AFTER CHURCH WHEN Mother's talking to a lady from the altar guild, I see Donna, trailed by Rick, heading our way. They sometimes come to our church. She told me his family goes to the United. I don't want to have to speak to Rick.

"Oh, Donna, hello," my mother says. "You two getting settled into your apartment?"

"Yeah, it's small though," Rick says. "Next year we hope to get a house."

"Have you made the tomato conserve yet?" Donna asks. "Rick wouldn't believe you could make jam with tomatoes."

"I'll be doing it this week. Come for tea and you can take some home with you. How about Wednesday?"

"That'd be great."

Donna smiles like my mother's invitation has made her day. I think it'll be less than great for Martin. But he did ask her to come.

WEDNESDAY, WHEN I get home, they're having tea in the living room. Mother has straightened things up. Our usual stacks of books are back on the floor-to-ceiling shelves, and she has set out the bone china cups on her grandmother's tea trolley. Donna smells of Chanel No. 5, her favourite perfume. She's enthusiastically describing how she's arranged her kitchen utensils. I would expect my brother to find this more than a little boring. He listens so intensely you'd think she was explaining Descartes.

"Gretchen, join us for tea," Mother says.

I drink my tea, eat two scones with tomato conserve and listen to Donna rattle on. She put the bone china away for special occasions. The blue Melmac's for everyday — plastic is so much more practical.

"I better be off," she says. "Rick expects dinner ready when he gets home. Did I tell you he's in charge of the used cars?"

As if we care.

"That's nice, dear," my mother says. "Here's a jar of conserve to take with you."

My brother says nothing, no doubt hoping Rick will be run over by a used car. We all get up to see Donna to the door. She hugs my mother, and unbelievably, gives Martin a quick peck on the cheek. Before he can react, she's out the door. "Gretchen, come see me Friday after school," are her parting words.

AFTER SUPPER I'M curled up on the couch with *Northanger Abby* when Martin says: "I knew it wouldn't be long till she was back."

"She came for Mother's tomato conserve." There's no sense agreeing with his fantasies.

"Gretchen, you're funny." He bangs his cane on the floor. He doesn't look amused.

Mother comes in with the teapot and tray. "Would either of you like more tea while we're studying?"

"Sure." I offer her my cup. I shouldn't have said anything to Martin. Now he's tapping his foot on the floor.

"And you, Martin?" Mother says.

"Not for me." He gets up.

"You're not leaving us, are you? I thought we'd work on Descartes tonight. *Cogito ergo sum*, how we know we exist."

"Not tonight, Mother. With the pain in my legs and elsewhere, I don't have any trouble knowing I exist." At least he doesn't slam his door.

"I do wish he'd be more sociable. He's been so moody lately. I thought Donna's visit would cheer him up."

Why on earth would she think that? It's a little scary realizing that I know more than my mother.

I don't visit Donna on Friday. When she waylays me at church I tell her I had to stay to talk to my Latin teacher. "It's tough going and I needed help."

"Well, come tomorrow after school. You can't be that busy."

I do stop by for a visit. She doesn't even mention Martin. She complains about how fat she's getting.

"That's not fat. You're growing a baby."

"Feels like fat." She shows me the pale green baby sweater she's knitting. "I couldn't choose pink or blue, though Rick's sure it'll be a boy. He wants a whole football team. One'll be enough for me."

Holding the tiny sweater, I think of my visit to see Sharon's baby brother. I envy Donna, until Rick comes in.

His opening remark is: "How's my roly-poly Pumpkin?" He gives her a big noisy kiss. Poor Donna, already fretting about her weight.

I get out of there as quickly as possible. I know one thing. Lin Slone wouldn't call his wife a roly-poly pumpkin. Lin would come in smelling of hay and horses and put his muscular arms around me. Stare deeply into my eyes and kiss me. He would lift my shirt and kiss my protruding belly too. No matter how long, I'll wait for my Lin Slone.

I SEE DONNA at church but avoid her apartment. I tell her I have to work really hard this year to prepare for the Departmental Exams. There are only six of us in grade thirteen. Judy Boyd and Sandra Green are great friends. They dress and act exactly like the Sweater Twins. They're always together, comparing clothes or making judgments. "Do you see that getup? Wonder what rummage sale she went to." I don't think either of them has a boyfriend. They gossip endlessly about who is dating whom and who's a slut. Judy'll go to Bible College. Sandra will be off to Normal School. I feel sorry for the kids she'll be teaching. The other two girls in our class are going into nursing. They're nice but I haven't got to know them. The only boy, Brian Jackson, is from the country and very shy.

Donna visits Mother and Martin occasionally but only once was she still there when I got home from school.

I've always liked my walk home, with or without Donna. To leave downtown, to watch the houses thin out, to come to the top of the hill and look down at Leaman's farm. This farm is my fantasy place where I'd raise my Welsh Cob ponies. From the top of the hill all you used to see were trees and bush and, in the distance, our old house.

I suppose I shouldn't have been surprised two years ago when he sold off the strip of land along the road. Now I stand at the top of the hill and see new bungalows sprouting like weeds. Only two are finished, but the whole strip's been levelled and every tree and shrub destroyed. They haven't attacked the main woodlot where the big trees grow, but the vine trees where Martin and I played have been bulldozed. Why wouldn't the new people want trees and wild lilacs? The house built next to our place, just across the road, has an Angelstone front. I call it Phonystone.

THE SNOW COMES early this year and Donna stops her visits. Too far for her to walk in the snow and she doesn't have her driver's license. I see her at church. We talk, say we should get together, but don't. She tells me the Christmas dance at the Briarhill golf club was a real hoot. Maybe she's forgotten how Martin feels about her. That would be for the best.

He gets moodier by the day. Stays in his room most of the time. I know he's working on his science fiction stories. He almost got "The Invisible Kitten" published. An American children's magazine wanted a few changes—not have the kittens killed, just almost hit by a car and almost killed by a dog. They said the story would be too upsetting for children.

My brother said: "Children need to be upset."

Mother said: "Childhood is the time to learn about nature and death. Doesn't hurt them to cry. That's how they learn empathy. Nevertheless, you should make the changes. Be worth it to get something published."

"Never," Martin said, "will I compromise my work."

I concentrate on school, much easier than thinking about my family.

Finally, I see Donna at church. She hasn't been coming very often. The baby's due in March and her belly's getting really big. She looks awfully glum and I feel guilty for avoiding her. After the service, I take her aside and say hello.

"How's school?" she asks.

"Boring. Donna, what's it like to be growing a baby? Can you feel it? Just before Tiger has her kittens, you can see her skin rippling as they move around in her belly."

"The cat's lucky. She only has to carry them sixty days."

"But what does it feel like?"

"The little bugger kicks and rolls around all the time so you can't sleep. And you get haemorrhoids, and you have to pee about ten times every night." She sounds really angry.

"But it must be exciting."

"I'll be excited when I get my body back."

"Won't be too long now."

"Yeah, thank God."

"Call me as soon as the baby's born."

"Come see me sometime."

"Sure."

I did intend to go to see her but I really am busy at school. We're already going over the exam papers from previous years. If you make three sentence errors on the English composition exam, you fail.

I've applied to Queen's University in Kingston, over two hundred miles from here. That's where Mother's friend Miss Talbot went and where Mother would've gone if she hadn't got married. Would Mother be happier working for a newspaper like her friend does? But then Martin and I wouldn't have been born.

ON AN EVENING in March, Mother's out splitting wood and Martin's in his studio. All winter they fought over heating his studio. She says we can't afford it.

"Why can't you write in your room?"

"You're a penny-pinching old woman!"

Finally, she bought him another small electric heater. He already has one in his bedroom.

The phone rings. Donna's all excited. "Just got home from the hospital. I have a baby boy. We named him Richard William, but we call him Billy."

At least they're not calling him Rick.

"Come after school tomorrow and see him," she says.

"I'd love to!" She sounds like her old bubbly self.

I'm about to run out and tell Mother and Martin but stop. He hasn't mentioned Donna in a while and I really hope he's forgotten about her. Mother'll hear about the baby soon enough.

The next day I go to Stedman's and buy a white baby nightie with blue embroidery. I can't resist buying the blue booties too.

When I knock on the door, she shouts: "C'mon in."

Her hair hangs around her like a shawl for the dark-haired baby at her breast. He's sleeping and sucking. Oh God, I want one. "He's beautiful."

She grins. "Yeah, he's a cutie when he's not bawling."

I show her the things I've bought and make us tea. She lets me hold him. He looks right at me with his bright blue eyes. I hope with all my heart that someday I have one too.

"How's Martin?"

"Okay, busy with his writing." The baby's eyes close and Donna lays him down in the wicker bassinette.

"I miss Martin. How's your Mother?"

"They're fine. I guess you're pretty busy now." I don't know how to tell her that I don't want her coming to our place, upsetting Martin.

"You told them I had the baby?"

"Not yet."

"Why not?" She sounds annoyed.

"Oh … they weren't in when you called and still asleep when I left for school."

"Your mother was sleeping in?" She stares at me.

"She has a cold." How easily I lie.

"I should give her a call."

"I wouldn't. She might be resting."

"Not like her to stay in bed even if she has a cold."

"She's not staying in bed. She just slept in." She doesn't need to tell me what my mother's like.

"Tell them about the baby."

"Of course." She'd better not call. Mother was up at six as usual. Donna will know I was lying.

Billy wakes up and she lets him nurse again. "I'm supposed to make him wait four hours, but why should I? If cutie is hungry, let him suck." She laughs and wiggles her nipple against his mouth. "Do you know what Rick said?"

"No." And I don't want to.

"'Save some for me,' he said."

The image of Rick at her breast makes me want to puke. I'm about to leave when Rick walks in.

"Hello, Pumpkin and Baby Pumpkin too." He gives Donna a big smoochy kiss. "Save some for me," he says.

Disgusted, I jump to my feet. I want out of there.

"Oh, didn't see you there. Hi Gretchen."

"Hi."

"Still hitting the books. You gonna be a teacher or what?"

"I don't know."

"How's your brother?"

"Fine."

"If I got in a car accident and ended up a crip, I'd shoot myself. He's braver than I am."

On the way home I think about Rick being in a car accident and ending up a 'crip'. He deserves it. That's a terrible thing to think. So, he'd shoot himself. He must think Martin should kill himself. My brother's done more with his life than Rick ever will. His poetry, his stories and he said he's started a novel. Rick's a real pill. "Save some for me." I can just hear her blurting something like that out in front of Martin. I hope she stays away. I do have to tell them about the baby.

At supper I tell them.

"Why didn't you tell me last night?" Martin asks.

"You were in your studio."

"So what?" He's tapping his foot on the floor.

I hate it when he does that. "Didn't want to interrupt you."

"News of Donna isn't an interruption." He scowls at me.

WHEN I GET home from school the next day, Mother's waiting for me. "Why did you tell Donna I had a cold?"

"I dunno."

"Honestly Gretchen, sometimes I don't know what gets into you."

That's for sure. "I don't want her coming here."

"Why on earth not?"

"She upsets Martin."

"He'd rather be upset than not see her at all. It's well documented throughout history that a writer's muse is often the woman he couldn't have."

I stare at her. Have no idea what she's talking about. Just like Mother to come up with some theory instead of just acknowledging how bad he feels. It almost sounds like lying. But who is she lying to? I am so tired of their dramas.

"I told him," Mother says, "Donna could be his muse. Gretchen, I want you to drive to school tomorrow and pick Donna up afterwards."

GOOD OLD GRETCHEN dutifully picks them up the next afternoon. Donna, as I knew she would, says: "Why did you say your mother had a cold?"

"I thought she did." We leave it at that.

Mother has put on a real spread. There's a lace cloth on her grand-mother's tea trolley which is loaded with butterscotch squares and brownies.

When we come in, Martin's standing in the doorway. "Martin, come say hello to Donna," Mother says. Donna hands me the baby while Mother helps her take off her coat.

Donna's wearing a red sheath dress that looks brand new. Her long hair is gathered back with a shiny red clip.

He comes to meet her, hugs her and doesn't let go. Buries his face in her hair. "You smell the same," he says.

I'm dying with embarrassment, but Mother just asks me for the baby. I hand her the sleeping bundle.

"Oh Donna, he's lovely," Mother says. She's not even looking at him. "Come and hold him, Martin."

"Yes, do, Martin." Donna finally wriggles out of his embrace. She hands the baby to Martin, tucking his free arm around the baby's body. Martin leans on his cane. "Hold him in the crook of your arm."

The cane clatters to the floor. The baby's eyes fly open. Martin leans against the doorframe. His hand traces the features of the baby's face. Martin looks like he's going to cry.

"Here!" Mother says, frowning as she picks up the cane. "Give me the baby and come sit down. So, how are you, Donna?"

Martin regains his composure, sulkily, but for once does as he's told.

"I'm pretty sore. I tore really bad. He's big—eight pounds. I sure won't be in a hurry to do that again."

Why doesn't she shut up and think about my brother's feelings?

"It's pain quickly forgotten," Mother says, "and such a healthy-look-ing baby." She takes off his bonnet and unbuttons his sweater. "Aren't you a beauty?" she says. "Gretchen, you take him. I'll serve the tea."

Little Billy stares at me with those big blue eyes. I sniff his hair that's soft like that of a newborn kitten.

Martin's staring at Donna. He ignores the plate Mother fixes for him.

"Well, I have some big news," Donna says.

"The baby's big news indeed," Mother says.

"No, we're buying a house. My dad's lending us the down payment, and Rick's dad is co-signing for the mortgage."

"That's wonderful, dear."

"And you'll never guess where it is?"

"Where?" Martin says hoarsely.

"Right across the road from here," she says. "We're buying one of the new bungalows my dad's building on Leaman's farm. It was already sold to some St. Thomas people but they backed out. We're going to be neighbours."

"Hello, neighbour." Martin says, leering.

I feel like kicking him. She's married, Martin. Leave her alone.

THEY MOVE IN a month later.

On my way home a few days after the move, I see her standing on her front lawn. Is she waiting for me?

"Hi," she calls. "I made coffee and Billy's sleeping. I'll have time to show you around."

She's so friendly, I feel ashamed. I want to be her friend but it makes trouble for Martin.

"What do you think of the carpet? Wall to wall, the latest thing."

The carpet is a bright aqua and matches the drapes. "You always liked aqua." At least she didn't pick fuchsia.

"Yeah, I got to choose it. The Waddells bought us the television — the cabinet's real walnut."

·"Nice."

"Let's have coffee. How do you like my new chrome kitchen suite?"

"It's pretty but what I love is the big window." I'm glad there's something I can honestly say I like. "You can see all over Leaman's farm."

"Yeah, makes me think of us riding the ponies. Your mother's going to teach me to sew curtains."

Has she already been over bothering my mother?

Billy wakes up and I get to change him. I'm amazed at the size of his privates. I somehow expected he'd have tiny ones like a kitten.

ABOUT A WEEK later, I come home to see my mother and Donna with the sewing machine up on the dining-room table. My brother stands in the doorway.

"Hi everybody," I say. "Where's Billy?"

"Rick's mother has him. Lucky for me she likes babysitting."

Donna's in another new dress — a pale green linen sheath. She's so dressed up.

Later, during tea, Donna talks constantly, describing every room in her house. Martin, who hasn't spoken since I came in, has that look of great concentration, as if he's memorizing every word.

"Gretchen's seen the house, but Mrs. Thorton, you and Martin should come to tea and have a look round. We finally got the pictures up. I put the photo of Rick holding his football trophy up beside our wedding pictures. The reporter for the *Port Erie Times* took it and gave Rick an enlargement. Rick's a real hunk in his uniform—wish I'd been around to see that game. Mind you, I would've been a kid in public school. Rick wouldn't have noticed me." She giggles like a ten-year-old.

"Sounds like you're getting settled in, dear," Mother says, smiling. It sounds like another one of her weird lies.

"How about coming over tomorrow?" Donna asks.

"I have too much to do," Martin says, limping to the front door.

I look out the window and see him heading for his studio.

"What did I say wrong?" Donna stands beside me. Her eyes look wet.

"Nothing, dear," my mother says. "He gets into moods. It's a stage he's going through." More lying. I'm surprised at how angry it makes me. Like Martin's a little kid.

"Will you come?" Donna asks.

"I'll talk to him. He doesn't leave the house much. Might be better if you come here. Your visits mean a lot to him."

I'm walking home from school doing Latin declensions in my head—a technique I've developed to avoid looking at the destruction of Leaman's farm. Only a month until exams.

Donna rushes out her front door. "Gretchen, I need to talk to you."

What now? I shouldn't be so unfriendly, particularly after the awful thing that's happened. "How's your mother?" Donna's mother had a stroke and she's only forty-two.

"She's home now, getting better. Brenda's looking after her. My sister's such a good student Mr. Podger says it's okay for her to miss as much school as she needs to. I try to help out but Billy's crying bothers Mom. "C'mon out in the kitchen and have some lemonade."

In his playpen, Billy's lying on his back and kicking his legs. "May I hold him?"

"Sure. Here's your Auntie Gretchen, Billy."

Auntie Gretchen? His dark hair has fallen out and a fine blonde down covers his scalp.

"Have a Rice Krispies square—made them today."

"Thanks. Billy's got a beautiful smile. You must love watching him grow."

"Love watching him sleep, which isn't often. Changing dirty diapers and cleaning up baby puke isn't much of a picnic. Rick's gone all day. I'm about to turn eighteen and should be out having fun."

"You went to the Briarhill Country Club dance."

"Yeah, but dating was more fun."

"What do you mean?"

"I loved all the sneaking around. Making out on the couch, scared his parents would wake up, catch me with my bra half off and my skirt up around my hips. Once you're married it's all just part of the routine."

She always tells me more than I want to know. "You said you needed to talk to me about something."

"Yeah, it's this." She hands me a letter.

Martin's done it again.

It's in braille. I sit down at the kitchen table and slowly trace out the words.

> May 10, 1957
> *Dear Donna,*
>
> *Tea, tea, tea, my mother's endless tea-making. Come to my studio. Bring some beer. Dragon Mother won't buy me any. Remember my twenty-first birthday? You missed my birthday this year. It's almost your day. Eighteen, my darling, all grown up.*
>
> *I wait and wait for you. My writing keeps me going. I'm well into the Joe and Cathy novel. Remember, I read you the first bit when you were here. Marsh Road is my serious work, quite different from the more commercial science fiction. Here's just enough of chapter five to get you interested.*
>
> Joe was fourteen when his sixteen-year old sister drowned herself in Eight Mile Creek. At least his parents

said she did. He didn't believe them. Maeve was terrified of water and never went to the creek with him and Cathy.

Joe figured she was murdered and he was damn certain he knew the murderer. Even as a little boy, he expected someday his father would kill him. When Bob was in a rage, he didn't just hit Joe with the belt. He used his fists. Once Bob threw him against the wall so hard, Joe passed out. The hole in the drywall is still there.

Bob slapped Maeve around but never beat her. In the weeks before his sister's death Bob raged at her, called her slut, whore. Mom asked Maeve how she could do this to us, bring shame on our family?

Did his sister have a boyfriend? Could she be pregnant? Rosie Jackson, who was fifteen but still in grade eight with Joe, got pregnant and dropped out to marry Larry Teal — big scandal, but no surprise there. Joe knew she'd done it with several of their classmates — not with him though, not with "Jigsy: dance us a jig, Jigsy"!

Maeve was so shy, she barely spoke. Still, something must've been going on.

Joe was shoveling out the chicken coop when he saw his sister walking across the hayfield toward the marsh. Her head was down, shoulders hunched. Maeve was scared of the marsh, said there were snakes.

He dumped the shit out of the wheelbarrow and started down the field. He tangled himself up in the long grass and cursed his jigsy-assed gait. Finally caught up to her.

Where you goin'?

Just walkin', she mumbled.

What's the matter with you, anyways?

Nothin'.

You got a boyfriend?

No! She turned and ran back to the house, leaving Joe standing there.

Two days later she disappeared.

Slut ran off with the boyfriend, Bob said.

Mom went around the house, weeping and praying. Oh, dear God, pity us.

Joe searched. That day he'd seen her walking she'd been heading toward the marsh. Maybe she was going to meet somebody. Had they taken the canoe? He kept it well-hidden in the reeds, but she knew about it. If she followed Eight Mile Creek to where it joins Big Creek, she could reach Lake Erie. But Maeve didn't know how to paddle a canoe. Maybe the boyfriend did.

When Joe found the canoe in its usual hiding spot, he was ashamed of suspecting his sister.

Three days later, he went back to the marsh, though he didn't know why he felt a clue was there.

He was wandering beside the creek when he saw the rubber boot. He knew instantly it was hers. Arsehole Bob made Maeve wear Joe's outgrown boots, even though one leaked and the back was split on the other. She'd decorated them with flowers drawn in red nail polish.

He found her a short distance away, lying face up among the reeds. His skinny sister was grotesquely bloated. Her eyes were rolled back, white, sightless, thick with flies. When he tried to brush the flies away, he gasped, turned and vomited. Maggots were eating her eyes.

He pulled off his shirt, covered her face, turned and ran, fell, wrenching his hip. Bawling like a little kid, he made his way home.

After the funeral, Mom told him his sister had drowned herself. When he ranted she wouldn't do that, Mom said, your sister was pregnant. Joe didn't know why that would make her do it, but Mom was crying so he didn't ask more. Bob told him and Mom never to mention Maeve again.

Joe suspected Bob of murder. Later he would suspect him of a different crime and wonder why he hadn't thought of it sooner. At fourteen he knew about the facts of life, but not about depravity.

Certain things kept bothering him. One, Maeve said
she didn't have a boyfriend, and he believed her. Two,
there was something about Bob that lurked around the
edges of Joe's consciousness.

The truth hit Joe one day in grade ten. The Dugans
were a big down-and-out family who lived in a shabby
house on Concession Road. The story was Ruth Dugan
was pregnant. He overheard some boys talking. Jamie:
My dad says her father did it to her. Ted: Granddad told
me in the old days the men would've tarred and feathered
him. Jamie: I'd go for that. The dirty bastard!

Joe felt goose bumps rise on his arms. Years ago,
when he'd got up to pee in the middle of the night, he
heard Maeve whimpering in her room and a threatening
growl, but not any thumps or smacks, and he knew Bob
didn't beat her.

Joe plotted murder. He'd do it for Maeve—for himself
too. But how? Bob was six foot two and three hundred
pounds. Joe was five foot three and weighed one fifteen.
He didn't think he could just wait for him to die. Bob
didn't deserve to live, in the first place.

*My darling Donna, I also plot and wait. What do you think
of Marsh Road? Hope it's not too bloody for you. The love
interest heats up in the next couple of chapters. Come see me,
my beautiful Donna. Bring beer for a thirsty man.*

"WHAT SHOULD I do?" Donna's reading over my shoulder.

"Pretty obvious what you shouldn't do." I'm tempted to scrunch
up the letter and throw it in the garbage.

"What?" She takes it from me and carefully refolds it.

"Like I said before, tell him to stop writing you letters."

"Okay. Do you think I should take him some beer?"

"No." What is the matter with her?

Billy's fussing and she stuffs the pacifier in his mouth. "But your
mother makes such a fuss if he asks her to buy him any."

"That's their problem, not yours."

Billy's still fretting. Donna bounces him up and down in her arms. "If he wants a beer, it wouldn't hurt for me to bring him some."

"Donna, you encourage him." Is she so stupid she doesn't know that? No, she's still teasing him. Flirting.

"To drink?"

"That's not what I meant. In the letter he called you darling."

"He shouldn't do that." She sighs. "But surely, we can be friends."

"Donna, you're married."

"So?" She frowns. "Doesn't mean I can't be Martin's friend. We were friends long before I met Rick."

I shrug. "I've got a Latin test tomorrow. Tell him to stop writing to you."

"Yeah, okay. I wish you didn't always have to rush off."

I DON'T KNOW if she told him to stop writing her letters. Except for taking Misty for a ride each morning, all I do is study. Donna's there a couple of times when I come home after school but I just say hi and go on upstairs.

There's a heat wave the week we write the exams. Mother says I can use the car. I don't want to. The mile-long walk clears my head. Walking down Leaman Road, past the new bungalows, past the older houses, and on the corner with Main, Grenville Public School, down Main, past the post office, the bank, Brown's Electric, the drugstore, the Quick Stop, and finally I'm in front of the high school. I feel something like love for the town, at least a sort of affection, like I can afford to care for it now that I'm leaving it behind. Each walk to each exam I feel freer. Free to do what? I'm not sure, but scared as I am, I want out.

And if there are any bullies these days on the streets of Grenville, I don't see them.

BACK WORKING AT the tourist camp. Putting in time till my real life begins, away from here. One night, it's just Mother and I on the porch and she says: "I wish Martin would stop pestering me to go New York or California."

"He could go on his own." I sip my tea. I wish just once we could drink our tea and not talk about Martin.

"Gretchen, you know he can't. We can't just spend the money like he wants to. His health will deteriorate sharply — he already has arthritis. His leg injuries are affecting his hip joints. Before I'm gone he could well be in a wheelchair."

"Mother, his legs aren't that bad — he walks for miles. He told me that, last night, he walked all the way out to the highway and considered walking to Port Erie." She ignores everything I say and rattles on.

"Gretchen, this is important. There'll be medical expenses and I want him to be able to stay at home. Not end up in some institution. I don't want you to have to look after him either. You'll leave this narrow-minded town, get a university education and live the life you deserve. But you must promise me you won't ever let him be put in an institution. Will you promise?"

"Okay." I push the porch swing with my foot. Screech squawk. What am I promising? I'll kill myself before I'm his servant. He's used up her life. He can't have mine, too. But still, poor Martin. I stare at the sky, pink and deep purple mingling in the west. I want to run away. I want to stay forever.

"Gretchen, would you like another cup of tea?" She's holding out our old Brown Betty.

I'll even miss the stupid teapot. "Thanks."

"Even now if he went away, he'd need a housekeeper and someone to drive him around. People would take advantage of him. And I can't go. My home is here."

"But Mother, long ago you wanted to leave Grenville and go to university."

"This place watches my back. My fortress, the one thing I've been able to hold onto." Her eyes have that sad, faraway look. "Strange how a place can take on a living form, become a presence. Even as a child, this was the only place that felt safe." She speaks softly almost as if she's telling herself a story. "My grandmother would drive up to the farm in her old Model T. Not many women drove in those days, but she did. She'd whisk me away against my mother's objections. I slept in what's now your room."

"I didn't know my room used to be yours."

"Yes, and I'd help her in the garden, not the back-breaking labour like at home. We'd pick a few tomatoes, rub the dirt off on our skirts, and eat them still warm from the sun. I'd help her tie up the tomato plants. She held them so tenderly, as if they were living creatures. There was no rushing on to the next thing. I think what I'm trying to say, Gretchen, is she took pleasure in whatever she was doing. With Ma life was a bad-tempered rush. If I'd be gathering the eggs, my mother would march into the chicken house. 'You think you got all day. Quit your dawdling. Those pens need cleaning.' Boy, I hated that chicken farm."

Strange, Mother and I sit on the porch, not her and Martin. He's out in his studio. He may stay there all night. She confides in me now.

"Ma told me I'd spoiled Martin. If I'd spanked him more often, he wouldn't have unlocked the balcony door."

I can't bear the look on her face.

"She told me it would've been better if Martin had died. She said that with him right there in the room, playing with his little cars."

"We had a lot of fun when Martin and I were little, before he went away to school. Remember all the hikes we went on and the campfires you made? You used to tell us stories. Were you happy then?"

"Gretchen, that was during the war, when your dad was away. He could've been wounded or killed. We were hard up. The army didn't pay much and we had so many medical expenses. Once I had to borrow twenty-five cents from my mother just to pay the gas bill. So humiliating. How would we have managed if something had happened to your dad? I'd have had to start teaching again. Who would've looked after Martin?"

"I didn't know any of that. Was Dad home when Martin had his accident?"

"No, they were about to be shipped out to England and he was in training at Petawawa. After the accident, he got leave and was home almost three weeks before the call came. Only lately, I've realized that must've been hard on him too. To leave when his son was still in a coma."

"You must've been so scared."

"Yes, and angry that he left." There are tears in her eyes. Mother never cries.

"He had to, didn't he?"

"Yes, Gretchen, he did." She wipes her eyes and swallows. "I was a silly young woman. There was a war on and a soldier has to obey orders. I was so unfair to your father. I thought he blamed me and wanted to leave."

"Dad didn't blame you. He said it was sad you blamed yourself. He told me accidents can happen to anyone. Dad fell off a porch roof when he was six."

"Martin's accident was my fault. I should've known he could unlock that door."

"You couldn't have known that. And anyway, most kids wouldn't have climbed up on the railing."

"I didn't know you and your dad talked about it."

"Once, on one of his business trips."

"Good that you had those times with him." She sighs again. "Your teen years have been hard, Gretchen. It'll be different when you get to university. I want so much for you to have the opportunities I didn't. And the war years weren't all bad. We were here, in my grandmother's house—she died just six months before Martin's accident. We planned to sell the house. But it was a comfort to me. I missed her so." She smiles. "But you're right, Gretchen. We did have good times. Martin was a happy little boy in spite of his handicaps. And so bright—the smartest child I ever taught."

Dark now and the wind rattles the lilac branches against the screens. "Think I'll head up to bed. We were busy at the camp today."

"Goodnight, dear."

"Night, Mother." I leave her sitting there in the dark. It's not like her —as soon as dusk comes she always turns on the lights; despite the cost. Says it makes a place cheerier, drives away the ghosts. I could go back out and switch on the light. But I can't make her happy.

Lying in bed, I'm too hot to sleep. Life is strange. I've always thought about the war years as a happy, innocent time. Martin and I were equals. His handicaps didn't matter. Never thought about what it was really like for Mother. I would've sworn she was happy too. Now I can see how she worried about Dad.

Then Dad came home and everything changed. There were arguments about Martin being sent to school. And then he went and I started school. There were no more hikes or campfires or storytelling. I don't understand why Mother spent so much time hoeing the garden or canning vegetables or raking leaves, always so busy. With Dad back working as an architect, they would've had more money. Martin was at school, so she should've had more time for me and for Dad. He played with me. Told me stories about when he and Aunt Maggie were children. If only he hadn't died.

Could Martin end up in a wheelchair? Will I have to look after him? No, that's just her worrying. At night, he walks for miles.

MONDAY, THE CAMP's frantic. There's a regatta on and everything's fully booked. My legs ache as I ride my bike home on the soft asphalt.

Canning season and the kitchen's steamy, Mother stirring and boiling. Rows of filled jars gleam in jewel colours along the counter.

Often, Donna's around, helping. Her canning outfit is short shorts and a halter top or a sundress and no bra. And Martin's there, usually in the kitchen doorway. Why would he stand there like that, watching, listening? He acts weird. Donna isn't there to visit him.

I wish she'd stay home. I asked Mother why she's over so much.

"We're canning together, splitting the batches. Donna's learning."

"Why isn't she home looking after her baby?"

"Rick's mother loves having Billy and I certainly don't mind the help. Canning's a lot easier with two people."

"Strange she's not helping her own mother, who's sick."

"Brenda's looking after their mother. Donna tries to help but they act as if they don't want her around. Awful when a mother plays favourites. No wonder Donna and Brenda don't get on."

"I wish you wouldn't work so hard." She has never asked for my help. Of course I would've complained if she had. She wanted me to enjoy being a child—play, go riding, read books, have the childhood she never had. As long as I was busy I wasn't expected to work. But Donna and I aren't children now.

"I'm hardly going to let the fruit go to waste." Mother frowned. "The garden saves us a lot of money."

Always harping about money. Martin says we have plenty, that she just won't spend it. He said $200,000 gives her an income of $10,000 a year. "That's only a third less than Dad earned," he said. How does he know what Dad earned? He added: "Ten is far more than most people live on in Grenville."

"So what's your point?" I said.

"We don't have to live like hick farmers."

"But she did all this work when Dad was alive."

"Our mother," he said, "is just a bit crazy."

She isn't crazy but I don't understand her.

Martin tells her to sell this place, says she could go to university.

She tells him: "Our lives are here. With the Great Books, we'll have the equivalent of a university education."

Despite an after-work swim I'm sweaty again. I think about a gigantic glass of Mother's lemonade and move faster.

The porch is empty and Mother's not in the kitchen. It's stifling. The big kettle, filled to the brim with peaches, is on the stove. So too are the sterilized jars. Where is she?

Martin must be in his studio. He'll know where she is.

I'm just by the forsythia hedge when I see them—Donna and Martin standing in the shrubbery by his studio door. For a moment, I think they're necking. But they're not. They're deep in conversation. Martin, a foot taller than Donna, is bent over, speaking earnestly. His dark curls almost touch her light brown hair. She's smiling up at him. He's holding her hand. If I didn't know she was married, I'd think they were a couple.

She's not flirting. Just looks happy. She's always so miserable at her place. Have I been wrong about her all along? Is she in love with Martin? Is it possible? But she's married and has a baby.

I'm about to say something, when I hear Mother calling. "Martin, Donna, I'm home."

"In a minute, Mother," Martin calls out, and goes on talking.

I sneak away without saying anything. I've no right to intrude. I always thought she was just teasing him. If she really loves him, does that make it all right? Of course not. What about little Billy? It's all too weird. I'd like to leave town tomorrow, first light.

"Where were you?" I ask Mother.

"I had to go to the store. We ran out of jar lids. Donna and I will just finish this batch. They're having tea in his studio. So hot in the house. Would you like to help, dear?"

"It's too hot. I'm going upstairs for a bath."

"Do that. Supper won't be for a while."

As I head upstairs I hear her calling, again: "Donna, Martin, I'm back."

RIDING HOME FROM work is better than yesterday but I'm still filmed with sweat. After dark Misty and I'll head to the beach and go swimming. My exam results came yesterday. I have a 74% average. Mother and I both expected it to be higher. I hope she's not too disappointed.

Donna, Mother and Martin are having tea on the porch.

"Taking a break from canning," Mother says. "Wash up and I'll pour you a cup."

I go upstairs and stick my head under the tap. Towel my hair dry. That feels better.

Nice on the porch. Our overgrown lilacs keep it cool.

"Have some pear pie," Donna says. "I made it."

"We've been busy," Mother says. "We started on the pears today. Donna's become quite the baker."

"At least now I can roll out pastry without it falling apart."

I would've thought Donna would grow up to be more like her mother who, if she weren't sick, would likely be sitting on the back patio with a gin and tonic.

"Your mother said you went to St. Thomas to get your clothes for university."

"We got more stuff than I'll ever wear."

"That blue taffeta with the gored skirt sure sounds swell. I'd like to see it and that one with the harem skirt too."

"Sure. I'll just finish my pie."

We go upstairs and I show her my trunk. It's new too — blue metal and paper-covered wood inside. My toiletries, socks and underwear, all new, are in the tray. I lift it all out and Donna gasps. I carefully unwrap the tissue paper.

"Wow, and your mother never used to buy you hardly anything."

"Yeah, the dresses are pretty, though I doubt I'll wear them. The skirts and blouses are for school, though I'd rather wear jeans. I bought a pair of Levi's in St. Thomas. Mother didn't approve. I'm bringing my old ones too."

"Your mother said there would be lots of dances."

"Yeah, maybe I'll go."

"Of course you'll go, you lucky duck. You know, Gretchen, sometimes I can't believe how my whole life got decided in high school. I was this kid who thought there were years and years of fun ahead of her."

"Don't you like being a mother?"

"I love Billy, and Rick too, but I wasn't ready for a baby or marriage. Oh, I wish I was going with you."

"Why are you canning and baking? You don't have to do all that."

"I like being here, talking with your mother … and Martin." Donna laughs. "The canning keeps my mind off other things."

"Doesn't Rick mind you being over here so much?"

"Why should he?"

"I dunno."

"He loves all the jam and pies."

"Still."

"Don't worry. Rick sees it as kindness to a poor crip."

"Donna, what an awful thing to say."

"I didn't say it, Rick did. He doesn't think of Martin as a man. I'm visiting a shut-in. Very charitable of me."

She sounds so bitter. I hate Rick.

I LEAVE TOMORROW. Won't get home till Christmas. How will I stand it?

I look around my room, mine as far back as I can remember. I wasn't quite two when we moved here. The red plaid curtains Mother made when I was eleven are faded pink now.

I go to my closet and from the back shelf pull out my threadbare old quilt. Mother sewed all the tiny squares together when she was a teenager. She told me which pieces were from her grandmother's worn-out dresses.

I put it in my trunk, under all my new clothes. Then the family picture on my dresser goes in. I'm ten here. It was taken when we were all dressed up for Grandma's funeral. Dad looks very much like I remember him, though I can't see any grey in his hair. The picture's in black and white. A little grey wouldn't show. The only other photo I have of Dad is his army one. We aren't much for photographs—Martin couldn't see them.

In his army picture Dad looks a lot younger than I remember him. Almost like a boy, a lot like Martin, except for the eyes. Dad's are clear and look right back at me. The photo was taken in 1940 when he was thirty-three. That would've been just a few months before Martin's accident.

Mother told me she didn't see him from between '41 and the summer of '45. That's too long to be apart, she said.

After his death she gave me his army picture and now I put it in my trunk with the quilt. The walls look bare—will it feel like my room when I come back?

Mother's still canning tomatoes and tells me to make the tea. She'll be out on the porch soon.

When I carry the tray out, I see Martin's reading. I pour him a cup and he mumbles "thanks."

I settle myself on the swing. Orange and mauve fill the sky in the west. I'll miss this place. I'm scared. Excited too. I wish I could bring Misty along. Board him on a farm near Kingston.

Mother said that wasn't practical. "Misty will be fine," she said. "I'll enjoy looking after him. He'll be waiting for you, Gretchen."

What will I do when I'm lonely? No warm pony to hug, take for rides.

Caesar lies on my lap, and I stroke his black-and-white belly. He stretches out and from the tip of his nose to the tip of his tail he's three-quarters the length of the porch swing. Hard to believe he was once a bedraggled little stray. He jumps off and mer-rows at the door.

Martin gets up and lets him out. "Have a good one," he says and laughs. He sits and picks up his loose-leaf binder, his hand moving swiftly down each page.

"What are you reading?" I ask.

"Just going over the first chapter of my novel."

"Is the book finished?"

"No, just beginning. Though I've got close to a hundred pages done in rough."

"I'd like to read it."

"Too racy for you, I'm afraid."

"Martin, I'm eighteen, all grown up."

He looks up and grins. "Eighteen you are. Grown-up? Not even close. But this part's mild enough. I'll read you a bit. Braille's slow going for you."

> "What's your name? The red-haired giant's words sounded more like a demand than a question, on Joe's first day of school. Jigsy, Joe answered. How clueless could he be, but at home he'd always been called Jigsy, because of the way he walked, weaving side to side like a drunk. Bob, his father, also called him Arsehole and Little Shit, but Joe knew those weren't real names. Stupid kid—didn't even know his right name. The teachers called him Joe.
>
> At recess Ted Englehart, the red-haired giant, knocked him down because he wouldn't dance. "Jigsy, dance us a jig!" Ted hollered. Cathy, her golden brown

ponytail bouncing side to side, marched over. Leave him alone, you big bully. She helped him up. "Joe, come play ball with me and Maeve." His sister, Maeve, was still in grade one, though two years older. She had trouble learning to read.

He and Cathy were friends from that day on. Along with Ted and Maeve they were the only children on Marsh Road. Cathy rode her bike over to his place and they hiked through the fields to the swamp. One time, Ted followed them on his bike. Go home, she said. And mind your own business.

Cathy and Joe were twelve when they built the raft from scrap lumber and logs. Not much of a raft, always floated at an angle. Nevertheless, it allowed them to explore Eight Mile Creek. The day they spotted the canoe, a perfectly good one floating overturned, Cathy thought they should tell somebody, but Joe said "finders keepers." The paddles were missing, but they used some old ones from the drive-shed.

Now they could explore the creek far into the marsh. Maeve never went with them. Scared of drowning, scared of snakes. Cathy learned to swim at Elginville beach where she went with her girlfriends, but Joe wouldn't go there. He didn't want people gawking.

Cathy says don't be silly, you're a good-looking boy. I like your dark hair and your blue eyes that look cold until you smile.

I like it here with just you, he says. I could learn to swim, if you teach me. Don't matter none the water's muddy.

Okay, try it. Take a big gulp of air and hold it. Go under, kick your legs and move your arms, wriggle like a fish, says Cathy.

He tries and by God, he's swimming. He's amazed how easily he can move under water, just like any other kid.

One bright September morning he and Cathy are exploring. They can paddle pretty well now.

Waving fields of cattails as far as the eye can see.
The swamp's noisy—frogs, insects, ducks, cawing crows,
and the call of a red-winged black bird. I like it, nobody
but us, Cathy whispers.

Me too. Joe smiles. Already at age twelve he notices
the rise of her breasts under the thin cotton blouse.

DOESN'T TAKE MARTIN long to bring sex into everything he writes. "Does Joe kill his father?" I ask.

"How do you know about that? That's not in what I just read."

"Oh ... um. Donna's told me a bit more about *Marsh Road*."

"What does she think of Joe?"

"I don't know. Do Joe and Cathy end up together?"

"That's still to be decided."

"Martin, do you ever wish we were children again?"

"You kidding? Childhood was hell."

I want to ask about all our hikes, campfires and Mother's story-telling. He's basing *Marsh Road* on one of her stories. What about when we still had our dad? I don't say anything. What's the point?

The sun's down now. Branches scrape the screens. Mother'll find us sitting in the dark. Order us to turn the light on. Mother, who is so frugal, is extravagant with light. Martin's world is always dark.

I GET OUT of bed just as the birds commence their predawn ruckus. Downstairs, I'm glad to see Mother isn't up. Slip on my sneakers and I'm out the door.

As I walk up the hill past the sleeping houses, the sky's dark, just a narrow band of pink above on the horizon. I've already said goodbye to Donna. Billy could be walking by the time I get home at Christmas.

Martin told me he sometimes writes from midnight to dawn. "Don't you get tired?" I said.

"I love it," he replied simply.

I hope someday I find work I'm that keen on. And someone to love. He loves Donna, always has. What will happen with them? I don't know, but he seems pretty confident these days.

I'm not in love with anybody and I don't have a clue what I want to do with my life. I know what I don't want: to spend my life as a servant, like Mother.

What does Mother want? She's most content in her garden. How carefully she pats the soil around the new plants. At least she has that. I want a lot more. I won't be an old woman filled with regrets.

Mother made a big lunch. I couldn't eat much. I helped with the dishes though she said she'd do them later. Took both of us to get my trunk into the car. Martin came with us to the station.

I waved until I couldn't see them anymore. Pressed my face against the cold glass and cried.

As the train clickety-clacks out the miles, I pull myself together. I've said my goodbyes,

I jerk awake. The train's starting up again. As we pull away from the limestone station, I see the sign — Coburg. I've never been here before. What would it be like to live in that blue house by the river or that brick one on the hill? I'll never know. I'm crying again. I want to live in all the houses, explore all the roads.

What will university be like? I don't know.

But that untravelled world — I want to travel it all.

GIRL IN A SHOE

PUSHING THE PRAM is exhausting. I see Mrs. Thorton mowing the lawn. I wave and she switches off the machine. I hope Gretchen's already home from school. I'm sure going to miss her when she leaves in September.

"Hi, Donna, have you time for a cup of tea?"

"Thanks, Mrs. Thorton. Billy finally went to sleep. You sure have a lot of grass to mow."

"And it grows so quickly in June. I'll let it dry and then rake it up for Gretchen's pony." She peeks in the pram. "So angelic when they're sleeping. They wear you out though, don't they? You look tired, dear."

"Yeah, he cries so much. Is Gretchen home?"

"No, she's writing her Latin exam. A cup of tea will do you good. We'll have it on the porch. I'll get the kettle on."

From the porch swing, I can keep an eye on the pram parked by the steps. I push the swing with my foot. The dear, familiar grating noise. Gretchen said when she was little, she named the swing Screechy. Gretchen and I are the same age but when she's not in school, she's riding Misty. Feels like years since I did things like that.

I hear the whomp of Martin's cane before I see him. My breath quickens. And he's here, his tall stooped frame, cloudy blue eyes, curly black hair. And I'm fourteen again. I smile.

Gretchen asked me in to lend me a book. He was reading a braille copy of Plato. He and his mother were studying Plato that summer. I first thought he meant the planet Pluto. How we've laughed over that. How flattered I was by the attentions of this older, handsome boy.

"Hi, Martin." I stand up.

"Hi, Donna." He pulls me to him. Hugs me.

Reluctantly, I pull away. "Martin, I'm married now." Though his cloudy eyes can't focus, I know he's looking at me. A long time ago he told me he just sees shadowy outlines. He grins.

"Little Donna, all grown up."

"What are you writing these days?"

"*Marsh Road* continues. Joe dreams of rescue."

Mrs. Thorton arrives with the tea tray. "Do sit down, Martin."

WHEN I GET home, I wheel the pram around to the back and haul it up on the deck, parking it under the kitchen window.

Better get the roast in, scrub the kitchen floor and wash the dishes. If the place isn't spotless, Rick's mother'll make me feel guilty. She'll be telling me once again how lucky we are to have this new house when we haven't even been married a year. And how good it was of Rick's dad to co-sign the mortgage and my dad to lend us the down payment. It is good, and we are lucky. Then, of course, I'll hear again how tough they all had it during the Depression. I haven't got time to think of all the things I should be thankful for.

I'm down on my hands and knees scrubbing. I should've said something to Martin about the letters. The latest came two days ago.

I sigh, get up and go in the bedroom. The letters are neatly stacked in the bottom of my underwear drawer. I take out the latest.

June 1, 1957
Dear Donna,

Bring me a beer and I'll read to you. Mother, after much prodding and gnashing of teeth, did buy some. But she keeps them hidden in the cellar and doles them out one by one with dire warnings about drunkenness and the squandering of one's time. Art is long, beer brevis. That deprivation is nothing compared to the deprivation of your company, my darling.

I write at least two pages a day and spend what's left of the day editing, just like Hemingway.

On his sixteenth birthday Joe's fuckin' arsehole dad bought 200 chickens and set him up in the chicken business. Money to be made, said Bob, who quit farming years ago to sell used cars in Elginville.

Joe hauls a burlap sack of cockerels to the chopping block. Spurs dig into his wrist as he forces the neck between two nails pounded into the block. One whack of his axe and the head flies off. The headless chicken runs in circles till it flops over. Joe gags — oh God, he hates the smell of chicken shit and blood. When the last chicken is headless, he gathers the dead bodies into the sack, leaving the severed heads in a pool of blood for the cats.

In the gutting shed, he hangs them by their feet above a trough to catch their blood. He goes to the house for supper.

Mom has made chicken pot pie. Joe smells only chicken stink and can barely eat.

Back in the gutting shed, he heats water, scalds, plucks and guts the bodies. He packs them into the old icebox. Once he has the sink cleaned out, he fills it with hot water. Plunges his face and arms into the scalding water and scrubs himself with harsh yellow soap.

Hey, Chicken Shit, keep your skin on! Bob stands in the doorway. You damn well better have that order ready for the hotel.

Later, lying in bed, Joe makes himself forget his day of slaughter and shit by remembering the time he and Cathy found the shack.

They pulled the canoe up on the muddy bank and went looking for elderberries.

The shack so sheathed in vines they almost walked past it.

Joe hacked the vines from the door. They must've been growing for years.

Sleeping Beauty's castle, said Cathy.

One big room, about 12 by 20, with a rusty cook stove, table, two chairs and an iron bedstead.

How'd they get it all here? Cathy asked.

Maybe in the old days there was a road. Joe looked out the window. Past the cedars, there's a steep drop leading down to the creek. We must've come up the back way, he said.

Yeah, the creek must circle around.

She found a tattered broom in a corner and swept the mattress. We could fix this place up.

They made elderberry sandwiches. The sour berries were delicious crushed between slabs of his mom's fresh bread.

This can be our fort, said Joe. Back then, he was still young enough to think of forts. Let's never tell anyone.

Our secret place. Cathy grinned.

Tonight, as Joe lies on his hard bed, he remembers those secret meetings and longs for Cathy, for only her sweet scent will drive out chicken stink, thoughts of unavenged Maeve and hatred of Bob.

Come, Donna, tomorrow afternoon. Mother has a library meeting. Rick won't notice a couple of missing beers. Come with or without beer but come.

Bees hum in the lilacs blooming for you, my darling.

WHY IS HE writing all that stuff about chickens? His mother must've talked about growing up on a chicken farm. I fold the letter into a tiny square like the notes school kids passed each other and stuff it in my jeans. Wouldn't matter if Rick saw it. He can't read braille. While Gretchen was at the pony track, Martin spent entire afternoons teaching me to use the braille typewriter. Our secret language.

Oh Martin, you have to stop writing me letters. Our story ends here.

GRETCHEN STOPS IN on her way home from school and I make coffee.

"He's growing too fast. He's already lost that new baby look," Gretchen says, kissing Billy's head.

"Not fast enough. I'll be glad when he's not crying all the time."

"Little babies make me think of newborn kittens. When I was little, I wanted to be a mother cat with a nest of kittens in the hay. The way the cat purred as they crawled on her belly. She seemed so happy."

I have to laugh. "You have an awfully romantic view of motherhood. A dozen stinky diapers a day, baby puke on everything. And the crying! That's the worst. But I don't want to talk about babies."

"Oh?" She's humming to Billy now.

"Your brother wrote me another letter."

"Did you tell him to stop like I told you to?"

"Not exactly."

"Why not?" Gretchen frowns.

"I figure he's lonely."

"Not your problem."

She sounds annoyed. She's supposed to be my friend. "He's always there when I visit your mother. I can't help seeing him."

"Well, maybe come over less for a while. I can visit you here."

"Your mother's been so kind to me. And since Mom had her stroke, I don't feel I have a mother."

"You told me she was better, getting around with the walker."

She goes right on cooing to Billy. Not paying any attention to me. "She is better. My sister looks after her, the kids and the house. But if I go there I'm just in the way. Billy's crying bothers her. She has no interest in her own grandchild."

"Must be because she's sick." She looks up from Billy for a second.

"Maybe, but she's never showed any interest in Ted and Laurie's baby either."

"That is a bit strange. Donna, I'm going to have to go. Mother doesn't like it if I'm late for supper. Please tell my brother to stop writing to you."

Gretchen always rushes off. She likes the baby but sometimes I feel she doesn't give a damn about me. Such a cold fish. I wanted her to read the letter and tell me how to handle Martin without hurting his feelings. Has she forgotten all the good times the three of us had together?

Rick won't be home till late. I wish he'd come home for supper like he used to but July's a busy month. Gets a burger from the Quick Stop and I can't be bothered making supper just for one. A peanut butter sandwich is enough.

Two hours later, after feeding, burping, changing Billy and listening to him cry for an hour, I'm relieved when he finally falls asleep. Thank God for gripe water. It's so hot that sweat's coursing down my face. I need a smoke.

Gretchen's still riding ponies. Doesn't even have a boyfriend. I'm not going to talk to her anymore about the letters. What the hell does she know about anything? Martin and I were friends long before I met Rick. Our friendship's nobody's business.

Damn it, is that Billy? If I don't go in, maybe he'll go back to sleep. Babies. Should've taken a closer look at Mom's life. I never wanted to be her. Brenda and me stuck looking after her babies. I swore my life would be different. What did I know?

The strangest thing is, I think Rick likes being married. His idea to get the station wagon. Time to settle down, he said. "Dad will make me a full partner soon."

This is the famous football hero talking, notorious for his partying. He smashed up his car once, walked away without a scratch. He drove his red convertible dangerously fast. Thought he could drive through the sand hills at Blackstone Point. Got stuck, but before he called his friend with the truck, we made love on the sand. That's my Rick. He used to call me darling. Now, it's always Pumpkin.

Butt my cigarette on a mosquito that's landed on the railing. I'm living Mom's life. What if I have a stroke when I'm 41? High blood pressure runs in families. Life can't just be growing up, getting married, having babies and dying. Where's the fun in that?

I shouldn't think like that. But how could she have a stroke at 41? Her leg looks like an old woman's—bulging veins, wrinkled skin and her ankles fat and shiny. The old Mom twirled for us in her little black dress. Them kissing. "Legs of a twenty-year-old," Dad said. It's not as if she's dead but she might as well be. A terrible thing to say but she's so unhappy. Did she intend to have five kids? Not me. Rick wants another one.

I got fitted for a diaphragm but he doesn't like me getting up to put it in. Says it ruins the mood. I try to remember to put it in every night. Sometimes I'm so tired I forget. Of course, it's okay if I've just had my period. I can't get pregnant then.

The sun's sinking. Gretchen would be admiring the sunset. All it means to me is soon Billy will be hollering for his next bottle. Oh God, let there be time for another smoke.

I'VE HAD A long hot shower. Rick's in there now. At the mirror, I admire myself in the red sheath dress I bought the week after Billy was born. Bawled the first time I tried it on — still looked three months pregnant. Oh Donna, you dope, did you think your belly would deflate like a balloon the moment the baby popped out? I look pretty good now. Lost most of the weight I gained. Lack of sleep or all that carrying laundry up and down the basement stairs is good for something.

Rick's mom picked Billy up at noon and is keeping him until tomorrow morning. I should appreciate her more but I get sick of her hugging Billy and saying: "How's my boy today?" He's not her baby.

"Pumpkin, you look good enough to eat!" Rick says, stark naked and dripping water all over the hardwood floor.

"Stop! You'll get water on me. Get dressed!"

"Yes, Mommy."

"Don't call me that."

"Okay, okay, be nice to me." He picks his towel up off the floor and rubs himself dry. His cock sticks straight out.

"Later, Rick. We have dinner reservations, remember?"

"Just a quickie please, Pumpkin?"

I grab his towel and swat his belly with it. "Meet you in the car." And I'm out of there.

RICK'S DRIVING TOO fast. Okay, he's mad at me. So I don't want it every bloody minute. Wham, bang, thank you ma'am. Not much fun. Sometimes he takes his time and it's good for me too. Other times I'm just so tired it wouldn't matter what he did. I spent an hour fixing my makeup and hair and what the hell, we haven't been out anywhere, alone, in months.

The car fishtails and my arm bangs against the door. "Watch it, Rick!"

"Sorry, Pumpkin. It's these damn gravel roads." He slows down.

"Gretchen and I used to ride the ponies along here."

"She plans on college, doesn't she?"

"Yeah."

"College wasn't for me, though my brother likes it. Who in their right mind would want to be a dentist — your hands stuck in other people's mouths all day? But he figures he'll make a fortune."

WE WALK HAND in hand into the pavilion — me in my red dress. Why didn't Rick wear his Levi's? He's always in a suit now, like his dad. There's a deejay playing the dining room where the dance floor is, but I like it better on the veranda overlooking the beach. We get a table right by the railing. We both order steak and fries.

"Once we rode the ponies along the beach all the way here," I tell Rick.

"Gretchen thinks herself too good for any hometown fellas."

"She's just shy."

"Peculiar, more like it. Hangs around too much with that poor crip of a brother."

"You don't really know either of them."

"Well, he's a creep, wandering around at night. Wonder if he peeks in people's windows? A blind peeping Tom, that's pretty funny."

"You're being stupid."

"Why are you bitching? Thought you wanted to come here."

"Yeah, I did."

"You know what? I sold five cars this week. First time my commission's more than my salary. Dad's not one to say much but he's pleased."

"That's good."

"I figure you just have to match the customer to the car. Like if Miss Ellerbeck, who's taught grade one since the ice age, comes in, don't try to sell her that groovy Chev convertible. She'll go for that stubby, 1948 Ford coupe I've been trying to get off the lot for the past six months."

Does he think I bloody well care what Miss Ellerbeck drives? "A whole year since we've been here."

"Yeah, we should get Mom to babysit more often. If things keep going this good, we'll double up the payments to your dad."

"Dad's not in a hurry for us to repay the loan."

"Well, I don't know, Pumpkin, but I figure with your mom ill ..."

"They're not hard up."

"I know that."

"Remember the last time we were here?"

He grins. "How could I forget? Thought a Ford V8 engine could handle the dunes."

I snicker. "A nice private spot where we got stuck."

"Worth it, having Dad bawl me out about the broken crank shaft."

WE'RE DANCING TO *Heartbreak Hotel* on a crowded floor and I'm not at all tired. Rick's arms around me feel good. I see the way women look at him. My Rick's a handsome guy. Tall, muscular, blonde crew cut. I smile at them—all mine, girls.

They're playing *Hound Dog* and we're jiving, stomping our feet. Rick left his suit jacket over the chair and has rolled up his sleeves. When I feel the music waking me up, it's like back in high school. He twirls me around, catches me, hugs me.

A GROCERY BAG on each arm, I trudge along Leaman Road. The tarry smell makes me sick. Why do I bother visiting Mom? I'm not wanted and Brenda manages just fine. The sun's too bright. You fool, not the sun or the tar making you feel like puking. Damn, damn, damn. How did it happen? Maybe that night when we got home from the pavilion? Couldn't have been then. My period had just finished. We danced and walked on the beach.

Rick hates my diaphragm, says he can feel it. That was the only time I didn't put it in. What about when Billy had that cold? Me up most of the night and Rick snoring away. Back in bed, I was half-asleep when he woke up and climbed on top. Did I get up and put my diaphragm in? I don't remember.

I can't have another kid. Rick'll be delighted. Did Mom intend to have another just a year after Tommy? I should ask her. Would she tell me the truth?

What the hell's the matter with me? I love Rick and my baby, but … but what? Like there's another life I should be living. Hanging out with my friends. Getting a real job. Sharon and I planned to find work in an office. She finished grade twelve and is working in Toronto. Imagine! Sharon, with her riff-raffy family. Their house looks like it's held up by all the add-ons. Have another kid, add a room. Dad calls it "shed style" building. She's the one who should've had to get married. But no, she has her own apartment in Toronto. Bet she flirts with her boss.

I've got to get home. I'll phone Rick's mother. Tell her I was sick. Rick can fetch Billy after work.

Go home. Take a cool bath. You'll feel better. I'll never feel better.

A WEEK LATER, me and Billy are on the Thortons' screened porch. I should be home. The house is a complete mess and Rick's brother and his girlfriend are coming for supper. Rick's bright idea. "Jimmy's in town with his new girl. I'll get some steaks."

I haven't met this girlfriend. No doubt another stuck-up college girl. When Mrs. Thorton invited me in, I should've said no.

She's gone to refill the teapot when Martin walks in.

"Hi, Martin."

He comes right over and hugs me. I feel his nose in my hair.

"Will you have a cup of tea with us, Martin?" Mrs. Thorton asks.

He lets me go. We drink our tea while Billy gurgles on a blanket on the floor. Only five months old and he can propel himself along on his stomach. "The baby's crawling right to you," I tell Martin.

He crouches down and runs his hands over the baby, gently touching his hair, his nose, mouth. A long time ago he asked me: "May I touch your face, so I'll know what you look like?" Why do I feel like crying?

Mrs. Thorton's talking about tomatoes. "There must be a bushel of ripe tomatoes. Why don't you take some home with you? Are you interested in canning any?"

"Could you write out the directions?"

"I'd really have to show you. Why don't we can together and split the batches? I've lots of jars."

IN THE DAYS and weeks that follow we can tomatoes together. I enjoy it.

Mom thinks I'm crazy. "Tinned tomatoes from the store are so cheap. Nobody bothers with canning anymore."

"Mrs. Thorton does."

"Those Thortons, a peculiar lot. Now you're married you should've outgrown them. Plenty of money, yet she dresses like a farm woman. Only farm wives do all that canning."

"Well, I like canning."

Mom never liked me hanging out with them. She didn't mind me going riding with Gretchen but didn't like me playing cards with Martin.

She's always been critical and since her stroke, she's worse. She has reason to be unhappy—the left side of her face droops and her unsteadiness means she has to use a walker. But she heaps praise on Brenda.

I get another letter from Martin. Mrs. Thorton must address the envelopes because they're not in braille. I don't like this. What if Rick had brought in the mail?

August 20, 1957

Dear Donna,

Tomorrow, when you're canning with my mother, come to my studio. I want to read you my next chapter. Enclosed are the first couple of pages, just a teaser so you'll want to know what happens next.

Joe figured the only good thing about being a fulltime chicken farmer was Fucking-Arsehole Bob bought him an old truck for deliveries. Joe was at the mill getting feed when he overheard Ted Englehart. 'Smoke chokin' me and it's blacker'n hell and about as hot, but I pulled Cathy and her mom out. All the time thinkin', that furnace gonna blow. Cathy's crying, but I get them over to the farm and they're gonna stay. Out of that firetrap. Faulty wiring most likely. Pretty swell this morning, havin' breakfast and still in our PJs. Cathy's real cute. Ted sniggered.

Joe wanted to rush over to Cathy but knew he wouldn't be welcome, at least not by Ted or her mother.

He cursed himself for sleeping through the whole thing, sirens and all.

Saturday, he and Cathy are in the canoe, paddling toward the shack. He tells her he wishes he'd been the one to rescue her.

She says 'nobody rescued me'.

But Ted said …

Ted's full of hot air. The only rescuing that went on was I had to haul Muffy from the back of the closet.

But you're staying at Engleharts?

Ted's granddad invited us to move in. He and my mother have been friends for ages.

You mean you're going to live there permanently?

Sure hope not. Mr. Englehart's nice, but Ted's a pest. When I finish high school, Mother wants me to go to university.

What do you want?

To stay right here forever. She stops paddling, trails her hand through the water. Laughs when minnows nibble her fingers.

With Cathy living at Englehart's, she comes over evenings as well as weekends. They head for the marsh and their shack. She brings her school books, helps him keep up. He will study on his own, do the Departmental Exams and escape the chicken farm. He'll go to university, become an engineer. Maybe he can win a scholarship. In school he always got the top mark in math.

He'll save his money from the chicken farm. The problem is Bob only gives him five dollars a week. His excuse is they need to build up the business.

Grade eleven finishes and Cathy starts grade twelve, Ted along with her. She says she doesn't know why Ted stays in school. He's too old and barely passes the exams. Joe could guess why he stays. Cathy tells him Ted wants to date her. She can handle him, or so she says.

Why don't you and your mother move out?

We can't, really. Her heart's so bad she had to quit her job and might need an operation. Mr. Englehart's going to pay for it and university for me.

Is your mother his girlfriend now?

No, nothing like that. He's 84.

Donna, come to my studio tomorrow and let me read to you.

I WANT TO go but I don't. Mrs. Thorton and I fill the wheelbarrow with the big tomatoes. A quick rub with her apron and she takes a big bite. "Warm from the garden, does that taste good!" The juice drips off her chin.

Now I know where Gretchen got the idea, sucking those warm tomatoes. She rarely comes to see me and I miss her.

I leave Billy with Rick's mother so Mrs. Thorton and I can spend afternoons making tomato sauce. Sometimes Martin stands in the doorway and eavesdrops. He makes me feel self-conscious and I feel like screaming: "Go away! I'm a married woman now."

When I tell Mrs. Thorton I'm pregnant again, he's standing there. He stares at me. Funny to say a blind man stares. But his intensity makes me blush.

"So soon," she says. "Still, it'll be nice for Billy to have a little brother or sister."

After canning all afternoon, I'm so tired when I get home I fall asleep right after supper.

Rick says: "Why are you wearing yourself out? We can afford to buy groceries."

"I like canning."

Rick's different now we're married. I think of that joke: "You don't run after the bus once you've caught it." It's supposed to mean that, if you let your boyfriend go all the way, he won't marry you. He got what he wanted. But I think there's more to it. Once a guy marries a girl, he doesn't have to court her. Gets what he needs without going to any bother. Before, he had to beg for it.

I miss the convertible. Canning with Mrs. Thorton keeps me from thinking about convertibles.

HER KITCHEN SMELLS of ripe fruit and boiling sugar. Late September and Gretchen's left for university. Mrs. Thorton has a bumper crop of pears.

The rows of jars filled with pale shapes floating in syrup make me think of babies floating in their mommas' wombs. Our feet are bare on these hot preserving days. I wear a loose sundress without a bra. Mrs. Thorton, in an Eaton's catalogue housedress covered by a faded apron, smells of fruit and sweat and Johnson's baby powder.

When we run out of sugar, I volunteer to go to the store but Mrs. Thorton says she hasn't been out of the house all day and could do with a walk.

"While I'm gone, why don't you have a cup of tea with Martin?"

Martin's on the porch and I suggest tea.

"Let's go for a walk," he says. "You can see how I've arranged my studio." He laughs. "My first step in leaving home."

Martin curses when he stumbles carrying the electric kettle. I notice he's limping hard and using his cane more.

"Let me plug it in," I say, placing my hand on his arm. He sets down the kettle and takes my hand. When he puts his arms around me, I know I should stop him. Wonderful the way his big hands so gently massage my back. He's kissing me and I'm kissing him back. He pushes down the elasticized neck on my sundress and kisses my bare breasts. I unbutton his shirt. He lifts my skirt and cups my bum. I unbuckle his belt and unzip his trousers. We end up on the couch.

I don't know why I don't stop him. Yes, I do. I don't want to.

You've only been married a year, goes through my head. But what does that have to do with Martin?

I don't know how much time has passed before I hear Mrs. Thorton calling us.

I scramble to gather my clothes. "Get dressed," I hiss at Martin, who sits there with a little smile on his face. I throw his shirt and pants on his lap and hustle up to the house.

"We had our tea out in Martin's studio. Really nice the way you fixed it up. I remember when it was just an old shed." Oh, my hair's all mussed and what if I smell of it?

"He needed a more private place to write," Mrs. Thorton says with a smile. "I guess we'd better get these pears done." She measures out the sugar while I put the jars on to boil.

Watching the pears bounce lightly as we add the syrup I look up to see Martin standing in the doorway. His shirt's buttoned up crooked. What if she notices?

THE HOT WATER running over my breasts and between my legs should wash Martin away but only makes me want him more.

What would Mrs. Thorton think of me? She's so straitlaced, a churchgoer who always puts duty first. She's devoted her life to Martin. After Mr. Thorton died, she could've found herself another husband if she hadn't been so busy tending to Martin. What kind of woman am I? I believe in my wedding vows. Once you're married, you're married.

I love Rick and little Billy but forgot all about them while I was with Martin. Thank God, I'm already pregnant.

I AVOID MARTIN for a long time. Canning season's over which makes it easier.

Then I get a letter from him.

Rick brings it in. "Here's a letter from your old boyfriend."

I'm glad Rick thinks Martin's a joke and shows no interest in reading his letters. It's not a letter, it's a poem.

The Harvest

Beyond the screen
bees harvest
windfall pears
while I kiss
each knob of your spine
hard bones
soft inner thighs
over-ripe pear's
slight perfume
is replaced
by your sweeter musk.
The bees and I
burrow and suck
and the air vibrates
humming through our bodies.
Bees tunnel pears
while we harvest.

EVEN RICK WOULD catch the gist of that poem — if, that is, he could read braille.

BEING PREGNANT WHEN we did it somehow makes it worse. All I do is mope around the house. I have morning sickness far worse than before. Even when not throwing up, I'm nauseous. And I'm getting huge. Always sick, I hardly eat anything.

Rick's kindness is horrible. As soon as he gets home from work, he plays with Billy. Some nights he even gives him his bath and puts him to bed. Once I've done the dishes, I just sit.

I GET ANOTHER letter.

> October 27, 1957
> *Dear Donna,*
>   *I miss you. Oh, how I miss you. I work hard at my writing, sometimes through the night. Here's a bit of the next chapter. Come see me and I'll read you the rest.*
>   In October, Mr. Englehart dies of a massive stroke. In November Cathy tells Joe about the possibility of her mother going to the Mayo clinic in Minnesota for open heart surgery not available in Canada.
>   In December Joe and Cathy snowshoe across the frozen marsh. He can handle snowshoes despite his lop-sided gait. The sun shines, the snow glitters and Joe gets a hard-on just thinking about being in the cabin with Cathy.
>   After he gets a fire going in the woodstove, they lie down on the bed and start fondling each other. They tug off each other's t-shirts. Their rule is no nudity below the waist. They don't want babies, they're planning on university. Cathy hasn't worn a bra and he fondles and sucks her breasts. He loves her small brown nipples and pushes his stiff cock against her.

Yanking out a package of rubbers from her jeans, she
tucks it in his hand. Standing in front of him, she pulls
down her jeans and panties and lies back down beside
him. He's so surprised, he can barely get his jeans and
boxers off. She kisses his cock and helps him pull on the
rubber. He tries to be careful, but she moans and locks
her legs around his ass. When he comes, it's like nothing
he's ever experienced, like being 100 per cent in his body
and 100 per cent out of it at the same time, like all the
stars have fallen through the earth, and he's fallen with
them. He can't describe it but has to. Being in her body is
the world being born.

In January, Cathy, her mother and Ted go to Minnesota
for her mother's surgery. Cathy and Ted come back married.

In some ways nothing changes. Cathy comes to the
shack regularly and they make love. They don't talk much,
but Joe asks, Did your mother want you to marry him?

Well, she said he would take good care of me. She
said the Engleharts are important people around here.
Ted's grandfather was a member of Parliament.

What did you want?

Mother would've died without the operation. I was
so scared.

Joe says, Bob showed me the money he's saving for me
—stacks of tens, twenties, fifties. He keeps it in a strong
box. When I get my money, we'll run away.

Cathy nods. Then she says, there's my mother to think of.

We'll look after her.

Okay.

Donna, please come see me.
Your lover, Martin

OH MARTIN, I can't deal with this. You're not my lover. And I don't
want to read any more of your stories.

I go to bed as soon as Billy does. When Rick comes to bed and tries to climb on top of me, I burst into tears. "Rick, I'm sick. Leave me alone."

"Ah, Pumpkin, it'll be okay."

He holds me in his arms and kisses me. "I'm gonna be sick." Untangling myself I rush to the bathroom.

When I get back in bed, I curl up into a tight ball.

He pats my shoulder and snuggles up against my back.

That's the end of it, that night. But the next night when he's cozied up against my back, he pushes up my nightgown, holds my thighs and pulls me up against him. "Don't worry, Pumpkin, I'll be gentle."

I just want to sleep, but if I object, he might get suspicious.

ONE AFTERNOON I'M sitting at the living room window when I see Mrs. Thorton walking up the hill toward downtown.

Martin's such a braggart. Must be proud of himself, finally got me to bed. At least Gretchen's away at university, so he won't be telling her. It's not the kind of thing even Martin would tell his mother. He never leaves the house so won't be blabbing it around town. Still, I better talk to him.

I pack up Billy and head over. Duck Martin when he tries to hug me. I sit in Mrs. Thorton's rocking chair and make a fuss over the baby: "Pat-a-cake, pat-a-cake, baker's man, bake me a cake as fast as you can." When Martin strokes my hair I shake my head and rock faster. I turn on Martin. "Okay Martin, it's over. Stop writing me letters!"

"Leave Rick, come live with me."

I stare at him. "Don't be ridiculous. I'm pregnant."

"Pregnant! That's wonderful." A big grin splits his face. Does he know how ridiculous he looks?

"I'll look after you and our baby."

"It isn't our baby, you jerk, and you knew I was pregnant. You were there when I told your mother."

"Don't worry. I like babies." He tries again to stroke my hair. I shake my head and rock faster.

"I'm three months pregnant."

"Let me hold you." Martin puts his hands out and I stand up and step out of the way.

"I'm going home."

"It's okay, I won't tell anyone," he calls after me.

I TRY TO make myself stay home. This fall is the dreariest yet. As the wind whips the leaves from the trees, I stand at my picture window, weeping. I don't like this image and I hate my stupid self. My saggy body, my aching legs, the ugly blue veins criss-crossing my thick thighs.

I'm so alone. The baby's always here but there's nobody to talk to. Gretchen's away. I can't talk to Mom, Brenda's always there. She quit school, says she'll go back when Mom's all better. Even if I could get Mom alone, what would I say? That I don't want another baby and I've been unfaithful to my husband? She'd call me a slut. Tell me I don't deserve Rick and the nice house I live in. I want to talk to Mrs. Thorton. That's my craziest thought yet. She'd be even more shocked than Mom.

God, Billy's driving me crazy. He's crawling now and gets into everything. We bought a playpen with wooden rails that reminds me of an animal cage. Billy shakes the rails and howls.

I can't stand it any longer and let him out. When I go to pee, third time in an hour, I hear a loud crash. There's broken glass everywhere, and Billy's wailing. He's pulled the lamp off the end table.

He's not hurt and I stick him back in the playpen. He screams and screams. I fix him a bottle and prop it up on a cushion so I don't have to hold it. I sweep up the broken glass, vacuum the carpet and, on my hands and knees, feel every square inch for bits I might've missed. We play on the floor with his toys for a while but I'm so bored with the same old red truck I consider a walk, even though it's raining. No walk. No nap either, as he slept from eleven until one while I caught up on some piles of laundry.

Billy bellows from his pen when it's time to get supper, so loud I long for earplugs. I turn up the radio. Hank Williams is singing *My Cheatin' Heart*. My tears plop on the potatoes I'm peeling.

Rick comes in. "Hi Pumpkin, I'm home. How's Little Sport?" He picks up Billy who promptly stops crying. "Let's play ball till Mommy has supper ready."

Mommy, I hate it when he calls me that. He should say to Billy "your mommy." He said: 'What's the difference mommy or your mommy?' I told him I'm not *his* mommy. But he just thought it was funny. Damn it! Am I going to end up like some housewife whose husband never calls her anything but Mother? Hell! Pumpkin's better than that. Supper's almost ready. In an hour I can put Billy to bed.

"**G**OOD THING WE got the station wagon, eh Pumpkin?"
Rick heaves the highchair into the back.

"The wheels of the car go round and round." I bounce Billy on my lap. Yeah, Rick, so generous of your dad to give us a station wagon when Billy was born. "Room for a whole football team," he and Rick joked. One kid's plenty, but here I am, nearly six months and thirty-five extra pounds along. What I wouldn't give for Rick and me to be back in his red convertible, *Hound Dog* blasting from the radio. Instead, I'm Pumpkin, a fat housewife with a baby on her lap and another in her belly. In high school I was Hot Pink Donna.

We're going to Mom's for Christmas Eve supper.

Brenda has done a turkey. My sister's a better cook than I am. Of course, she's not pregnant. Poor Mom's quiet at supper. Dad tries to jolly things along. Even opens a beer for me.

We exchange gifts. I got a mauve angora twin set for Brenda and a Norwegian wool vest for Dad. Tommy and Stevie love the Meccano sets. I'm excited when Mom starts opening her gift — the red satin housecoat.

She bursts into tears. I go to her, thinking she's overcome by our generosity. It was the most expensive robe I could find.

She pushes me away and sobs: "You think I need another housecoat? I suppose you think I spend all day in one!"

"Now Mom, it's okay." Brenda puts her arm around her. "Donna didn't know you get dressed every morning just like the rest of us."

Since her stroke she's been in that ratty chenille thing every time I drop in.

Mom heads toward her bedroom. Her walker makes it slow going.

"She throws temper tantrums for no reason," Dad says. "Just ignore ..."

"Christmas is a bad time for her," Brenda says. "How would you feel if last year you were out dancing and now you're using a walker?"

"We better get Billy home to bed," I say to the room in general. Nobody objects.

We aren't going home to bed. We're sleeping over at the Waddell's house so that we'll be there first thing Christmas morning. They want to see Billy open all his Santa gifts. They've created a grandkids' room —brand new crib, highchair, change table—all for Billy, their first grandchild.

DRESSED AS SANTA on Christmas morning, Mr. Waddell takes about fifty pictures while Billy, who has no idea what's going on, rips the paper off the presents. Each time Mr. Waddell needs to put in another roll of film we all have to stop and wait until we can resume our poses. He wants to record every moment of Billy's first Christmas. Both he and his wife have tears in their eyes. They bought Billy a fire truck, the kind a kid pedals like a tricycle. It's metal with a windshield that could be-head a small child. Billy tries to climb on and falls. Mrs. Waddell comforts him by sticking another damn cookie in his mouth. The third one. He promptly throws up all over the shiny gifts. She ignored me, of course, when I said he was too young for cookies.

Rick gives me a sewing machine tied with a big red bow. "Pretty nice, eh, Pumpkin?

"It's Singer's top model," his mother says. "You can even do embroidery on it. Be great for baby clothes."

I bet it was her idea. What am I? Her baby-making machine?

ON BOXING DAY, I go to Martin's for tea. When Gretchen greets me at the door, she's wearing old jeans and a ratty sweater. I expected her to look more sophisticated.

I hear Martin's cane before I see him. My heart pounds.

"Hi, Donna." He's wearing a black t-shirt and blue jeans. His glossy dark hair curls over his cloudy eyes. He smiles. Craggy face, but it's his full, warm lips that give me goose bumps.

"How about a poker game?" Martin says.

They've already set up the table with the braille cards and chips.

"Go ahead," Mrs. Thorton says. "I'll keep an eye on Billy."

It's like old times—a cozy room with kids just playing cards.

LIFTING BILLY OUT of the buggy I see that miraculously he's sound asleep.
I'll have time for a nap, the best Christmas present anybody could give
me. Rick's still out with his brother, shooting rabbits. Just as I'm stuffing my mitts in my coat pocket, I feel something there.

An envelope with my name, printed in braille. Damn it!

December 25, 1957
Dear Donna,

*Merry Christmas, my darling. I know we won't be able
to talk with my mother and sister here. When we play poker,
my mind won't be on the game. I will savour each moment I
can smell your sweet body.*

*Christmas Eve I stayed up all night writing. Let me
bring you up to date with "Marsh Road".*

The chickens have become psychopathic killers. A
disease produces sores on their combs and makes them
bleed. One drop of blood on another chicken is enough
for the whole flock to gang up and kill it. The infected
chickens fight back. More blood.

Joe grabs each chicken and scrubs it down. If it has
no sores or pecks, he tosses it into the unused cow stable
part of the barn. He's plugged in an electric heater. He
bags the wounded ones He knows he should bury them,
but Bob told him they go to the newly opened
southern-fried chicken restaurant. Money to be made,
he said.

In spite of the sub-zero temperature, Joe's soon
oozing sweat. Two hours later he wipes both chicken
blood and his own from his arms. When he spreads bales
of straw, he sees the chickens have dried nicely. They
peck at the straw and not each other. He turns off the
heater and returns to the scene of the massacre. He
shovels the shit and dirty straw into the wheelbarrow and
dumps it on the manure pile.

He's dumping the third load when Cathy climbs out
of her red Chevy. I brought the snowshoes, she calls out.

Joe leaves the overturned wheelbarrow. Won't Ted notice you missing?

He's off killing deer with his buddies.

In the gutting room, Joe washes his face and arms in the sink and changes into fresh clothes. As they set out across the untouched drifts, he scoops up the glittering snow and scrubs his face—breathes in the fresh scent. He still stinks of chicken. Cathy will tell him he's imagining it.

Cathy snowshoes ahead. Her red scarf and brown ponytail dance in the wind. He would follow her to the ends of the earth.

I CAN'T HELP it. I like his stories. I'd love to be snowshoeing across a marsh right now.

Oh, there's another page.

Dear Donna,

You can't have forgotten our afternoon together. The humming bees burrowed pears while we loved. You have no reason to feel guilty.

We loved each other long before you met Rick. All those summer afternoons when you learned braille and shared your smokes with me. You stayed with me. Though you didn't care about schoolwork, you studied hard with the Brailler. We have a private language that this town can't read.

It's only the crazy notion that pregnancy means you have to get married that has chained you to Rick. You must have faith, I will look after you. You're far too intelligent to spend your life with a man so inferior. He'll never make you happy. You have a right to be happy.

Gretchen leaves on Sunday and Mother has a Bible study meeting Monday afternoon. Please come see me.

Your lover, Martin.

I FOLD THE letter up quickly and shove it in my pocket. How dare he call himself my lover? What if he told Rick? What if Rick kicked me out? Mom wouldn't let me come home. I'm six months pregnant and as big as a cow. How could I get a job? My ankles are so swollen, even walking is painful. What would happen to Billy?

And Martin look after me? That's a joke. Fantasizes he'll write a bestseller and move to New York.

I knew what would happen when I went with him to his studio. It's almost like I didn't care. He held me and I let him. God, I know it was wrong. I'm so damn stupid.

I crawl into bed and wake to Billy hollering. Don't remember the whole dream, only that I was lying in a field of sweet clover and there was an open jar of pears. The bees were sucking them.

Rick calls to tell me he'll be home late.

I start a bath for Billy. Throw in lots of toys. I slide down onto the floor mat while he plays and rest my head on the side of the tub. When I'm pregnant, my cheeks get chubby. No wonder Rick's always joking: "How's the big Pumpkin doing? Do you think it'll be twins?" If Martin could see me, he wouldn't call me his beautiful darling.

Heaven forbid—twins! I'd slit my wrists. "C'mon, Billy," I say, "Time for bed." When I try to pick him up, he shrieks. I lay my head back down on the tub's edge. I'm afraid I'll fall asleep and Billy will slip under the water. Feel myself dozing off and jerk awake. When I haul him out of the tub, he kicks me in the belly. "Quit that!" I tuck him under my arm. I'd like to smack his plump pink bottom, but don't.

He screams while I'm diapering him and getting him into his sleepers, only stopping when I put him down on the floor while fixing his milk. Once he's in his crib with the bottle, I kiss his forehead and turn out the light. I'm thankful he can hold his own bottle now. He's a pretty smart baby.

After emptying the tub I take a hot shower, struggle into my nightgown and check on Billy. He's fast asleep.

Finally, I can go to bed. The wind howls. We must be getting more snow. Tonight, I'm grateful for this bed, this warm house. I think about poor people and wish every pregnant woman a warm room. The window rattles and I pull the quilt up over my head.

I barely stir when Rick comes in. I'm too tired to speak or open my eyes. He gets into bed and curls against my back. Cozy, though he smells of beer and sweat. Just as I'm dozing off, he pushes up my nightgown. "Rick, I'm too tired," I mumble.

"Hunting all day. I'm horny." He has me pinned in a bear hug and he's pushing up against my bum. He nips the back of my neck.

"Leave me alone, I'm tired!" I try to shrug him off.

"Shhh." He holds my thighs and lifts me up so he can get it in. What the hell do I care? I go back to sleep.

At five a.m. I carry Billy into the kitchen to fix another bottle. I almost trip over the pile on the floor — Rick's hunting clothes. Would it be such a strain for him to put them on, or even near, the washing machine? I put the baby down to crawl, throw the muddy clothes down the basement stairs and slam the door.

When I open the fridge I'm greeted with a skinned and gutted rabbit. I'm tempted to tuck it into bed with Rick.

D AVID'S BORN JUST three weeks after Billy's first birthday. Thank God Rick's mom takes Billy to her place twice a week. At least the new baby sleeps a lot and doesn't have colic. When Mrs. Waddell takes Billy I sleep all day, just waking up to feed David, change him and put him back in his crib.

MRS. THORTON INVITES me over. I haven't visited in months and they haven't seen the new baby. Rick's mom bought us a double stroller so now I can take both babies out. Mrs. Thorton told me Gretchen's home from university. That's good. I'll hang out with her and avoid Martin.

Gretchen and her mother both greet me at the door.

I hear the thud of Martin's cane. I haven't seen him since Boxing Day. When I get David out of his blankets to show him around, Martin insists on holding him. He stands there rocking the baby in his arms. Tears run down his cheeks but he's silent. My crying is loud wailing and choking noises.

Mrs. Thorton's embarrassed. "Martin, give me the baby and sit down for your tea." She takes David and Martin turns and leaves the room.

I stand there not knowing what to do.

A FEW DAYS later I get a letter.

> May 15, 1958
> *Dear Donna,*
>
> *Stayed up most of the night reading On the Road. My studio was so cold I wrapped up in two quilts. Frost last night and it's the middle of May. Mother doesn't approve of me spending the night out here. Is she afraid I'll escape?*
>
> *Chilly enough to imagine myself heading for Chicago but stranded somewhere in the hills near Pittsburgh with my thumb out and no ride in sight.*

I finished the book at four and went outside just as the birds were waking up. Even with the rain it was warmer outside.

I walked into Grenville. Mother's had a fit the few times she's spotted me coming home just before dawn. Easier walking at night when there's no glare, no shadows to trip me up. I can hear a car coming, feel its wind as it passes by. My thin-soled runners tell me I'm on the gravel shoulder.

With the town sleeping, the road, every crack and bump familiar, belongs to me. Sometimes I get as far as the highway and imagine walking the couple hundred miles to Windsor and then crossing over to Detroit. Don't worry, it's just fantasy.

I've walked this road so many nights for so many years. Summers when the crickets are as loud as the Quick Stop's jukebox and the grass has that spicy smell after there's been no rain for weeks. And I've walked at five a.m. in lilac season in a misty, perfumed rain with all the birds chorusing their chirping, cooing love.

Last night the rain changed to a steady drizzle, soaking my jacket. As I walked past your place, I thought about sneaking into your house to carry you away as you slept.

The honeysuckle hedge by the Leaman place is just coming into bloom. In their hayloft I would so gently lay you down. And what would you do when you woke up and found yourself spirited away?

Your lover, Martin

P.S. Listen to the new Patsy Cline song:
"I'm always walking after midnight searching for you
I walk for miles along the highway
Well that's just my way of saying I love you."

I TRACE HIS words with my finger.

IT BOTHERED ME thinking about him walking along the road while I lay beside Rick. Though I have no reason to think he comes near our house, I'm going to lie in bed wondering if he's outside.

The best thing to do is to talk to him.

Monday, when I see Mrs. Thorton walking up Leaman Road, she has Gretchen with her.

Once they're out of sight, I wrap the baby up in a blanket and head over.

I knock. No answer. I open the door. It's never locked. "Martin, you in the house?" I step inside. "Martin!" Maybe he's in his studio. Against my better judgment, I head past the forsythia hedge into the grove of lilacs. They're in full scent. My breath quickens. I shouldn't be here.

Our yard is neatly mown grass and two trimmed trees. The one next to ours is exactly the same, one king maple and one blue spruce.

Here, the lilacs have been growing forever, their overgrown branches so long and twisted I have to shove my way through to his studio door, keeping the baby clear of the unwieldy branches.

He flings it open. "Donna, you've come and brought our baby!"

And before I can stop him, he's hugging us both. I pull away. "Now stop this nonsense! You know he's not your baby. You knew I was pregnant."

"Don't worry, darling. You're here. That's all that matters." He grins and reaches for me.

I move aside. "Martin, I came to talk to you about your wandering around at night. Your mother worries."

"I know where I'm going. C'mon in. Sit down and I'll make tea."

"Okay, just for a little while." I do have to talk to him. He has to stop this nonsense about David being his. I sit in the desk chair. That way he can't sit beside me. I cuddle David.

Martin plugs in the kettle. Lifts the teapot down from the shelf. I'm always amazed at how easily he does things, like a sighted person.

"Come over to the couch. You'll be more comfortable."

"I'm fine here."

"You're wearing your Chanel No. 5, aren't you?"

"Yeah, I am."

"I like it."

His handsome face goes all serious. Rick never notices my perfume, even though he's the one who gave it to me. Did the saleslady tell him it's a popular scent?

Oh, Martin, you remind me of Heathcliff in *Wuthering Heights*, which we read during my last year. That book was so different from the boring stuff we usually read. Don't look sad, Martin. I would like to lift your dark curls off your forehead and kiss that sadness away. Oh God, how can I think that? Talk to him. "Martin, you know David's not your baby. You write beautiful poetry. Your name will live on in your poems."

"Don't talk nonsense, darling." His raises his eyebrows. "The substitution of art?" He laughs, such a bitter sound. "You're talking like my mother. Donna, I've read the most wonderful book, *On the Road* by Jack Kerouac. I'll lend it to you. Not the braille copy Mother made. Here's the original."

He hands me the book. He knows where everything is. He picked it right off the shelf.

"How do you know which book is which?"

"*On The Road* has a paper cover with a chewed spine, courtesy of Caesar Cat, I suspect. Us crips have to be observant."

"Don't call yourself that."

"Why not? It's the truth. I believe in calling a spade a spade."

"It's not the truth. You're a smart handsome man."

He runs his fingers over my face, and I know I must get out, right away. I push his hand away. "You woke up the baby." I lift David out of his blankets. He opens one eye and whimpers. "I have to feed him. I better go." I wrap him up quickly and push past Martin. He just stands there.

"Don't go. You didn't come to see me for three months and five days. Then you came but we had no time alone together. Been such a long winter." He sighs, reaches out, and takes my hand. "Don't go, Donna."

I pull my hand out of his. "Martin, if you went to church, you'd meet people. Stop wandering around at night. Go downtown in the daytime, talk to people, have a coffee at the Quick Stop. You turn your back on everyone."

"Not on you, Donna." He laughs but it's a sad little laugh. "Oh, Donna, you're the one I want to be with. Take the book. Read it."

"Fine!" I take it and gather book and baby to my chest. I practically run out of there.

THAT VISIT DIDN'T accomplish much, and sure enough, three days later I get another letter.

> June 4, 1958,
> *Dear Donna,*
>
> *In regards to you and Mother telling me to keep writing: that each publication is a living heir, that each poem I sign with my name is keeping my name alive, me being the last of the Thortons because if Gretchen ever has children, they'll have some man's surname. Poems are my children, you both say.*
>
> *Poems are not my children. Poems are my excrement. Most people don't know that all they leave behind is shit.*
>
> *The town council wants to build a sidewalk on our land and then bill us for the cost. Mother says we can't object even though the deed shows it's our property. Mother's getting old and is afraid to offend the council. I'm not. This is my house, my land, and when Mother dies, I'll have the money to get married.*
>
> *In the meantime, I'd better get a book published, because Mother may well outlive me. I'm putting together some of my science fiction stories to send to Ballantine Books in New York. They published Arthur C. Clarke's Childhood's End, one of my favourite science fiction novels.*
>
> *Gretchen's not in Mother's will. With the $10,000 Dad left her for university, she has no need of an inheritance. Soon she'll be a teacher and they're well enough paid. She's inclined to hold on to her money but she'll pass me a twenty if I nag. Conscience money.*
>
> *The Sand Press in California is going to publish "The Harvest" in an anthology they're putting together. I have achieved an underground reputation but the pay is bad. I need to find a magazine that respects my work and pays accordingly. I'm going to have to use a simpler style but the audience will still have to be reasonably intelligent. Sand Press doesn't pay much but at least they understand intelligent writing. When Mother dies I'm going to sell this place and*

go to California. Not fair she won't give me a share of the money. Why didn't Dad leave me $10,000? Of course, what did he care? He sent me away to that school as soon as he got home from the war.

All sorts of great writers go to California: Ginsburg, Kerouac. You'll like it there, could go to the beach year 'round.

It's three a.m. and from the sound of that wind we're getting more rain.

Here's a little poem for you.

Branches thrash the windows
while the wind's roar drowns
the clicking typewriter
my cold companion who
swallows my thoughts
and spits them out
in puny turds.

My fingers ache from
these rough keys and
will never find release
till they play
upon that other keyboard
where they can tap
each knob
of wrist, of spine, of rib, of hip
till they are stilled
by you.

Come to tea tomorrow, Donna.
Your lover, Martin.

I READ THAT letter twice and he doesn't mention David. With luck, he's accepted David isn't his. I don't know why he's still lending me books. How could he think I have time to read? I read a bit of *On the Road*. It's about a bunch of drunks. I return it to Mrs. Thorton at church.

I'M HELPING MRS. THORTON with the rhubarb jam. This fruit and sugar mixture has to cook longer than most jams. When she takes a turn stirring, Martin takes my arm and tells me he wants to show me something. I pull away but follow him into the living room.

"Has Rick figured out about David?" he whispers.

"You jerk! Rick is David's father. Count the months."

"He was premature, wasn't he?"

"A nine-pound baby premature? You have to be kidding."

AND THAT WASN'T the end of it. Generally, Martin ignores kids, but this one time, when David's about five months old and playing on the floor, Martin kneels down beside him on the blanket and offers him a rattle. He strokes the baby's head and says to me: "David has my curls."

"Rick's curls!" I say.

Martin just smiles. He's ridiculous.

I'M SO BUSY with the kids that for days at a time I forget about Martin. I hope he's forgotten about me.

The cold weather comes and I hardly leave the house. Not worth the struggle to get the two of them into their snowsuits.

The days are a blur. Every one's the same and weeks can pass without me noticing. Other times an afternoon feels like a year. Christmas comes and goes. I don't visit the Thortons on Boxing Day, say I have the flu. I don't even see Gretchen.

Then suddenly it's spring and my birthday. Rick takes me out for dinner. So tired all I want to do is go home and sleep. I'm 20, what the hell, lost in piles of dirty laundry and screaming babies.

"**S**TOP THAT!" I grab Billy and smack his bottom. Oh God I can't stand this. Now they're both crying. "Don't you dare kick your little brother!"

Jesus Christ, I hate this. I envy my brother hitchhiking out to Vancouver. Just took off. Sent me a postcard of a place called Kits Beach, where people loaf around sitting on logs. I'd love to sit on a log on a beach far from here.

Ted's living like those guys in that book Martin's always yakking about and trying to get me to read. I have visited the Thortons a few times, but I'm careful not to be alone with Martin. I told him those guys were a bunch of losers, abandoning their wives and girlfriends and driving drunk or hitchhiking back and forth across the United States. Just like Ted who left Laurie and his little girl and hitchhiked out to Vancouver.

"Here, spit it out. What's he got in his mouth, Billy?"

"Don't know."

I dig around in the baby's mouth and pull out chewed-up grass. At least it wasn't a rock this time.

"How about I put you guys in the stroller and we'll go for a walk?"

"Walk. No stroller. Big boy."

"Well, okay, but you hold on to the stroller. No running off." Three o'clock. In four more hours I can put them to bed.

"Let's go visit Auntie Laurie."

Billy helps me push the stroller for one minute before he takes off.

"That's it!" I grab his arm. "You get in the stroller!" I force him into his seat, and he kicks the baby. They're both bawling again.

I see Laurie's place up ahead. A winterized cottage her dad bought for them. What's she doing up on a ladder?

"Hi! That's no job for you."

She climbs down, dripping with sweat, splattered with green paint, and her face is scarlet. "Hi, guys." She gives me a hug.

Billy's in full tantrum mode, his feet rhythmically kicking the metal footrest.

"What's the trouble, Number One Nephew?" She crouches down beside him.

"He hates the stroller."

She undoes Billy's harness and lifts him out. "Why don't you go out back? Arlene's playing in the sandbox."

Billy trots around to the backyard. He obeys everybody but me. I fix David's blanket. He looks like he's about to fall asleep. "House painting's a man's job, Laurie."

"I don't have a man," she says.

"Have you heard anymore from my ass of a brother?"

"Nope, just the one card."

"Laurie, didn't you paint the house last year?"

"Yep." Using her sleeve, she rubs the sweat off her face.

"How can it possibly need painting again?"

"Either that or throw myself down the basement stairs," she says, grimacing.

"What? "

"Can't you guess?"

"You mean ..."

"Yeah, your dear brother left me with a bun in the oven."

"Oh, Laurie!" I hug her and feel her body tremble. "Painting the house won't help."

"Did the trick last year."

"Oh. What if you fainted and fell?"

"There's an idea."

"Laurie, think of Arlene. She needs you."

"I know. That's why I'm not having another one."

Screams from the backyard. "I'll see what they're up to."

"Be with you in a minute," she says hammering the lid on the paint tin.

"He hit me with the pail." Three-year-old Arlene, holding a metal sand pail, stands with her hands on her hips and observes Billy yelling and stomping on the lawn.

I can't help but laugh. She's so indignant—like an offended housewife. She's a chubby little blonde. "Enough now." I pick up Billy and hand him a pail and shovel. "There are plenty of toys to go around."

"Want that one."

"Hush." I plunk him down in the sandbox.

"He can help me dig a ditch," Arlene says sweetly.

When Laurie comes out the back door, carrying a tray-load of Kool-Aid, Arlene runs to her.

"My little helper," Laurie says as Arlene hands us each a plastic cup.

Billy'd be more likely to throw them at us. "Your Arlene's so well behaved."

"Yes, she's my sweetie."

Would it be different if I had a girl?

WE'RE ON OUR way home when Mrs. Thorton calls out: "Donna, come in for a cup of tea."

The baby's still sleeping and I park the stroller next to the porch. Mrs. Thorton hauls a big cardboard box onto the porch for Billy. He climbs in and out. Then puts his rubber dog in. "Lie down," he says. "Be good." He can be such a cute little guy.

Mrs. Thorton heads to the kitchen. I sit down in the slatted rocker and watch the bees floating in the lilacs. Already lilac season again. This whole past year's a blur. David's over a year old. I'm living someone else's life. Donna Evans, the centre of every sock-hop, has disappeared. Donna Waddell, mother of two and wife of Rick Waddell, co-owner of Waddell Ford, is someone I loath.

I see Mrs. Thorton at Martin's studio door. Bet she's telling him to join us. I feel a tightening in my gut.

She has just poured the tea when Martin emerges from his studio. His trademark black turtleneck and blue jeans. His curls almost reach his shoulders.

He walks unevenly across the porch. Touches my hair. "Hello, Donna."

"Here, Martin. I've just poured you a cup," his mother says.

"I've been rereading *On the Road*," Martin says. "Did you ever finish it?" He stares so intently at me.

"They're a bunch of drunks, running from one woman to another. I returned the book to your mother last fall."

"Why'd you do that? Do try and read it. Oh, Donna, the drunken escapades aren't the point of it at all. It's a spiritual quest." Martin whacks his cane on the floor.

What's he getting so worked up about? "Spiritual—that bunch of drunks? They reminded me of my brother."

"What?" He's practically shouting. "You must've been half asleep when you read it."

"Don't argue, you two," Mrs. Thorton says. "Have some more tea, Martin, and don't pick on Donna."

No SURPRISE WHEN a couple of days later I get another letter, this one with a parcel.

> July 3, 1959
> *Dear Donna,*
>
> *Do have another look at On the Road. You must understand, it isn't the details of the plot, such as what girls they're with, that are important. What you must see is that these young men want to experience it all, throw themselves wholeheartedly into life, to be free.*
>
> *Run of the mill people get dull jobs and think their hick town is the centre of the universe. There's a world out there to experience and they live their whole lives never touching it. Kerouac and his friends roam the country, soaking it all in.*
>
> *Look at page 9: "the only people for me are the mad ones, the ones who are mad to live, mad to talk, mad to be saved, desirous of everything at the same time, the ones who never yawn or say a commonplace thing, but burn, burn, burn..."*
>
> *Do you get it? Note that "mad to be saved." Now do you see the spiritual journey?*
>
> *Ah, Donna, you and I must set out on our travels. Life is too short for you to spend it with a used-car salesman.*
> *Your lover, Martin*
> *P.S. Find enclosed On the Road. This time read the whole thing.*

When do I have time to read anything? Does he think I lie around eating chocolates?

NEVERTHELESS, WHEN RICK's working late and both kids are actually sleeping at the same time, I turn the television off and open the book.

I skim through the part I'd already read. Then Sal meets this Mexican girl, Terry, and I get interested.

They meet on a bus. She's fleeing her violent husband. She's had to leave her kid with her folks. Sal and Terry fall in love and plan to go to New York as soon as they can earn a little money. When they can't find work in Los Angeles, she takes him to her hometown, Sabinal. She thinks her brother will help them. Everybody drinks too much and can't find work. They move into a cotton picker's tent that rents for a dollar a day. Sal picks cotton and Terry and her little boy help. They earn enough for groceries and the tent. He'd earn more if he didn't do idiotic things like taking naps: "My face on the pillow of moist brown earth." I can just hear Gretchen saying something like that. She and Martin romanticize everything, just like Sal does.

He plays with little Johnny while Terry mends their clothes. There's a lovely scene where he's resting while she and Johnny draw pictures in his notebook. Sal says he's a man of the earth just as he always dreamed of being. The weather's getting cold so Terry and Johnny move in with her parents, who disapprove of Sal. He stays in a farmer's barn and she brings him food and blankets. They make love. He says he'll have to leave. He doesn't tell Terry that he's wired his aunt for money. Terry says she loves him. He says he'll see her in New York. She's supposed to drive to New York with her brother in a month. Sal says they both know this won't happen.

He takes a bus where he meets a girl and necks all the way to Indianapolis. He appears to have forgotten all about Terry. She was just an adventure for him. He talks about adventuring in the crazy American night.

When he gets home he stuffs himself on everything in his aunt's icebox. He uses the money he's been sending from California to buy her an electric refrigerator. I guess he sent her money before he met Terry. I must've missed that part. He could've used that money to bring

Terry and her little boy to New York. He doesn't even mention Terry again.

I throw the book across the room and go to bed.

About a week later, I'm having tea with the Thortons and Martin asks if I finished the book.

"No. I've read quite enough about that jerk, Sal, and his crazy friends."

"What do you mean?"

"And you told me it's a true story, that it's actually Jack Kerouac's life and his travels."

"Yes, and he's one of the greatest living American authors. Why would you call him a jerk?"

"Look how he treated Terry."

"Terry?"

"The Mexican girl he lived with and said he loved."

"The book's not about plot. It's about the writer experiencing all there is. He can't stay in California picking cotton. He spends the next year writing."

"But what about Terry? He may well have left her pregnant. How's she supposed to manage?"

"Donna, you're hung up on plot. It's Kerouac's spiritual journey that's important."

"He's a jerk."

"You just don't get it. How can you say that of a man who writes of 'the ragged ecstatic joy of pure being?'"

"And how much joy did Terry have in her life after he left?"

"Forget Terry. The book's not about her. It's about the meaning of the road. Kerouac writes 'the road is life.' You just don't get it." Martin strides around the porch, clunking his cane.

"Now, now, Martin," his mother says. "Do sit down. Those boys are young cads, but they're also searchers after life's meaning. So both you and Donna are right."

That night when I'm frying chicken and trying to stop Billy from stuffing David into the cupboard under the sink, I long to be back on that porch. A different world there. I think about how Martin would love to join Sal and his friends on the road but can't because he's blind. That life does have its appeal. Like my brother sitting on a log at Kits Beach. That life's not possible for Martin, or me.

And what about the babies? The women get stuck with the kids, the laundry and the sink of dirty dishes. Like Laurie, like me.

MY HEAD ACHES so and David's screaming in the back-yard. Damn it. Billy must've pushed him down again. A miracle David ever learned to walk. I better get out there but the shrieking shoots right through my brain.

I scoop Billy up before he makes another run at David. "Time for lunch." Only eleven, but who cares? The sooner they have their lunch, the sooner I can put them down to nap.

"THERE YOU GO, night-night." I lower David, clutching a bottle, into his crib. He'll be asleep in a few minutes. "C'mon, Billy, night-night time for you, too."

"No!"

"Stories first, c'mon." I give him a piggyback ride to his room. "Shoe, shoe." He grabs *Nursery Rhymes* and turns the pages. "Shoe," he crows triumphantly. "Read."

I look at the woman beside her shoe house. She has one of the kids over her knee and is giving him a spanking. I sigh.

"Read," Billy demands.

> There was an old woman who lived in a shoe.
> She had so many children she didn't know what to do.
> She gave them some broth, without any bread,
> and whipped them all soundly ...

BILLY HOOTS AND kicks his feet in the air. "And sent them to bed!" he shouts. "Read again!"

"Settle down now."

"Read shoe."

"Go to sleep." I get up and pull the drapes closed. "Here's your zoo blanket." I kiss his nose. "Night, night." I close his door firmly behind me.

Before I've reached the couch I hear his door open. I lie down and close my eyes.

"Howdie Doodie show."

"Go back to bed."

"Howdie Doodie."

I grab him, smack his bottom, and carry him back to his room.

I'm back on the couch. There was an old woman who lived in a shoe. That silly rhyme needles my aching brain.

"Howdie Doodie."

· I groan.

"Howdie Doodie!" His mouth goes into a pout, and in a minute he'll be yelling.

I drag myself up off the couch and turn on the television — some news show. Billy plunks himself down on his tummy in front of the set. "Not so close. You'll ruin your eyes." I pull the drapes.

"Howdie Doodie?"

"Not yet." He lies there staring at the screen. I stretch out on the couch. There was an old woman …

A COUPLE OF days later I'm headed to Laurie's house with the children. I feel terrible, almost a month since I've seen her.

When she opens the door, I'm shocked by how thin and pale she looks.

"You okay?" I'm trying to hold Billy's hand and carry a drowsy David.

"Yep. Hi, Billy." She swings him up in the air. "Here, let me take the baby. You've got your arms full."

I gratefully hand over David. "I'll unload the stroller."

"C'mon, Billy, let's go find the toys," she says.

As I'm getting the stuff out, I hear Billy laughing. Laurie's so good with kids.

When I go in the house, she's carrying David and dancing Billy around in a circle. "What's all this?" she says.

"I made too much jam last fall. That pear conserve's really good."

"Looks yummy and there's cherry, Arlene's favourite. Billy, you want to colour with Arlene?"

Arlene's on the floor, colouring on a brown paper bag. I catch Billy as he makes a grab for her paper.

"Billy, I've got one for you, too." Laurie slits open another bag and spreads it on the floor. Billy accepts a tin of crayons and stretches out on his tummy.

Miracle of miracles Billy colours happily with Arlene and David falls asleep. I gratefully accept a steaming mug of coffee and light a cigarette. I pass her the pack. "Laurie, you're really thin. You're not sick, are you?"

"Nope, not pregnant either. Still bleeding though."

"You should go to the doctor."

"Why bother?" She shrugs and lights her cigarette. "I shouldn't smoke. They're too expensive. Doctors cost money, too. But I'll go, if it doesn't stop. After all, you bleed for quite a while after having a baby. Not as if I used a coat hanger or anything like that."

"So it worked?"

"Moved a lot of furniture, too."

"Any word from my brother?"

"Nope."

"He's a selfish prick. What are you going to do?"

"I clean houses three days a week and take Arlene with me. Once she's in school, Dad says I can work in the store."

"That's two more years."

"One year and ten months." Laurie laughs. "Maybe Ted'll come back."

"You want him to?" Surely not.

"Good question. I miss him though. Playing house without a husband's no fun. We had some good times."

"For at least a year he didn't even have a job. You could meet somebody new."

"Nobody wants you once you have a kid."

All the way home I think of that "Nobody wants you once you have a kid." I'm lucky. Rick wants me and we have plenty of money. Poor Laurie. Martin wants me too. Better not think about that. Ted's such a bastard. Of course he may not be Arlene's father. Laurie's famous list. Not fair my parents made Ted marry her just because he was twenty-one and the others were high-school kids. But poor Laurie.

On a hot July day I sink gratefully onto the porch swing. David's asleep in the stroller, and Mrs. Thorton has Billy with her in the kitchen.

"Relax while I make us some tea," she said.

I could sit here forever listening to the bees buzzing in the orange blossom. There's a breeze and the branches scrape the screen. I hear a cardinal and a distant train whistle. At home I never notice the birds. The kids make too much noise.

I stretch out on the swing.

I hear Martin's cane. He's smiling as he bends and kisses the top of my head, his curls brushing my face.

"How are you, Donna?" He moves the swing back and forth.

"Tired," I say with a sleepy smile.

"Wish I could lie down beside you."

At that moment Mrs. Thorton appears with Billy trailing behind her. I sit up quickly as Billy hands me a serviette. He's quite civilized around Mrs. Thornton. She makes it look so easy.

"Sit down, Martin," she says. "We'll have our tea."

He scowls at her and sits in the rocker.

"How's the writing going?" I ask him.

"Been raining for days and Marsh Road's flooded. Joe's up to his knees in mud, shit and dead chickens." He gives me a wicked grin.

Bet he's trying to gross me out. "Can't you write a happy story?"

He lifts his eyebrows and smiles. "Bob blocks the doorway, 'God-damnuselesscrip, every dead chicken comes out of your hide.'"

"Martin, that's enough! Billy doesn't need to hear you talking like that." Mrs. Thorton gives him a thunderous look.

With a scowl, he subsides and doesn't say another word.

The next day I'm having lunch alone. Not that I mind—no spilt milk, no screaming kids. Rick's mom has them.

I'm lighting a cigarette when I hear Rick's key in the lock. Damn it, he'll expect me to make him lunch.

He has the mail with him. "Hi."

"Hi Pumpkin, thought you were going to cut back on the smokes." He shuffles through the bills and just my luck, there's a letter. "Here's another one," he says. "Open it, I'm curious," and hands it to me.

I recognize Mrs. Thorton's writing. She does the envelopes and the letter will be in braille so there isn't any real danger. "It's my letter."

"Sure and you're my wife," Rick says with a grin.

"You're jealous?"

"Of a crip? Not likely, but I'd still like to know what he's writing to my wife." He's not smiling now.

"Really none of your business."

Rick snatches the letter out of my hand and tears it open.

"Rick, damn you, give it back!"

He laughs and holds it out of my reach. There isn't much I can do —I'm five two and he's six one.

"What's this—some kind of code?"

"It's braille."

"Hold on a minute, there's another page. It's in English." He sniggers. "Looks like a poem."

Oh, hell, must be a piece his mother sent to a magazine for him.

"Listen to this. On the hill they pray for their lost moon. Let her be made whole again. Ohmah, ohmah, ohmah." He's laughing so much he can't go on.

"Stop that."

"Sorry, but it is funny, the poor bugger thinks he's a poet."

"Not funny. Give me my letter."

"Okay, okay." Rick hands it over. "Sorry, but it's so pathetic, all these letters."

"You don't open other people's mail."

"Jeez, I said I was sorry. Anyway, how does he manage to type?"

"A Brailler."

"What's that?"

"A typewriter that does braille."

"Can he read just tracing the dots?"

"Yeah."

"How come you know how to read it?"

"I learned when we were kids."

"Must be a slow process. Why would he bother? I guess he doesn't have much else to do—stuck there with his old mother. Maybe a blessing he's blind—at least he can't see himself. You'd think his mother would have him wear dark glasses."

"Why?"

"Those weirdo eyes. I bet he's in love with you." Rick chuckles.

"Don't be silly. He just needs somebody to talk to, write to."

"I was talking to the guys at work about Martin's letter writing. You know Gary?"

"Sure."

"Well, he's taking this psychology course by correspondence. Wants to be a social worker—a bit of an oddball. He was telling us about Freud—that head doctor who's always writing about sex."

"I know who Freud is."

"Gary said Freud would say it was, what did he call it, sublication? No, sublimation! Poor Martin wouldn't be able to do it with a girl so he writes you love letters." Rick looks pleased with himself.

"Waddell Ford mustn't have much business."

"What?" He frowns.

"Or you guys would be too busy to gossip about Martin."

"Look, I feel sorry for the poor bugger."

"And that's why you opened my mail?"

"Jesus Christ, Pumpkin, I said I was sorry."

Why would he think Martin ugly? His opaque eyes add mystery to his face and his mouth is so expressive. That tiny smile when he's amused. His sneer when he's hearing about the town's latest stupidity. His face goes still when he's touching me. He has a handsome face, high cheek bones, a long thin nose. Black curly hair and such white, clear skin. Strong well-muscled shoulders and arms. Gets a lot of exercise dragging that leg.

RICK HAS LEFT for work and taken the boys with him. He'll drop them off at his mother's. I have a dentist appointment for a root canal. I've time for a second cup of coffee and a smoke.

I fetch the small duffle bag from the back of my closet and take it out to the deck. With the unzipped bag on my lap, I touch the letters. There's quite a bundle now.

Sometimes Rick can make me so mad. Now every time he sees one of Martin's letters with the mail he'll hand it to me and go "Ohmah, ohmah, ohmah," and laugh out loud.

When I get mad, he'll say he's sorry. Just pretends to be sorry.

Rick hasn't opened another letter and usually I get to the mail before him.

What am I going to do with all of these?

"Silorian Flight" was the poem Rick read. Martin sent it to me because a science fiction magazine accepted it. I'm surprised his mother types such poems. Sometimes I think it's dirty, but then I reread it and think it's just sad. A magazine called *Fantasy in Orbit* accepted the poem, and a month later, *Galaxies Unlimited* took one of his Silorian stories and paid him $50. He shouldn't have bought me a silk scarf with the money. Not that Rick notices what I'm wearing.

There was one piece he sent me about a Silorian man and a Tercheran girl doing it. He was smacking her ass and as he hit her he was watching the bruises "bloom through her pale translucent skin." I tore that up, the only piece of his writing I've destroyed.

I'm no prude. I don't mind an off-colour joke. Rick told a good one the other night about an old man and a specimen bottle. I laughed so hard I thought I'd pee my pants.

Martin's stuff is disgusting and a little weird. And he's not like that. He's a very sensitive person.

I can't throw out Martin's writing. It means so much to him. What a poor audience he has in me. I don't understand poetry.

I've said to him: "If writing causes you that much pain, why bother?"

He's constantly sending the stuff he writes out to magazines and having it rejected. Only a few of his stories and poems have been published. When "Silorian Flight" was accepted, he showed it to me. He was so over the moon about it he didn't notice I wasn't saying much. The magazine looked like some guys put it together in their basement.

"I'm breaking into the San Francisco market," he says.

"What did they pay you?"

"They pay in copies. Only the mags published by the universities have money and they're controlled by the tight-assed establishment."

If I wasn't worried about hurting his feelings, I would tell him: "You're crazy. You knock yourself out, go through hell waiting every day for the mail, hoping one of these magazines nobody in Grenville has even seen will take a poem or a story for which they pay you practically nothing. Does that make sense?" I know what he would reply. I've heard it often enough.

"Damn it, Donna, I'm a writer and I'm starting to earn money. That fifty dollars from *Galaxies Unlimited* is just the beginning. Science fiction is pop fiction. Someday my serious work, my novel, will be published. Then we'll be in the money."

"Okay," I said to him. "You want to be a writer. Get out in the community, meet people and listen to them. Write about real people.

He laughed but then began to sulk, raging about Grenville — its dullness and stupidity. He doesn't make much sense. He doesn't understand that people would treat him just the same in New York, or anywhere.

DAMN IT, RICK should've stayed home to help tonight. I'd heard people talk about root canals. Now I know how it feels. I'm on my hands and knees cleaning up the bathroom floor. I left Billy for one minute to fetch clean towels and he managed to empty the shampoo bottle on the floor. I shouldn't have given him a bottle to get him asleep. Rick told him only babies have them. But he sees David having one and wants one too. What the hell, if it gets him to sleep? And if Rick doesn't like it, he can put him to bed. I could've used some help tonight, but oh no, Rick had a Kinsmen meeting. He's such an upright citizen. Oh God, my mouth hurts. Two painkillers and off to bed. Feel like swallowing the whole bloody bottle.

AFTER MIDNIGHT WHEN Rick climbs on top, I smell his beery breath. I'm too tired to fully wake up and too tired to respond. He must think I'm asleep. Guess it wouldn't bother him if I was. No need to stroke or pet me. No need for compliments. His idea of an endearment is to call me Pumpkin. Thinks it hilarious when I complain. "My funny little Pumpkin," he'll say. Martin calls me Star, the North Star that leads travellers home. I think of Martin's hands touching me.

A few quick thrusts and Rick's done.

THE NEXT AFTERNOON David sobs while I hold the frozen peas against his swelling cheek. Billy stands in the kitchen doorway. I leave David in the rocker, snatch up Billy and give him a couple of good smacks on his behind. "Your cars are not for throwing! You do that again and they all go in the garbage!"

Thank goodness Rick's mom's picking the kids up at one.

THE PLACE IS quiet at last. I need to scrub the kitchen floor—the mixture of pea soup, milk and cracker crumbs looks like puke. I should know better than to give David a cup. But he wants to do everything Billy does.

The floor can wait. I'm going to bed.

I stand in the doorway and survey the rumpled bed and the pile of Rick's clothes on the floor where he shed them last night. I don't go in. I'm tired, but suddenly, not at all sleepy.

Maybe I'll go over and help Mrs. Thorton. She always makes me feel better. I bet she's canning tomatoes.

I walk over and knock on the screen door. "Anybody home?" No answer. I go in. If she's in the kitchen, she might not have heard me.

She isn't. I'll check the garden.

"Mrs. Thorton, you out here?" It's hot for September and dried-out vines sprawl on the ground. Ripe tomatoes are as big as grapefruit. But no Mrs. Thorton. I pick a tomato, rub it on my jeans. Take a big bite and juice squirts and runs down my chin.

"A thief in the garden." Martin touches my arm. I didn't hear him come up behind me. My arm tingles and I suck in my breath.

"Hi, Martin, where's your mother?"

"She took some vegetables down to old Mrs. Green. Come to my studio and we can split a cold beer. My dear mother gave me a bottle before she left. With nagging she allows me one a day. Teetotalers are haunted by the spectre of alcoholism. I bet most of the men in this town have a couple of beers a day."

"I thought she'd be canning."

"C'mon, Donna, you're not scared of me, are you?"

"Of course not. A cold beer would taste good." I smile and feel the return of that naughty kid I was for so long. "Rick's mom has the boys. I'm free."

"Wonderful, you're free." He touches my mouth smeared with tomato juice. With his hand he wipes the juice from my chin. I take that hand and we walk to his studio.

EIGHT-THIRTY AND Rick still isn't home. Then I remember he said that after he closed up he was going to another Kinsmen meeting. They're planning a kids' baseball tournament. Most nights we eat right at five and he goes back to work to close up at seven.

I struggle through bath-time. Billy likes having a bath with his little brother but as usual he ends up hurting him. I make Billy get out and he runs, yelling, all through the house. I ignore him which, I've discovered, works better than spanking.

David goes willingly to bed right after his bath. I read Billy *Peter Rabbit* though he wants "shoe" as he calls that stupid rhyme. I'm sick of that old woman. I fix Billy a bottle, and he throws it across the room. "Big boy!"

I read *The Little Engine that Could.*

He doesn't go to sleep and is now snuggled up against me as we watch wrestling on television. I know it's not good for him, but I like it, and I'm too tired for more stories. Rick still isn't home.

An hour later, I tuck Billy into bed and get myself a beer. Why the hell not? Rick and the guys always go for a beer after their meetings. I take my drink and smokes out on the deck. Not much cooler, but a soothing breeze keeps the mosquitoes at bay. I won't think about this afternoon.

Mmm, cold beer sure tastes good. Is Martin in his studio longing for a second beer? I could take him one. Donna, you know that would be stupid. You had no business going there. Don't think about it. There are no solutions. Hell, you're a married woman with two kids. What were you thinking of? Not thinking. For a change, doing what I wanted.

All these bloody rules about how you're supposed to live your life. Poor Martin with his one beer a day and she won't even buy him cigarettes, afraid he'll burn down the house. I left him my pack. I know she means well but poor Martin.

I've been through it all so many times. I have two kids, couldn't get a job. Martin doesn't earn anywhere near enough to support a family.

Mrs. Thorton thinks I'm such a good wife. What a laugh.

"So young and managing two babies and a house. You even find the time to can tomatoes. You're an old-fashioned girl, after my own heart. You work so hard and still bother with us, your old friends. Why don't I call Martin and we'll sit down and have tea?"

She wouldn't think so highly of me if she knew. Says I'm his muse. Wouldn't be pleased if she knew what else I am. I finish the last of the beer and butt my cigarette on the railing. Go to bed, Donna, go to bed. The kids'll be squalling by six.

I go in the bathroom and insert my diaphragm — no more chances.

ON A LATE September morning when the King Maple outside my window is scarlet, I climb out of bed and pad into the kitchen, thankful the kids are still asleep. With luck I'll have a peaceful cup of coffee on the deck. The warm fall days are numbered.

The coffee has just started to percolate when the first wave hits. I run to the bathroom and throw up. I crouch, sobbing and holding the toilet bowl. Only one thing can make me puke at the smell of coffee.

No, I can't bear it. So bloody stupid! Rick hates my diaphragm, but I do insist.

There was that once with Martin. Can't be. What are the odds?

I'm not having another one.

I TRY JUMPING from the top of the deck steps a few times. Nothing happens. When I'm not looking Billy jumps and badly bruises both knees.

"You jumped, Mommy," he says, sobbing.

I give him a big hug and that's the end of my jumping.

I can't paint the brick and stone house. Anyway, I don't see how that worked for Laurie. There was an old woman who lived in a shoe. Oh, God, how'll I handle three. Maybe it'll be a girl. One like Arlene.

RICK, OF COURSE, is delighted. "Pumpkin, you pop them out like hotcakes," he says. He should try it and he wouldn't be saying "pop them out."

I gain more pounds with each pregnancy. By three months along, I look like Billy's roly-poly clown that you bop on the head and it springs right back up again. I should've bopped myself on the head before I let this happen again.

I've avoided the Thortons. When I did go over for tea, I wore baggy clothes. After a couple of months I told her I'd just found out I was pregnant. Don't know why I'm worrying. Still, when it arrives I'll say it was premature.

Of course, Martin has written.

Oct. 26, 1959
My darling Donna
 The rain beats the leaves from the trees. My cane sticks in the mud. Usually I hate fall, the harbinger of winter. Because of you this drear rain becomes a spring shower. You have tricked the seasons. Autumn's ripe tomatoes are enchanted. Juice dripped from your chin like communion wine anointing my hand.
 Marsh Road *continues:*
 Bob's drinking more, hitting Mom more, and she's praying more. At twenty, Joe's five nine and 145 pounds. Still no match for Bob, he's getting regular beatings and five dollars a week.
 Frequently, in the evenings, Bob unlocks his strong box and shows his son the stacks of bills. Now, there are stacks of hundreds.
 All yours when I'm gone.
 I need stuff now.
 What ya need?
 Decent clothes, my own car.
 What, you wanna go courtin'?
 Maybe I do.
 Jigsy goes a courtin'. Jigsy goes a courtin'. He roars with laughter. Then sobers. Gotta face life, son, no courtin' for a crip. Work hard and the chicken farm will see you fed in your old age. That Cathy Englehart just comes over here because she pities you.

For ten more years, Joe works the farm and puts up with the beatings. Cathy's mother dies, but Cathy doesn't leave Ted. She says, How could I support myself? Let's enjoy these times we have together. I love the marsh and our secret home.
 All that keeps Joe from following his sister's example are his visits with Cathy.

Been over a month now, Donna. Please come back. The
remembered smell of your skin sustains me. After your
visit I wrote all night. I love you, Donna. You are light
and warmth in my dark world.

OH, MARTIN, IT'S all lovely in your head, but dammit, that's not reality. Why won't you understand I can't just leave? What about Billy and David? And now there's going to be another one. Oh, I hope it's a girl.

Rick wants a big family. He's a good father. Martin couldn't support me—thinks his mother wouldn't mind if the children and I moved in with them. She'd tell me to get home to my husband where I belong. Maybe in Toronto and London people get divorced, but not in Grenville. Mrs. Williams is the only divorced woman I know. Her husband owns the drugstore. She wears clothes far too young for her. Behind her back, everybody laughs.

If I did find a job, Martin couldn't look after the kids. I don't think he's all that fond of children. Always saying: "Couldn't you get a sitter?"

Mom would call me a whore. She so admires Rick.

Worse than that, Rick would get custody because I'm immoral. He'd remarry, easy for him. I see how women look at him. Laurie wasn't so smart either. She had to have a hysterectomy. Now she'll never have more children. She cried when she told me. "Why do I care?" she said. "I didn't want this one. But I still dreamt of someday being happily married with a baby in my arms."

I only dream backwards, all the way to high school. Oh, God, why is everything wonderful in the past? The dance hall at Blackstone Point. Rick twirled me around in my red-dotted circle skirt. I loved red—halter top, net crinoline, even my panties. Rick wore tight Levi's and an open-necked shirt with the sleeves rolled up. My handsome boyfriend with his tanned arms and sun-bleached hair. Old Spice and male sweat.

When we danced, they made a circle around us and clapped. A hot, humid night. I could smell the lake through the open windows. "One, two, three o'clock rock." So, so happy. Jumping with happiness.

We walked in the dunes and could still hear the music when we lay down together on the sand. Did I love him? Yes, yes, yes. Or did I love the music, my red panties, the warm sand?

Skinny-dipping. We heard voices and ran out of the water and into the dunes. We never found those red panties. They must still be there— an old rag buried in the sand.

Things used to be good. Babies change everything. Not just the babies. "You don't run after the bus once you've caught it." He complains I fall asleep right after supper. Okay, that's true, but not always. Some evenings I'm leafing through *The Ladies' Home Journal* while Rick listens to the hockey game. If he'd just hold me then, for a little while …

ON A DAY when I'm six months along, the doorbell chimes. Billy and David are fighting over the dump truck. Nearly two now, David's hitting back. I'm the size of a cow and long only for sleep. The doorbell again. "Sharon! How lovely. Been a long time." Yeah, lovely. Like I want her to see me like this.

"Too long. I don't get home that often. And when I do, Mom and the kids monopolize my time. Well, how are you?"

"C'mon into the kitchen. I'll make tea." Pretty obvious how I am. She, on the other hand, looks like a million dollars. Her red hair is piled on top of her head. When she slips off her fur coat and slings it over the back of a chair, I see she's as slim as ever and her breasts just as pert. "I better hang that up. You don't want the kids slobbering on it."

"Yeah, these little monsters might do it harm." She scoops up Billy and David and gives them big smoochy kisses. They hoot like maniacs. "Hey guys, look what I brought you." She pulls a set of rubber cars from her shopping bag—expensive ones made by Tootsie Toy.

" A lot safer than metal," she says.

"You shouldn't have spent so much on them."

"I haven't seen you guys in ages," she says.

"You have a mink coat, lucky duck."

"Well, it looks like mink. I'll be paying in instalments for the next three years. You look tired, Donna, and you're having another one."

"I'm fine," and I burst into tears. She hugs me and I manage to stop blubbering. "Sorry about that."

"Why are you having one right after the other?"

"Not that easy not to."

"Haven't you guys heard of rubbers?"

"Rick wouldn't use them, even before we were married. Says it doesn't feel the same."

"Big deal! You should make him. Anyway, get yourself fitted for a diaphragm, I did."

"I have one but some nights I'm so tired I forget. You're not married and you were able to get a diaphragm?"

She grins. "In the city doctors don't care if you're married."

"Oh, Sharon, I envy you. How's the job going?"

"Great." She gets down on the floor with the boys. They scoot the cars across the kitchen floor.

"You must like kids," I tell her.

"I do, and that's why I'm not having any. I don't mean you shouldn't have babies, if you want them. This is a nice place for kids. You and Rick must be doing okay."

"Yeah, after David was born Mr. Waddell made Rick a full partner."

"Glad to hear he's settled down. Marriage must agree with him."

"He's settled down all right. Even joined the Kinsmen. He's a proper pillar of the community."

"That's good, isn't it?" She gives me a puzzled look.

"Sure. I'm just tired."

"Maybe hire a part-time babysitter."

"Rick's mom takes them three afternoons a week."

"That must be a help. Do you see much of Gretchen?"

"She's away at university. Her mother and I are friends."

"How's Gretchen's brother doing?"

"He's a writer. He writes poems and science fiction and he's working on a novel."

"Wow, I had no idea. Must be a lonely life though."

"I guess so." I better shut up. She's the one person who might guess. "A lot of people have it tough. My mom needs a walker to get around."

"So young to have a stroke."

We have tea but run out of things to talk about. Sharon plans to drop in on her mom before driving back to Toronto. She has her own Volkswagen Beetle. She promises to come again. I don't know whether I'm glad or sorry to see her go. I want to wear a purple mini-dress and a mink coat and work in an office. And go out on dates and dash around in a cute red car.

When we were kids hanging out at the pony track, I never thought Sharon would be wearing mink and working in Toronto. She came from a family of ne'er-do-wells with too many kids. Her sister Gloria got pregnant at thirteen. Sharon was a tough girl who went with older boys. But she didn't have to get married, I did. How come she's done so great?

I HAVE A baby girl, Katelyn Louise. And thank goodness she has brown eyes like mine and blonde hair like Rick. Labour was a lot easier, only four hours.

There won't be any more. The Pill's brand new, first year legal in Canada. I heard about it from Sharon. She was here for her dad's funeral. She married a lawyer—showed up for the funeral in a black Lincoln Continental. Old Dr. Stewart said the Pill hadn't been tested well enough. To hell with him. I told Rick I was going to shop and visit Sharon in Toronto. His mother babysat. I went to see Sharon's doctor. No problem.

Rick agrees the Pill's better than the diaphragm and said I could stay on it for a couple of years. That's what he thinks. I'm on it for life.

I've lost most of the weight I gained. Pulling off my nightgown I stand naked before my mirror. Life is what you make it. I reach my arms up over my head. I hear the boys squabbling over something. I keep right on doing leg stretches. Rick has all the kids with him in the kitchen where he's making pancakes for Sunday breakfast.

We went to Cleveland for five days. Left the kids with his mom. While Rick was at his convention, I shopped. Boy, did I shop. We went dancing. I was still wide awake when we got back to the hotel. We both drank more than a bit. I sat on his lap and we fooled around like teenagers.

I love my babies and I love Rick. I really do. We had a great time in Cleveland.

I stretch my arms up, up. Reach for the ceiling. Touch my toes. Faster, faster.

That's enough exercise. Run my hands down my sides, my thighs. My smooth thighs. Love my body again. Lift my full, still-perky breasts. Massage them a bit.

Well, bod, you're doing all right. Yours may not be as perky as a teenager's and your belly's not as flat, but I love you still.

Rock, rock, rock around the clock. Did it matter what boy swung me around? See me, see me, that was my song. Gorgeous me.

"Pumpkin, for heaven's sake! Get your clothes on before one of the boys comes barging in."

I turn and face him. "What do you think, Rick? Have I got the old bod back?"

"You look fine, Pumpkin. Plenty of mileage in the old girl yet." Rick chuckles.

We hear a yell and a loud thud.

"What now?" Rick says. "Hurry up. Pancakes are ready." He closes the door behind him.

I stare at the closed door. "Damn you." I pound the door with my fists. David's shrieking in the kitchen. I lean against the door but Rick doesn't return. Doesn't hear me.

WE SIT AT the head table for the community centre's opening celebrations. Rick has won an award for raising the most money. He donated twenty dollars for every new car he sold. Been a record year for sales. He says it's important to have an indoor rink for the kids and is already teaching Billy to skate. Wants to start a boys' hockey league. He's been invited to join the Lions Club.

I'm wearing a black silk sheath and weigh one hundred seventeen —same weight as in grade eleven.

Gretchen's home for Christmas and she and Mrs. Thorton are here. She's wearing a beige car coat and a plaid skirt. Still hasn't learned how to dress. I saw Sharon come in earlier with her mother. I must try to talk to her as we're leaving so she can see the real mink Rick got me for Christmas.

No surprise Martin hasn't come to the dinner. He's become such a hermit. He doesn't realize that makes people think he's strange. I don't visit the Thortons much. And when I do, I take the children. With the boys running around there's no chance of him getting me alone and that's the way I'm going to keep it. There's a column in *Ladies' Home Journal*, "Can This Marriage Be Saved?" I read every issue. I'm going to save my marriage.

Of course Martin's still sending me letters.

Here comes the mayor. The speeches will be starting. Rick's speaking after dinner. Never nervous, my Rick. When he gets up to speak, every woman in the room will be looking at him.

WHEN WE GET home, I'm not at all tired. Take a quick shower and pull on my hot pink nightgown, another Christmas gift from Rick.

I climb into bed, and he's waiting for me. It's over a little too quickly — still it's good.

I WAKE UP and look at the clock — two a.m. Rick's snoring loudly beside me with one arm stretched across my chest. His arm's heavy and I push it aside. Wish I could sleep like that.

I'll make tea. That'll help me get back to sleep.

I put the kettle on and go in the boys' room. I fix David's blankets and remove the hockey puck from Billy's hand. Other kids take a teddy bear to bed. His father's son, all right. His thick blonde hair has a slight wave to it. Going to be a real lady-killer. Both boys have their daddy's blonde hair.

By Katie's crib, I admire my perfect baby girl in her perfect pink room. Rick painted the walls but I did everything else — pink and white ruffled curtains and a matching comforter. She has her balled fists up above her head like she's about to challenge somebody to a fight. With those brothers, she better be a toughie. I'll skin them alive if they ever lay a hand on her. The blonde fuzz she was born with has fallen out, and her hair is coming in black curls. Doesn't mean anything. My dad's hair is dark.

The tea's not working. I wander into the living room and stare out the window. There's a light on next door. Martin must still be up.

I feel bad about avoiding him but it's the right thing to do. After a few pages of my library book, I lay it aside. I sneak in our bedroom and from the back of my closet pick up the duffle bag.

At the kitchen table, I light a cigarette and pull out the unopened letter that came almost a month ago. I'd promised myself I wouldn't read it.

November 29, 1960,
Dear Donna,

Winter's coming, the dead time of the year. Come talk to me and listen to a story. Here's a bit to get you curious.

Joe comes in from the barn to a familiar sight — Bob face down in his own puke. A dark stain on the seat of his trousers — oh great, the bastard has shit and pissed himself again.

Mom grabs Joe's arm. Jigsy, we've got to get him up. He could choke like that.

Joe's my name.

Don't fuss. Help me turn him. She's struggling with Bob's shoulder. Years back she would've turned, undressed and washed him and with Joe's help got him up on the couch. Since Maeve's death, Mom has become a wizened-up hag.

Joe turns away. He needs a shower and Cathy's waiting by the creek. Ted was home for a whole month with pneumonia — so drunk he'd turned his truck over in a water-filled ditch. Unfortunately, he didn't die. Fortunately, he's away on business, but tomorrow afternoon Cathy and Ted are flying to Vegas. Joe and Cathy only have tonight.

As he leaves the house, Mom grabs his arm and begs: Help me.

He shakes her off.

Cathy and Joe haul the canoe up the bank and climb the hill to their cabin. The shack is stuffy. Cathy pushes up the window and leaves the door open. Look what I brought us, she says.

He watches her bent over the bed, covering it with a red and purple Indian bedspread. He wraps his arms around her and pushes his stiff cock against her ass She laughs softly and turns to him. They fall on the bed and make love with frogs serenading them. They drink Chianti and feed each other small oranges from China. She brings the world to him.

Early in the morning they paddle back. He kisses her goodbye and she's home before the sun has dried the dew on the grass.

Joe changes into his overalls in the barn, where he keeps a spare pair. Filling the water containers, he hears shouting and steps outside in time to see Bob chase Mom across the yard. He catches her by the well and slams her down. Joe hears the crack and runs to her, crouching beside her.

Bob stands over them.

Joe sees blood leaking from her ear. You killed her!

Goddamnit, out of my way Chicken Shit! Bob shoves Joe aside, picks up his wife and staggers back to the house.. Bob's still wearing his stained trousers. When he lays her down on the couch, blood pools by her ear.

Joe runs to the phone and calls the doctor.

Dr. Simmons arrives and Bob tells him, she fell on the well curb. Must've slipped on the wet grass.

When the hearse comes to take her away, Joe still hasn't spoken up. He curses himself for that.

The next day he drives to the police station and tells the whole story to Sergeant Stevens, the officer on duty.

Stevens is having none of it. What a story, you little shit. It was an accident. You better get on home. Your dad hears such crap, he'll whip your arse.

Joe should've known the police wouldn't help him.

He says nothing during the funeral or after. If only he could talk to Cathy, but she's in Vegas.

Bob has his drinking buddies back to the house, Sergeant Stevens among them. Joe doesn't go in the house. He gets in the canoe and paddles through the marsh.

Outside the cabin, he sits in a decrepit lawn chair. He stares down at Eight Mile Creek, as if Cathy might miraculously appear.

He remembers playing with Maeve and the barn kittens. She built elaborate hay barriers to hide the

kittens from Bob. She always called him Daddy. Mom
called him 'your dad'. Respect your dad, she'd say.

Honour thy father and mother. How should I honour
you, Mom? Some night, when Bob's sleeping, sneak in
and behead him like I do the chickens? Forgive him. Joe
can hear Mom saying that and that he "didn't mean to".
He does love us. His temper just gets the better of him.

When Joe returns to the farm a week later, he goes
straight to the barn, believing the chickens have been
without food and water for a week.

The chickens are fine and Bob's gutting young
cockerels for the restaurant order. About fuckin' time you
got back on the job, Bob says.

Joe, cursing himself, gets to work. If he leaves with
nothing, he'll be leaving Cathy too.

STOP SENDING ME this stuff. I don't want to hear any more about Joe
and Cathy. Get it through your head, Martin, I'm not leaving Rick. I
love Rick and my kids. What kind of role model would I be for my
daughter? How can I even think about leaving? Just crazy middle-of-the
night thoughts.

LAURIE'S GETTING MARRIED today. So easy to let the years slip by without noticing. Arlene's seven, nice kid, a real credit to Laurie. My ass of a brother's still somewhere out on the west coast. Sends Mom a postcard about once a year.

Laurie's dad paid for her divorce. I wish I felt her troubles were over. Wayne Bracken's fifteen years older, a widower with four kids, two-year-old twin boys and two girls, the oldest five. His wife was walking home when she was killed by a drunk driver.

Laurie says she's glad he has kids. "You know I can't have any more."

I said: "What about money?" She told me they'd manage. I don't see how. They're all going to live in the winterized cottage. Wayne's a salesman for some vacuum cleaner company. At least this year he is. Before that he worked at the quarry. He has a reputation for drinking. I know one thing—I'm glad I didn't end up in a winterized cottage with a bunch of shitty-assed kids.

Why's Katie yelling? "Billy, help Katie find her shoes. Grandma'll be here any minute." Rick's mom is good stuff. Not many women would want three noisy kids messing up her house.

"No! NO! *NO!*"

"Mommy, she won't put them on." Billy, kneeling next to the squirming Katie, is offering her the pink sandals. He's so sweet with Katie. He'll even play tea party with her.

"Want Mickey Mouse!" Katie yells.

I grab her Mickey Mouse runners from the closet. "Here, stop yowling and get them on." I swear Katie, at three, acts worse than Billy ever did and I thought he was a little monster. So much for me having a sweet little girl like Laurie's Arlene. Let's hope Katie will outgrow this monster phase, just as Billy has.

"Hello there. Donna, why's Katie crying?" Mrs. Waddell barges right in. Would it kill her to ring the bell?

"Just a fuss over her shoes. They're all ready to go. Billy, where's David?"

"Don't you know where he is, dear?" Mrs. Waddell has picked up Katie and is whispering something in her ear.

"Grandma has a surprise!" Katie says.

I find David in his room, busily drawing. His bulletin board's covered with lovely magical creatures. "Grandma's here."

"How long will you be gone?"

"It's Auntie Laurie's wedding. You're staying overnight at Grandma's."

"I could stay with Arlene."

"No, no, c'mon now. Grandma's waiting and she said she has a surprise. Where's your stuff?"

David picks up his pajama bag and follows me out. Why does he always look like he's being led to the guillotine? He's just as handsome as his brother. But Billy got all the confidence.

In the sudden quiet I take a deep breath. I suppose truly good mothers aren't so keen to have a day away from their kids. Katie's the main problem. Now that Billy's in grade one and plays more with other children, he isn't always bugging David. But Katie moves from one tantrum to the next. And her brothers always give in to her, which doesn't help. Rick gives in to her, too. If she wasn't so pretty, she wouldn't get away with it. She has big brown eyes and black curly hair that hangs in natural ringlets around her face. And such white skin, not a freckle on her. Those black curls so like Martin's. Don't even think it. I can't help it, every time I look at Katie I see Martin and my heart aches.

Life is funny. Laurie, who grew up in one of the big brick houses downtown ends up in a shabby old cottage with too many kids and Sharon, who came from such a place, marries a Toronto lawyer.

If Rick hadn't married me, I could've ended up like Laurie. I'm pretty damn lucky.

Time for a smoke and a quick cup of coffee before Rick gets home. I carry my coffee into the living room, sit by the window and watch the road.

Weddings depress me. The reception'll be at the Legion. Tacky paper streamers and heart-shaped balloons. Bingo tables gussied up with white cloths. Long speeches and bland food. People'll say wonderful things about Laurie and Wayne, most of them lies. Rick will yak-yak with everybody there. Always the salesman. I'll be stuck with the old married women and we'll talk about our kids. The young couples will dance.

There's Mrs. Thorton heading downtown. She's carrying a thick brown envelope, no doubt another of Martin's manuscripts. I wonder how he is. Sure like to see him.

No, I wouldn't. I know what would happen.

I order myself to take a shower and get to work on my face. Curious to see how that new shade of eye shadow goes with my nail polish.

After my shower I stand naked before my mirror. Maybe I'm not quite that *Playboy* centrefold hidden in his underwear drawer. Damn it, Rick, look at me, sometime. I look pretty good.

I spread my dress out on the bed. Got it in St. Thomas—midnight blue, backless with a swirly skirt. I drag over a chair and pull down the duffle bag. Cradle it in my lap. Leather against bare skin.

No letters for months and then one came a few days ago. I'd put it away unread. Now, I tear open the envelope.

> May 15, 1962
> *Dear Donna,*
>
> *You have forsaken me. As Christmas approached I was sure you would come. You came when Gretchen was home, but you didn't come to me.*
>
> *I hated December, but grey January even more. My small heater kept my studio just above freezing. Day after day icy rain thrashed the bare lilac branches against my windows. To shut out their constant scraping, I turned to my typewriter. Let me bring you up to date with Joe and Cathy.*
>
> With Mom gone, Joe stays away from the house as much as he can. Bob spends most evenings at the hotel but when he's home, out comes the strong box. He counts his money in front of Joe. You goddam chickenshit, you'll be rich someday. Your old man takes good care of ya. After locking the money away he drinks himself into unconsciousness. Joe, in his narrow bed, curses the old drunk to hell but does nothing, not for Maeve, not for

Mom, not for himself. He remembers his high school Shakespeare. The coward dies a thousand deaths. He curses himself most of all.

As he dumps the grain into the troughs, his lower back and legs ache. The last few years, wet weather bothers him more. He's looking forward to a hot shower and bed.

The hot water streaming down his back feels so good, he stays until the shower runs cold. He pulls on a ragged t-shirt and sweatpants and gobbles down some bread. Washes it down with a beer. Bob'll come home too drunk to notice one missing. He climbs into bed and pulls the quilt up over his head.

Goddamchickenshitprick, get up and make my supper! Bob has him by the shoulder.

Fuck off, would ya?

You little shit! Think you can swear at the old man? He punches Joe in the ear. Git downstairs before I give ya a lickin'.

Ear ringing, Joe stumbles down the stairs, Bob right behind him.

What do you want? Joe stands by the stove.

Fry me up that big old steak I bought.

Joe unwraps the bloody brown paper. He turns on the element and adds a little butter to the pan.

Bob cracks opens a beer. Speed it up, chickenshit.

Joe flips the steak onto a plate and smacks it down on the table.

Bob saws into the steak. Goddamnchickenshit, this fuckin' meat's raw! He hurls the plate and it bounces off Joe's head..

As Joe heads for the door, Bob sticks a foot out Joe goes down, hard. Bob kicks him in the back until he runs out of breath.

At eye level with the wood box, Joe grabs the hatchet and staggers to his feet.

He sees the frying pan out of the corner of his eye and

ducks it, making for the door. He's not fast enough.
Bob's got him by the back of the neck. Joe turns and
with all his strength swings the hatchet.

He stares as blood gushes from Bob's throat. He has
time to notice the blood's a brighter red than a chicken's
before Bob crumples to the floor. His head lies at a
strange angle, nearly severed. Joe drops the hatchet.

Wailing, he runs to the barn, rubbing his blood-
splattered clothes. Finally, he thinks to grab a canvas tarp
and a roll of twine. Hugging them to his chest, he staggers
back to the house. Spreading out the tarp on the kitchen
linoleum he rolls the body onto it. Blood spurts from
Bob's throat and he shrieks, falling back on his ass. He
vomits. Shaking uncontrollably, he wipes his mouth with
his t-shirt and ties the body securely in the tarp.

Sweating heavily in the rain, he drags the body to
the well. He notices the tarp is stained a bright green,
from the last time he touched up the porch. Christmassy,
he thinks. Shocked at his own thoughts, Joe shoves the
iron cover aside and with a strength he didn't know he
had, heaves the body over the edge. There's a terrible
thud and splash. Joe peers in, sees only limestone walls
and dark water. He shivers and rams the cover into place.

No more shaking. Good. Grabbing the hatchet, he
smashes the padlock off Bob's closet door. Whacking
open the strong box he pauses to look at the stacks bound
with rubber bands. For an instant he sees Bob's pudgy
fingers caressing the bills. Joe drops the hatchet and
turns away.

In the shower, he can't get rid of the blood rimming
his fingernails. He puts on his good pair of jeans and his
only dress shirt. The buttons won't fasten. Pulling on the
sweater Cathy gave him last Christmas, he kicks his stained
clothes under the bed. Throws his backpack stuffed with
money onto the passenger side of his truck and starts the
engine. He turns it off and sits for a minute.

Joe lugs the gallon jug of gas into the kitchen. Blood, so much blood. He pours the gas on the wood box and drops in a lighted match. The flames whoosh up. He hasn't noticed how cold he was and runs for his truck.

Driving toward St. Thomas, the shaking's back and he can barely stay on the road. A couple of miles outside the city, he turns down a dirt lane to the old canal. He drives the truck right to the edge so the front tires rest on the low curb.

Joe thinks back to another time, when he'd sat here contemplating driving into the canal. That was the night Bob stomped on his hand, breaking three fingers. The thought of Cathy brought him home. Someday, when he inherited the farm, he'd sell it and they would run away.

What now? He has murdered his father.

The rain's back, too, beating on the windshield.

My lovely Donna, spring is here. Winter's cold is gone, not forgotten. I've filled a jug with lilacs, a promise to myself that spring always follows winter. The lilacs bloom for you, too, my darling. Come soon. Don't let Joe die.

OH, MARTIN, STOP with the scary stuff. You should've finished *Marsh Road* years ago or forgotten about it. Why don't you stick to science fiction? You've just had two more stories published. I liked the one about the lovers escaping the moon colony. Hate *Marsh Road*. Not my fault what happens to Joe. You made up the whole thing—it's your story. Leave me out of it. I'm going to a wedding with my husband. My children are safe. There will be dancing.

THE BARN 1982

MY HEART THUMPS. How could I let a baby starve? He's in the hamper — maybe not too late. I'm out of bed and rummaging through the laundry.

Oh God, what's the matter with me? Just a stupid dream. I climb back in beside Rick — on his back with arms flung out, like a kid. If only I could sleep like that.

That awful feeling of forgetting something I was supposed to do. Think and think and watch the clock. 2:01. Doze off and jerk awake. 2:20, 2:31.

Leap up at the first ring. There's been an accident — David and his fiancée were driving back from Toronto tonight.

Or my little granddaughter Claire. She had a stomach ache — her appendix? Billy wouldn't listen to me.

My hand shakes as I grab the receiver.

It's Mrs. Thorton. "Martin has fallen and can't get up. Can you come over?"

"Be there in five minutes."

I'm just pulling on my jeans when Rick sits up, rubs his eyes. "Pumpkin, what's going on?"

"It's okay. Mrs. Thorton's having a bad night."

"Huh?" he says. "I didn't know she was sick."

"Go back to sleep. I'll be home soon."

"Yeah, okay." He flops back down, grumbling something about how they should both be put in a home.

I grit my teeth and close the door quietly behind me.

A cold drizzle slaps my face. I can just make out Mrs. Thorton's porch light. Her beacon. How many nights has she sat on that porch waiting for Martin? At least he's not wandering around at night anymore.

Maybe I should've brought Rick. Last time I had a hard time getting Martin up. His embarrassment makes everything harder.

The moment I open the door it's obvious what's happened. Martin's been drinking, tried to get to the bathroom and slipped in his vomit.

Poor little Mrs. Thorton is trying to get him up. She has become old and frail. Martin's slurring his words, can't make out what he's saying. Finally understand he wants us each to take him under an arm and lift. Mrs. Thorton grabs hold and is all set.

"Don't," I tell her. "You shouldn't be doing this. You're nearly eighty." He's urging us on. "C'mon, jus' balance me."

Balance, my eye, he's a dead weight. "Martin, your mother's not supposed to lift heavy things."

"Not liff, jus' balance."

"Don't," I tell Mrs. Thorton. "I'll call Rick."

"Donna, you liff me," Martin says.

I ignore him.

RICK AND I get Martin to his feet and then onto the bed. Martin's fuming, but I don't care. Would he care if she broke her hip or had a heart attack trying to help him? I want to stay and clean up but she won't hear of it. Her humiliation makes everything harder, too.

A FEW DAYS later I get this in the mail:

> January 10, 1982
> *Dear Donna,*
>
> *I'm sorry the party got out of hand the other night. I should've had you over to drink with me and the evening would've had a better finale. Better luck next time, eh!*
>
> *Well, Rick finally saw the inside of the writer's lair. When we were kids and he thought he could push me around, bet he never dreamt someday he would be a car salesman and I'd be a writer. What did he say about all the books? I assume he never enters a library.*
>
> *Why don't you come over this afternoon and let me make it up to you? I made Mother get me a good bottle of Scotch. My penny-pinching mother usually gets that cheap rye which is why I got sick.*

*The rain, the wind and the wolf are pelting these old windows.
Maybe they'll blow this house down which might not be a bad
thing. Mother's at a prayer meeting, asking forgiveness for their sins.
Poor old woman, what does she need to pray for? She never had
time for sinning. I wouldn't mind if the house fell in and buried me.*

*If you come, I'll demand the sun to shine and this house
to stand forever.*

DOESN'T IT ENTER his head she might be praying for him? I won't go to
see him. It would just be another fiasco. The last time we tried, he
couldn't get it up and I was unnerved by the intensity of his frustration.
I told him it was the booze, that when Rick's had too many beers he
can't either. Martin ranted about football players making terrible lovers
as they haven't any brains and love's in the head as much as the cock.

I said: "Let's just cuddle."

"If I wanted cuddling, I'd cuddle one of the cats."

I got up and left. Didn't know what else to do.

AS THE DAYS and weeks go by, I try not to think about him. I babysit
little Claire. We colour together and roll in the snow. She loves hearing
about the snow forts her daddy used to make.

THIS MORNING, THERE was another letter. While Rick watches the hockey
game, I lock myself in the bathroom and open the letter, overwhelmed
with dread.

February 25, 1982
Dear Donna,

*All hell's broken loose. Gretchen's moving back home. I
can't believe it.*

*She's quit her job. Already sold her house. Never said a
word to me about it. Doesn't seem to realize this is my house.
She must be meaning to stay. Damn.*

GRETCHEN'S COMING HOME. She's certainly needed. Mrs. Thorton can't
manage any longer.

But what if Martin and Gretchen talk? As kids they were so close. A long, long time ago, 1953, when I met the Thortons.

I'd seen a horse at the place up the hill, a few blocks away. Their house, I soon discovered.

I rode my bike up there and fed the horse carrots and apples through the fence. That's how I met Gretchen—she wanted to lend me a book.

I never read any books except for school. But said I'd like to and that's how I got to see inside her house and meet Martin and their mother.

Martin was hunched over a book, his fingers tracing the words.

"This is my brother, Martin," Gretchen said.

He looked up. I saw his unfocused eyes and knew something was wrong. It was a year before Gretchen would tell me he had fallen from a balcony when he was five. When I first asked, her eyes would slide away from mine, as if everything about her family had to be kept secret.

He said they were studying Plato's *The Apology*. Later I would understand he was referring to himself and his mother.

Martin left the porch and hobbled outside, bending over the flowers. He came back with a rose. Said something about art and nature. Then he said: "For you"—and handed it to me. Ah, Martin, I fell in love with you right then.

I say "hobbled." That sounds pathetic and there was nothing pathetic about him. He was a good six-feet tall, with curly black hair that accented his clear, pale skin and those cloudy blue eyes. A bit spooky, but not pathetic. The way he smiled made me think of somebody much older than eighteen. My brother, who burped and farted at the dinner table, was eighteen.

She's coming home. Oh, Gretchen, I wish we could turn back the clock.

I LIGHT ANOTHER cigarette and check the doors are locked. All the letters are spread out on my bed. I cry every time I read the first one.

> August 28, 1956
> *Dear Donna,*
>
> *You must understand why I couldn't attend your wedding. As a non-believer how could I enter a church? Mother said you looked lovely. Your loveliness I do believe in. Even my sightless eyes know how beautiful you are.*
>
> *I wanted Mother to take you our roses. She said it wouldn't be proper to arrive at church with an armload of flowers. Mother worries a good deal about what is proper. If I'd been there, I would've piled all the roses from our garden at your feet. They're blooming more ardently than ever, as if they know it's their final hurrah before frost.*
>
> *Do come and see the roses. Their sweet perfume reminds me of you. I am waiting, not patiently. As I've told you, I'm not known for humble patience.*

EACH TIME I read this, it all floods back—living above Brown's Electric, waves of nausea every morning.

Martin, I wish you had come with your armload of roses and dropped them at my feet, just at the moment Rev. Everet said: "Does anyone know any reason this couple should not be wed?"

I imagine the thump thump of your cane as you stride up the aisle and the gasps from the congregation. Your tall stooped frame, craggy profile, cloudy blue eyes. Should you have worn a black cloak for the occasion?

You wrap me in your cloak, lift me into your arms and march right back out of there. What a picture we make, me in my white dress, clutching fresh roses!

And then what? When your prince comes, he's supposed to carry you off to his castle.

Poor Martin, you didn't have a castle. And for that matter, you couldn't even have picked me up. Your limp was already too bad.

The wind howls, and the rain pounds the window. Gretchen must be having quite the drive from Ottawa. God, keep them safe. Mrs. Thorton doesn't need any more tragedy.

I light another cigarette.

Why was I so damn miserable that fall? Why in the hell didn't I settle down like I was supposed to? Rick was a good catch.

Lots of women carry on as if pregnancy is the greatest thing in the world. I remember Gretchen the summer she was pregnant with Owen. She walked around with that smile on her face as if she'd just fallen in love. That's how some women act, like they're in love with their unborn babies. I loved and resented mine in equal measure. Every day.

Once, she told me in giving birth she went to the centre of life, of passion. Blood and shit and you're torn open and there's life in all its glory. That's Gretchen all right. What nonsense!

Too bad when we were 17 she wasn't the one with a bun in the oven.

Back at the window I sip my coffee and watch their place. The rain has turned to wet, driving snow—Leaman Road's ankle-deep in slush. Is Martin in his studio tapping away at the Brailler? Is he drowning Joe and Cathy?

A mini-van pulls up. I can barely see through the sleet but it must be Gretchen. The roof rack's piled high. She steps out and now I see Owen. He's as tall as his mother.

Owen's fourteen. Don't really know him, though he comes with his mother each summer. He's always been shy, a lot like Gretchen as a kid. I've no idea how the divorce affected him.

GRETCHEN, MY LONG-AGO best friend, what will you think of me?

The summer we met, we helped out at the pony track. Then she got a job there and was so keen on it. I preferred hanging out in their barn with the loft swing. Had a seat wide enough for two.

We made that swing go so high we could touch the boards lining the roof. On wet days as the rain drummed on the metal sheeting, the orchard and gardens flashed by in colourful squares — like my View-master.

Gretchen, like Martin, writes poetry. The poems are in magazines, those same ones he sometimes has stuff in. Magazines you never see in a store. Only once, she showed me one. In the poem the boards are bending away from the barn and crying in the wind like children. Eerie and a little crazy.

She was always a bit peculiar. She didn't want to grow up. Once that first year I was married, she told me: "When Martin and I were children we were happy. Had school with Mother and went on hikes."

"My mom would never have taken us on a hike."

"She read by the campfire while Martin and I went exploring and made up stories about the Juperians."

"You both have great imaginations."

"The Juperians were tiny aliens who used to live on one of Jupiter's moons. Their moon had been knocked out of orbit by a meteor and had drifted through space. Martin and I, along with a small band of other Juperians, built a flying saucer to escape the doomed moon and landed on Earth. I can still hear Martin as a kid saying 'doomed' and 'drifting.' So much drama."

All these years later at the oddest moments, like sitting in church, I'll remember her saying: "When Martin and I were little children, we were happy."

RICK'S LEFT FOR work. Wish I had a job to go to, even working in the drugstore like I did as a teenager. Rick says the poorly-paid jobs I could get would just mess up his income tax.

Is it too soon to go see Gretchen?

Well, what do you know—there she is, coming from downtown. Odd. Nothing's open this early.

I run to the door and wave. "Hey, stranger, long time no see."

"Hi, Donna, I was going to stop in but thought you might not be up."

"Good to see you." I hug her. "You were downtown?"

"Wanted to have a quiet look around," she says, hugging me back.

"Coffee's on, or I can make tea. I know you guys always have tea."

"Coffee, please. I haven't been home twenty-four hours and I'm already sick of Mother's endless supply of tea."

"Just throw your coat over a chair." I pour us both a coffee and we settle at the table. She looks exactly the same, skinny and not a hint of grey in her dark hair. "Endless tea?"

" All my life, Mother's been sitting me down to a cup of tea and telling me all her worries about Martin."

"How is he?"

"Drinking too much. I knew it was bad and she's having a hard time." She stirs and stirs her coffee.

"I should've told you."

"I could've come sooner."

"Martin wouldn't want me to interfere."

"It'll be good for him to have Owen around. Make him start think-ing about somebody other than himself. Owen's really good at Scrabble." She gulps down her coffee. "Donna, I'm thinking of getting a horse. Maybe two. Owen's interested. How about you?"

"Haven't ridden since we were kids."

"It's not something you forget. It'd put that big empty barn to some use. I went out this morning and sat on my swing and it reminded me of happier times. I'd get a couple of quiet old horses."

"Oh, Gretchen, I would love that!"

OUR VISIT WASN'T awkward at all. Maybe I'm silly to worry about what Martin might tell her. He can't have said anything. Maybe he won't.

She hates "mother's endless tea," she said. Funny that—because that endless supply of tea has been my comfort all these years. If I were granted a last wish, it would be having tea with Mrs. Thorton. Horses. Wouldn't that be something, riding again?

ALMOST A WEEK since Gretchen's visit. I'm so restless. Too many smokes and too much coffee. If I went over there how would Martin act? That sad ending to *Marsh Road*—what does it mean?

The letters are still in my closet. Wouldn't be so bad if they stayed there but once again they're spread out before me on the bed. I don't think Gretchen's read much of his novel. He used to call her a prude.

Marsh Road went on and on through so many chapters—seemed it was always raining, the chicken house flooding, chickens buried in mud and shit. Then, after all these years, just a few days after Gretchen comes home, he sends me the ending. Depressing read; should've stuck to his science-fiction stuff, which was actually published, though to little or no pay.

Would things have been different if Martin could've gone to school in Grenville? Gretchen told me some bullying went on when they went downtown or the beach. She claimed Rick was one of the bullies. I doubt that. He's really good with kids.

As I told my kids, teasing and being teased is part of childhood. Stick up for yourself.

Another cigarette. Katie calls them cancer sticks.

Funny I once thought the boys might bully her. Katie's everybody's darling. Still Rick's little princess. He better not give her a car for graduation. There were times I was jealous and times I was scared. Katie looked too much like Martin.

Katie acted like I was her rival. Still does.

The other day she said: "I'm sure as hell not going spend my life as a stay-at-home housewife." She doesn't have a clue how I've spent my life. Thank heavens.

Gretchen and I were best friends and as we got older her isolation bothered me. Martin and I urged her to go the dances, even if it was just the after-school sock-hop.

High school was exciting but I still needed the Thortons. They were different and made me curious. They had braille cards and a Scrabble game with raised letters. It was fun learning braille.

I'd entertain them with tales of the crazy things kids did at school. Martin listened to my stories and asked questions. Gretchen listened as attentively as he did. You'd think she went to a different school.

He always approved of my school antics. Mr. Baxter's math class—must've been grade ten. Didn't have my homework done and I sassed him. "You give us too much. We still have to do the decorations for the Valentine's dance, you know."

"Is a dance more important?"

"You can bet your boots it is and a lot more fun." I got a detention.

Martin laughed, said I had guts. It was heady stuff having a boy four years older listen and approve of every word I uttered.

That day Gretchen missed school, I stopped at her house to see what was wrong. Martin said she and their mother were at the dentist. He suggested I wait.

"Do you want to play poker?" I said. I was a pretty good poker player, though Martin usually won. Luck does play a large role in poker but he could outwit luck—quickly figuring the odds of getting the cards he needed.

"What are you wearing?" he asked. I described my new circle skirt, aqua felt with black piping.

"Piping?"

"Trim dividing the sections."

"I've always wondered what you look like. May I touch your face? Then I would know."

I let him. His fingers lightly circled my eyes, touched my nose, brushed across my lips. I closed my eyes. His hands stroked my neck. When they reached my breasts and stayed there, I did nothing. He couldn't see my big smile. His lips were moist and warm against mine.

He didn't do anything I hadn't already done, just the same innocent fooling around I'd been doing since I was thirteen. Afterward, I wondered what the hell? Ian was my boyfriend. When Ian fondled my tits, I didn't get all hot and tremble-y, like with Martin.

I didn't want Martin for my boyfriend. What would the kids at school think? My stomach feels queasy—too much coffee and too many smokes. Should go for a walk. I gather up the letters. One slips out and I pick it up.

> Nov. 20, 1965
> *Dear Donna,*
>
> *From my studio I watch the shadowy limbs bend and sway. I'm the man chained in Plato's cave watching shadows. No metaphor this.*
>
> *I'd like to get this place winterized. It's damn cold. Needs a better heater. Fat chance of that. Mother rattles on about the high cost of electricity. At least it's quiet. She's been at the piano again. I'd like to take an axe to it. She's either playing it or bemoaning the fact I'm not. "And you had such talent as a little boy." That's based on my playing the melody for Silent Night when I was six.*
>
> *Remember in the last chapter I sent you Joe killed his father. Here's the next bit.*
>
> The rain thrashes against the windshield, obliterating the canal. It was self-defence. No one would believe him.

OH, MARTIN, I'M not in the mood for *Marsh Road*—too much of a downer. I sigh and fold up the letter. A couple of years earlier he'd written about Bob's death. Then no more. Yet here he was back at it.

Get your raincoat. A walk, remember? Who feels like walking in this dreary weather? Maybe a nap.

I stretch out on the bed and close my eyes.

Was the carrying-on with Martin all my fault?

After Gretchen got her driver's license, it became more complicated to keep my two lives separate.

Gretchen wanted me to go to the drive-in with her and Martin.

Said she could get the car. I thought it would be fun, the three of us going out together.

When we got there, Martin told Gretchen to get in the back, and she went without a word. He moved over into the driver's seat, put his arm around me and kissed me. I pushed him away. "The movie's starting." He talked all through it. Such a know-it-all! Still is.

She never said anything the whole bloody evening. Why did she ask me to go? Like she was setting me up for a date with Martin. She knew Ian was my boyfriend.

Often that fall Martin wanted the three of us to go to the Quick Stop. That should've been okay. Gretchen never hung out there but when Martin wanted to, she would agree to drive. I wasn't leading him on. I had a boyfriend. But their dad had just died and I thought it was good for Martin to get out more. At home he seemed a man, not a boy. So smart, all the books he'd read. And music too. Knew all the bands and titles of every song. Walking in the garden he was a handsome, romantic figure and his blindness and limp only added to his aura.

At the Quick Stop he was weird—"Can this two-bit place change a twenty?" He smacked the juke box with his fist.

How could I have done things differently? Oh hell, there's the doorbell.

It's Gretchen. "Rotten day to be out," I say and hang her wet coat over the back of a kitchen chair. She doesn't dress much better than she ever did—jeans and an old parka. I don't think I've ever seen her dressed up. She could afford a mink if she wanted. Teachers are well-paid these days. But of course she'd agree with my Katie and feel sorry for the little animals.

"Hope you don't mind me dropping in unannounced but I just had to get out of there."

"I'm really glad to see you.' I concentrate on measuring out the coffee and then need three tries to hit the ON button.

"Your hand's trembling. Donna. You okay?"

"Just too many smokes."

"I should've phoned first."

"Oh, Gretchen, you don't need to phone. I'm so glad we're neighbours again."

She stares out the kitchen window.

I stand beside her. We're silent for a bit. I feel I know her well, though I've hardly seen her in years. "Remember us riding Misty and Prince out there?"

"Those were the good times." She sighs again.

"I've been worried about your mother."

"Me too. She sits around moaning about poor Martin. I try to change the subject, get her interested in Owen. After all, he's her only grand-child."

"How's Owen liking the school?"

"Not bad. It's much improved since we were there."

"How's Martin today?"

"As usual, working himself into a rage talking about when we were young."

"When we were young—what do you mean?" Oh God, what has he told her?

"Donna, you don't know what it was like. My mother's friends were as bad as the bratty kids. They'd come right up to us on the street and pat Martin on the arm or on the head and say, not to Martin, but to Mother: 'How's the boy today?' Old Mrs. Granger, how we hated her. 'Our prayer group is praying for the dear boy every Thursday night.'"

"I suppose she meant well," I say, getting down the mugs.

"As Martin often said, why didn't the old bag pray for rescue from her boring little life? Mmm, thanks. Coffee's delicious."

"You sound angry too."

"Hated them all.

"Did you hate me?"

"Of course not. You were the one friend we had but you did play with Martin's feelings. No big deal for you to go with us to the Quick Stop, you so pretty and popular. You have no idea what it meant to him. How afterward he analyzed every word spoken there. Asked me all these questions about the decor, the jukebox."

"Back then, did you and Martin talk about me? After going to the Quick Stop, what would he say?"

She laughs. "One time he said: 'Bet not many guys taking Donna there have a twenty to spend.' He thought himself on the top of the social pinnacle being there with you, the prettiest and most popular girl at Grenville High."

"I wasn't that pretty or popular."

"Oh yes, you were." She gulps her coffee. "I'd better be off."

"You just got here."

"Mother doesn't like me to be away too long and I've got to get some groceries."

"Lugging groceries all that way? Why didn't you drive?"

"I love walking."

"In this weather?"

"The wind and the rain clear my head," she says.

She sounds just like Martin.

We finish our coffee, and she rushes off.

I light a cigarette. I did understand how much getting out meant to him. I just didn't know what to do about it.

The grand finale wasn't long in coming. Funny how a small incident could take on such importance. He had talked us into going to the dancehall at Blackstone Point.

He had his dad's flask. Gretchen was pretty riled up about that. I don't think Mrs. Thorton knew he had it. I made him put it in my purse. "Martin, this is a slow one." Dancing would get his mind off getting drunk. If he came home drunk, his mother would think it was my influence.

We walked jerkily around the floor with me trying to get him to keep his hands to himself. A game. He'd put his hand on my ass and I with a wriggle would yank it up to my waist. A sparkly ball hung from the ceiling, flashing on the dancers, on us. My black taffeta skirt rustled and his dark curls brushed my cheek. More than okay, perfect.

The disc jockey switched to a fast one and after a minute or two of that, Martin and I fell. Gretchen made a big fuss and insisted we go home. I guess we embarrassed her.

I light another cigarette. Better be my last. And get some windows open. Rick'll be on my case again.

After that, people started asking me if I was dating Martin Thorton. I knew they thought he was weird.

Ian and I had broken up that fall. And just like that, I was a social outcast. I avoided the Thortons. Why didn't I turn to Martin?

In some ways, he intimidated me. I'd started confirmation classes. Gretchen, Martin and I were on the porch when I asked him why he didn't go to church. He went on and on quoting the Apostles' Creed and making fun of it. Said people were stupid to get confirmed and the church just wanted their money.

I went to church to be with my friends. There were some cute guys in the senior class and they all went to Young People's Group. We did fun things like wiener roasts and baseball games. The meetings were discussions about religion—right up Martin's alley. If he hadn't been so high and mighty, he could've gone and enjoyed himself. Who knows what's true? Like the stuff they taught us in school. In grade three we made relief maps out of asbestos mixed with water. Everyone believed that asbestos was just fireproof insulation. Now they're tearing it out of the walls of the high school.

Oh my God! I completely forgot that Jimmy and his hoity-toity wife are coming for dinner.

They set themselves above other people. Martin does that too. Making fun of Rick being a car salesman or golfing or us for going to church. Selling cars is an honest way to make a living. And what's wrong with playing golf? He'd say: "Rick out chasing his little balls again?"

So maybe Martin knows all the words in the English language. What good did it ever do him? He and Gretchen never knew how to have fun.

Both of them lorded their book-learning over me. They aren't actually superior—they don't know the simplest things, like that going to church is the normal thing to do.

Even when I was a teenager I knew what I wanted. Lots of friends and a regular life. Martin couldn't give me that. Oh, come on, Donna. What I'm avoiding admitting even to myself is that I didn't turn to him when Ian dropped me because Martin was handicapped, because everyone thought him weird. I loved him. I was so bloody stupid.

How can you be attracted and repelled at the same time? And there was attraction, far more than there'd ever been with Ian. Ian was just a boy. But right from that first day when I was fourteen and met Martin, the things I'd felt for him were different, and strong.

Then I met Rick. I'd gone into the Quick Stop on the way home from school and was sitting with a girl from my class. Her boyfriend stopped at our booth and Rick was with him. I recognized him from his picture hanging in the school foyer. Star quarterback and now, at twenty-one, he was even better looking. "Mind if we join you?" and he pushed in beside me. With his muscular thigh against my leg, my gut went all quivery.

He asked me to go to the show Friday night. The following Monday, when he picked me up after school in his red convertible, I went from being scorned to being envied.

Things just happened with Rick. We dated, we made out—I let myself go with the flow.

Getting married should've been the happy ending.

Better get the beef marinating. Going to try that new recipe for stroganoff. Apple crisp for dessert—quick to make, and I can dress it up with ice cream. Oh damn, I forgot to get the meat out of the freezer. I'll have to thaw it in the microwave.

Now it's soft and brown on the edges and still frozen solid in the centre. The mallet will fix it. I like pounding meat.

I'd like to make Mrs. Thorton a nice dinner, look after her. She's been a second mother to me and more a grandma to my kids than my own mother. Mom's never had much time for kids and her stroke made her bitter, self-centred. How nasty she's been to Laurie and little Arlene, her own grand-daughter. Once Ted left, she completely ignored them. If I said: "Look, Arlene's your granddaughter," she'd say: "Maybe she is, maybe she isn't." Mom never paid my kids much attention either. Brenda and Frank's girls get all the love. Of course they all live with Mom and Dad.

When Billy was a baby and we moved here, I started hanging out with the Thortons again. I so want Gretchen and me to be friends again. But Martin's so angry. And what's he been telling her?

ICY SNOW SLANTING on the windows. Gretchen's been home nearly two weeks and we're still having winter. Billy, Ruth and Claire are still in Florida. I miss babysitting Claire.

Another cigarette. I know damn well I should be smoking outside but it's freezing cold and I'm sorting the letters in the order in which they came. Do I think I can file my life by letters? I run my fingers over the bumpy words and think of Martin doing the same. Braille's interesting, how the words stand out. I like to touch his words.

A person can get starved for touch. Rick likes sex. But touch is more than turning to each other in bed with the lights out. Something as simple as him running his fingers down your arm, or tracing the features of your face and saying: "You're beautiful." Martin never got tired of touching me.

> July 1, 1968
> *Dear Donna,*
>
> *When are we going out in the Mustang again?*
>
> *Driving down the back roads, a beer in my hand, and the branches thwacking the side of the car. Finally "on the road." Jack Kerouac's kind of place— "journeying in the crazy American night."*
>
> *Naughty of me to tell you Marsh Road would be dry in July. As kids we used to hike there, use the vines to climb those mossy trees. I'd terrify Gretchen with ghost stories of lost elderberry pickers.*
>
> *You so scared we were going to get stuck in the mud. And bad boy me hoping we would.*
>
> *That Mustang's a great car. I'd like to work on the assembly line in Detroit. As the car parts passed through my hands, I would imagine the shiny Mustangs, today's covered*

*wagons, carrying lovers across America, Jim Morrison on the
radio singing "Light My Fire."*

*You should always wear pure silk undies. Cool silk—
warm skin. Your tits rising to my touch as I slipped off your
bra. Ford had lovers in mind when they designed those
reclining seats. Crickets and frogs sang in the ditches while
your sweet smells mixed with that of the Mustang's leather
upholstery.*

*Come on baby, light my fire. Oh Donna, come back. So
many roads to explore, so little time.*

I HAD CLEANED the car as soon as I got home. One door was scratched
and of course Rick noticed. I said Billy must've been playing with a stick.
Some mom I was, blaming the kids. Some wife too—Rick bought me
that red Mustang to taxi the kids around. Only took Martin out that once.
I'd taken the new car over to show it to Mrs. Thorton. Rick was at a Lion's
meeting and the kids were staying over at the Waddells. Martin begged
me to take him for a ride.

Hadn't seemed that risky. Rick would've thought I was being kind
—taking the shut-in out for a drive. Martin talked me into driving
back to the swamp. Nearly got stuck trying to get turned around. He
was laughing and singing along with the radio: "Girl, we couldn't get
much higher ..."

Oh God, what an idiot I am! Right from the first time I felt terribly
guilty. I swore 'never again'—convinced myself it was just a bit of left-
over teenage passion, teenage rebellion.

The sleet has turned to rain, miserable rain. Oh, to turn back the
clock. Get in my Mustang, pick up Martin and drive and drive.

You're crazy, Donna.

I did feel sorry for him but that wasn't why I went back. I needed
him and don't know why. I had Rick, my kids.

He was threatening to sue some poetry magazine that asked him
to do several book reviews and took only one.

"How's your novel coming along?" I said to distract him.

"Latest bit's right here." He reached for the stapled pages on the end table.

"Read to me." I loved him reading to me in bed, the intimacy of it.

Propping himself on one elbow, he traced out the words. Late afternoon light outlined his craggy profile.

He read about Joe and Cathy in the car getting nowhere. They had tried to get to Detroit, planned to fly to Mexico, but the police were after them. They heard on the radio Joe was wanted for questioning about a suspicious fire and his father's disappearance. They travelled the back roads and he kept on through the rain and the muddy roads, and Joe and Cathy, and hiding out in the bush. Our bed got colder and damper and as the sky darkened, the shrubs pressing against every window turned black.

No light on and he kept reading, his fingers tracing the words in the dark, until I felt we were lost on some long gravel road. He was too worked up by his reading to be cold.

All I wanted was to go home to my loud kids and Rick, to my warm snug bungalow with broadloom rugs, a plump couch and the TV blaring *I Love Lucy* reruns.

Joe and Cathy were sleeping in his car. They had stocked up on provisions and had stolen blankets from a clothesline. Cathy said: "I have to get home—I need clothes and I'm running out of my birth control pills. You said we were just going for a drive in your new car." "Darling, you worry too much, we've lots of money." "Oh Joe," Cathy sighed, "just tell the police the truth." "They don't care about the truth," he wailed. She tried to comfort him.

I especially remember the line: "Cathy's warm, caressing fingers reached for his cock." All I could think was poor Mrs. Thorton having to read that.

I'm surprised Mrs. Thorton didn't edit out the vulgar bits. Though really, the sex stuff in his stories was pretty tame compared to some I've read.

Often, he lent me books—trying to educate me, I guess. He got all fired up over Henry Miller's *Tropic of Cancer*.

July 7, 1973
Dear Donna,

*Read this book! Forget making beds, forget baking
peanut butter cookies and throw the squalling brats a hunk
of bread. Read this book!*

*Henry Miller is the greatest American author ever. His
book Tropic of Cancer was banned for 30 years.*

*Miller said he was going to make a book out of all the stuff
that had been left out of literature. He wrote about what he was
really thinking. If he was walking along a Paris street, wondering
how he could still have an erection when he hadn't eaten all day,
that's what he wrote about. Not like that moron Wordsworth
babbling about brooks and daffodils when he was probably
thinking about his cock and what to do about his sister.*

*Before Miller, books were written about so-called great
events. The Second World War. A football hero. A fantastic
murder trial. The Black Death.*

*Miller dared to write what was in his own mind so
powerfully you could smell the women's bodies. While
walking in the rain, he dared to reveal what the world had
become after almost two thousand years of Christianity.*

Why are you still reading this? Go pick up the book.

I DID TRY but must admit I skipped parts. Miller could go from something simple like his wife saying: "You're a great human being," to a
real flowery passage—something about the equator and the Garden
of Eden. He'd lose me completely. I didn't much like the main character, who's apparently supposed to be Miller. He might be giving us the
inside of his mind but what was in it was a lot of disgusting talk about
women. Except his wife, Mona—I think he really loved her. In one
place he talks about a great void opening in front of him when he thinks
of her. No surprise to learn that she left him.

Martin wanted to be like Miller. Strange really, because Martin's
the most romantic man I've known. When he used words like fuck, cock,
cunt, he made them something other than swear words, unlike Miller
and his *Tropic of Cancer*.

Rick caught me reading *Tropic of Cancer*. I was surprised he'd heard of it.

"What, you're reading that dirty book? Gary had that with him at work. When business was slow, he read us the juicy bits."

"Gary? Waddell Ford's book expert?"

"Why do you make fun of Gary?"

"What did the genius Gary have to say?"

"He didn't have to say anything. I've got ears. That Miller guy's got a sewer for a mind. Did you borrow it from Martin?"

"Yeah."

"Guess that poor crip reads about it, because he doesn't get any."

I knew better than to say anything.

Disturbing to think of Mrs. Thorton, who never even says damn, reading *Tropic of Cancer*. She did though, recording the whole thing on tape for Martin. She said: "Henry Miller is a significant piece in the literary puzzle and it's important that Martin has all the pieces."

Oh, the arguments Martin and I had over Henry Miller. I said any man who would describe a woman's vagina as a dark unstitched wound has to have some pretty weird notions about women.

"You just don't get it. Miller worshipped women. He saw the whole of the world in a woman's cunt."

"Call it a vagina or I'm leaving." I got sick of Martin trying to talk like Miller.

"All right, all right," Martin said, laughing. "Vagina — the meaning of life is in a woman's vagina. That's not insulting, is it?"

"No, just silly."

The scene where Miller's watching his friend with the prostitute really made me mad. His friend can't reach a climax and he keeps ramming the woman. They make fun of her because she's hungry and they won't give her anything to eat and call her a starving cunt, as if it's her fault. Laugh at her owing back rent and leaving her baby in the country. He says most prostitutes have a baby in the country. In the Thirties, long before the Pill, I imagine many of them did have kids their relatives looked after. It's all a joke to Miller and his pals. They just want to get laid. And they're mad because she's obviously not enjoying it. Why would they expect her to?

MARTIN SAID: "You don't know what he's talking about. The whore symbolizes the society that has lost any passion it ever had. That's why he talks about war and the man in the trenches. Wars are fought over money because all the passion has gone out of people's lives. That's why he keeps talking about the fifteen francs."

"I still feel sorry for the girl."

Martin raised his voice. "You're missing the whole point of the book. It's not some soppy novel about a starving prostitute with a baby in the country. It's an analysis of all of human history."

I still think Miller was a jerk!

I LIE IN bed and listen to Katie's high-pitched laugh. What do you bet Rick's making pancakes? Always does when she's home for the weekend. Last night when I asked her who she was dating, she laughed and said: "I'm between men at the moment."

"Oh honey, I'm so sorry."

"Mom, no tragedy."

"I know you'll find someone. You're a pretty girl."

"Mom," she said. "I'm not looking."

"But you are twenty-three."

"So? I don't intend to get married until I'm at least thirty."

"What about children?"

"Not sure I want any. And I have plenty of time. Lots of women have their first one at forty."

"Well, I wouldn't want to see you left behind."

"Mom, you're a friggin' riot. 'Left behind?' When I get my degree, I'm going overseas to teach. You think this hick town is the centre of the universe. Didn't you ever want to see the world?"

"Your dad and I are planning a trip to Europe."

"Being a friggin' tourist, that's not seeing the world."

I FLUFF UP my pillow. Love sleeping in. For so many years I didn't get a chance to. Katie reminds me of Martin. Stop it, Donna. Don't go there. Those black curls against unfreckled skin. Rick and the boys have freckles, so do I. But it's more her facial expressions. Her funny little smile when she's being sarcastic. She has my brown eyes and small nose. She's tall, but so are the boys and Rick. What are the odds?

Shouldn't worry. Martin doesn't even look much like Martin now. He aged so early, his hair completely grey by thirty-five, going bald and a reddish complexion — broken blood vessels from the drinking.

Only in his forties and looks like an old man. Rick's still a good-looking guy.

Might as well get up. I pull on my silky red housecoat and head to
the bathroom.

The hot water pounds my back, somewhere between a beating and
a caress. Washing away my sins.

I pull off my shower cap and brush out my new perm. Not a grey hair,
thanks to my hairdresser. Carefully do my face. Takes longer and longer
to make myself presentable.

"Good morning, Pumpkin. We saved you some pancakes."

"Just coffee for me." Rick's wolfing down a plateful loaded with butter and maple syrup, ignoring what the doctor said about his cholesterol.

"Katie, you're up bright and early."

"Mom, you look ready for a bridge party."

"And your shirt needs an iron."

"I don't iron." She laughs.

"Well, you should." I pour myself a coffee and sit down. Listen to
them discussing the features of the latest Fords. She and Rick are a pair.
He approves of everything she does. He wasn't like that with the boys.
I could bring her down a peg with: "Funny how you look like Martin
Thorton." But I'd bring myself down too, much further down.

THEY'VE GONE DOWNTOWN. Rick wanted to show her the new models
and I reminded her she was home to study. She ignored me. He better
not even think about giving her a car.

I lock the door. I get out the letters and continue my sorting. I'm
only going to keep the non-incriminating ones.

Here's a funny one.

> April 9, 1969
> *Dear Donna,*
> *Caesar's in trouble again. Mother's determined to cut
> off his balls. She's offended by that phrase. 'Why do you have
> to be so vulgar? Why can't you just say have him neutered?'*
> *It's Mrs. Johnson complaining this time. Caesar pissed
> on every door to her house and beat up Huggums, her poor*

*cat. He's deballed, declawed, only outside on a leash and so
overweight she has him on a diet and pills three times a day.
Caesar would've been doing Huggums a favour if he'd
killed him.*

*Caesar's stretched out on his back on the windowsill in
my studio. I've told him he'd better lay low until the old
hags calm down.*

MARTIN DOES LOVE cats. There'd often be five or six living there. People
still dropped off their unwanted kittens by the barn. Mrs. Thorton
would call the Humane Society and Martin would rage: "Mother's sent
another batch to the gas chamber!" Such drama.

Caesar lived to be eleven, which, with all his wandering, is amazing.
He got run over right in front of their house. He'd been smart about
cars but no doubt age was slowing him down. Martin, on one of his night
walks, stumbled over him. I asked him how he could be sure it was
Caesar. "Even with his head crushed, I knew him." He'd buried him next
to the studio. "It was a good quick death. Not a bad way to go. He felt
life—had his moments of eternity," was all Martin said.

Why am I thinking about dying? Even his humorous letter about
Caesar depresses me. Get busy and straighten up the kitchen.

I clean pancake mix off the stove, the counter, even the floor. Rick's
a big kid who never learned to clean up after himself. I load the dish-
washer and make a fresh pot of coffee.

Martin has always been unbelievably stubborn. Even as adults we
had heated arguments about religion.

"Don't you see it's just a bunch of comforting lies?" he would say.

This one raised my ire. "You said yourself that you can't prove or
disprove the existence of God, so what makes you think you know? There
could be a heaven and some spirit that cares about us and looks after us."

"Rubbish!"

"It could be true and it helps people get through life. That's what
faith is. To not believe in anything must make it awfully hard to live."

"I believe in you."

"You'd be better off believing in God." I stormed off. I'd had a still-
born baby two months before. A little girl—I would've had another

daughter. He knew about that. For a long time I hadn't wanted more children, but in my thirties when Katie was ten, I did think it'd be nice to have another one. I hoped for a little girl—Katie needed some competition. Rick, of course, was delighted. I got pregnant right after going off the pill. When I told him he came home with roses and champagne. We were so happy. The children too, well the boys, that is. Katie said I was too old to be having babies. Ten years old!

This pregnancy was nothing like the others. Rick and the boys waited on me. They barely let me get supper and didn't let me wash dishes or scrub the floors. I sat with my feet up and a cup of tea.

Eleanor Jane Waddell was born with the umbilical cord wrapped around her neck. Perfectly formed little girl, reddish blond hair—a lot for a newborn. I hope with all my heart that she's with God, safe in heaven.

I don't think about religion all that much but I believe faith is what gets people through life. Martin never thinks all that much about what other people need.

I got a letter from him after Eleanor died. A sympathy card? No, it was another chapter of Joe and Cathy in the rain on those back roads, fleeing the police. I knew it would end badly. Why couldn't he let them escape to Mexico? Why didn't he write something to cheer me up? He knew my baby had died. But I'd just said it: Martin doesn't think all that much about what other people need.

Why am I keeping the *Marsh Road* stories? All they do is depress me. But they're harmless. It's the personal letters that incriminate me.

And they hold my memories.

One Sunday afternoon Rick had taken all three kids to the driving range and I was visiting Mrs. Thorton when Mrs. Granger from the Altar Guild arrived. Martin, Mrs. Thorton and I were on the screened porch.

"These are for him," she said, offering Mrs. Thorton a flower arrangement from the morning service. Gorgeous—hyacinths, iris, daffodils and tulips. "I know he loves flowers."

Mrs. Granger was blocking the doorway so Martin couldn't escape without at least asking her to move. He picked up a book and never looked up the entire time she was there.

"We bring them to all the shut-ins in our congregation to brighten up their days."

When she finally left, Martin got up and knocked the flowers to the floor. Guess who got to clean up after his tantrum?

"Martin, she meant well," his mother said as she scooped them up. "Just sit down and have another cup of tea."

She thinks tea solves all problems, just like Gretchen says.

"Old busybody. I'm not in her bloody congregation and I'm not sick either." His cane knocked over a chair as he left the porch.

"You have some tea, Donna. Poor Anne's eighty-five and I'm sure she appreciated flowers when she was laid up with her broken hip last winter. And Martin *is* a member. We had him baptized. The day'll come when he'll regret turning his back on the church. And I've told Anne how much Martin loves flowers, that he can identify any flower by smell and how when Martin was a little boy he'd walk around the garden sniffing and naming all the flowers."

Mrs. Granger was just trying to be kind and had no idea she came across as condescending. Martin complains the church people don't talk to him, just to his mother. 'How's the boy today?' But how can they talk to a book in front of his face? Her bringing flowers had nothing to do with the truth of the existence of God or the virgin birth.

I followed Martin into his room and tried to talk to him. Before I could open my mouth he said, "The church is a pile of shit and altar flowers stink of it."

"Mrs. Granger's a poor old lady. Why couldn't you just accept the flowers?"

"For the same reason the teenaged James Joyce couldn't take Easter communion."

"What are you talking about?"

"Not serving what you no longer believe in."

"This is about being polite to an elderly lady."

"No, it's about integrity. Even when Joyce's mother was dying he refused to get down on his knees and pray though she begged him."

"The prick."

"You don't understand."

"No, I don't. You insult an old lady and now you go on about some dead author who has nothing to do with our church or town."

A few days later I got another letter and just shook my head.

Sept. 1, 1972
Dear Donna,

You went away mad. I want to try to explain. You said James Joyce has nothing to do with All Saints Anglican in Grenville. Maybe you would understand if I told you about my discovery of Joyce.

I was eighteen and out of school. So glad to be free of it. They were such a bunch of Pollyannas.

The Great Books Foundation, a brain wave of the University of Chicago, started book clubs. The idea was to get the public to read "great" books. Of course, they had a tight-assed idea of what was great. Needless to say Henry Miller wasn't on their list. Leaders (semi-intellectuals like my mother) went to training sessions and started groups themselves. There were prescribed readings for each year the club operated. In year three some of the authors were Plato, Aristotle, Euclid, Lucian. St. Thomas. Calvin, Voltaire, Gibbon and Freud. Pretty heavy stuff I think you would agree. Along with the club meetings that I didn't attend, there were weekend conferences and I went to one of those. One of the books was A Portrait of the Artist as a Young Man.

It's hard to explain what that book meant to me. I'd read a lot of so-called great books. 'Is that idea or essence, which in the dialectical process we define as essence or true existence — whether essence of equality or beauty or anything else — are these essences, I say, liable at times to some degree of change?' I tried hard to understand what Plato meant. The philosophy books challenged my intellect, but Joyce's book spoke to me as a man. He wrote as we think — not in syllogisms, but with a line from an old rhyme — 'Pull out his eyes. Pull out his eyes' — followed by the way the sheets feel when you're a small boy wetting the bed. It's like he entered my psyche — I wet the bed at the School for the Blind. I knew him. He knew me.

I'd never read anything like it. He wrote about the church, the priests and their long sermons, promising hell to terrify

*children into belief. Joyce almost became a Jesuit. He was
saved from the priesthood by the smell of cabbages in his
mother's garden. That may sound crazy, but what he meant
was appreciating what's right under your nose. Not denying
the world out of some sense of guilt. He knew he had to be
free to find his own way. He had to be free of the priests and
of his mother who belittled his revolt— 'you'll come back to
the church when you're more mature.' That's the sort of
thing my mother says. When Joyce refused to take communion,
a door opened for me—somebody knew how I felt. And I
knew how he felt. I was closer to him than I was to anyone
in my family, school or town. And that kind of leap,
occasionally repeated with other books, is not dependent on
whether the author's alive or dead or whether I ever met
him. That leap is an idea or an image having a reality, a
power of its own. Image is better because idea is too much
of the intellect, and what I'm talking about is something too
visceral to be called an idea.*

*Now do you understand why I couldn't take those bloody
flowers? Come Tuesday. Mother's at her library board meeting.*

I HAVE READ and reread this. I don't know why since I don't really know
what he's talking about, but he was so fired up about it. I want to understand Martin. All I really know is he thinks his mother wants to control
him. But she's actually trying to look after him.

Once Martin clung to me and said: "In all the universe's empty space
only this makes life possible." Even after sex he couldn't stop thinking.
Most people just do it.

Maybe I should've thought more about what we were doing. It's like
I was two people. I was the young woman caught up in Martin's spell, but
I was also the young woman at the supper table listening to Billy telling
his daddy about sports day at kindergarten. How he'd won four ribbons.
Such a sturdy little fellow—a miniature Rick.

David, on my lap, was lining up his zoo animals along the table edge.
I wanted to hold us there, to stay in that moment forever. I liked the
woman in that picture.

I liked the woman who camped at Algonquin Park with her husband and teen-aged kids. At night they heard a bear outside their tent and they sang boisterously to drive him away. The family joke became that we were such terrible singers even bears ran from the sound of our voices.

I'm not too fond of the woman who visited Martin's studio. But I'd get another letter like this one and I'd go back.

> June 20, 1974
> *Dear Donna,*
>
> *To get inside my studio I must push aside the branches growing over the door. Sleeping Beauty's castle, but my love isn't here today. All the windows are open and I swear you can smell new growth after last night's rain. Some bird is piping 'Dee, dee, dee' and the raccoons are keening in the wood lot.*
>
> *Remember the last time I read to you, it was late fall and Cathy and Joe were travelling the back roads. Here's the next chapter.*

EVEN BACK THEN I knew *Marsh Road* would end badly and it bothered me more than it should've. I was beginning to wonder if I could trust Martin. Yet, in spite of all that, there's something magical about his letters. Like he's offering me a whole other world. Sleeping Beauty's castle and a lover keening for me. Heady stuff right from the beginning. When I'd just moved to Grenville and met him for the first time and he went out in the garden and brought me a single red rose, I was just a silly girl, but I knew even then he was somebody special.

Other women I know, like Laurie, read Harlequins. I didn't need romance novels. I had a dark mysterious lover who wrote romantic letters and was always waiting for me.

L AST NIGHT RICK asked: "Have you been over there? How's Martin doing?"

"I can't bear to see him."

"Poor chap. You've been a good friend to him. We should both go over some evening."

Rick wouldn't be so sympathetic if he knew just how good I've been to Martin.

Oct. 7, 1975

Dear Donna,

Mother just brought in the mail—another rejection slip. I need to get out of here. If I were in California or New York, I could make the contacts to find a publisher. Or is that just a dream?

That the estate's growing isn't a dream. Even though Mother's pretty secretive about finances, I know it's nearing $300,000. She does know how to pile up money but doesn't know how to spend it. Just as well—more for us.

I've been working hard. If you remember, Joe and Cathy are on the road, holed up in a scummy motel. Here's a bit to get you interested.

In the rearview mirror, Joe spots a police cruiser. As he speeds up, he hears the siren.

He swerves onto a narrow gravel road. The car fishtails. The police aren't far behind.

He's doing close to eighty when he turns onto another gravel road. The car nearly slides into the ditch, but Joe spins the wheel and keeps going. Good traction, he laughs.

Cathy screams: 'You're going to kill us!'

Not a bad way to go. He grins. They'll never catch us.

Don't you wonder whether Joe and Cathy die on that gravel road in the rain? Donna, come see me.

THAT LETTER'S DATED 1975. Even then I found Martin's novel scary. It was plain that Joe and Cathy were meant to be him and me. "Not a bad way to go." I don't know which bothered me more—his expectations about me, or his attitude toward his mother. Did he know he was waiting for her to die?

He's so bloody selfish. The force of my anger surprised me.

Feb. 12, 1979
Dear Donna,

 Sorry your visit was ruined. My mother sat there talking about the garden and the church. You must've been bored. She used to know when to disappear. It's hard to see her go downhill—she had a sharp mind.

 She's beginning to accept her disabilities. Money that should've been reinvested wasn't. She simply forgot the dates. At last I'm looking after the estate. What a muddle! But I'm getting things in order.

 Mother's memory has gotten so bad she can't remember which bills she's paid and which she hasn't. Her eyesight's still good, so now when she gets the mail I just tell her what to do. Once I get power of attorney, I'll sign the cheques. She can be my eyes. I can do everything else.

 It's still a battle—she begrudges me the money for a bottle of booze.

 Come Thursday afternoon. She'll be at the church.

THE PART ABOUT her being his eyes infuriates me. He uses her, doesn't give a damn about her needs.

For years things progressively got worse. It seemed Martin was always yelling and swearing at his mother. He doesn't respect her. If he acts like that when I'm there, what's it like when I'm not? I'd dropped in to get Mrs. Thorton's green-tomato mincemeat recipe. Rick loves mince pie, and as always, she made a pot of tea.

"I'll see if Martin'll join us." She set down the tray, and I heard her knocking on his closed door.

"God damn it." I heard him say. What's he going on about, not tea surely?

"It must be right there on your desk," she said, and I got up to see if I could help.

"Damn. You've been messing with my stuff."

"I have not."

"You were in here."

"Of course, I was cleaning."

"What the hell for?"

"You were complaining about dust." She pursed her lips.

"Put things back where you find them."

"I carefully put everything back," she said.

"Like hell you did or Chapter 20 would be here."

"I'm sure it is."

"You're sure. I'm sure you're going senile."

"You better watch it or people'll think you're getting odd."

"Her mind's going," he said to me.

Mrs. Thorton tried to squeeze past him. "I'll just have a look."

"Get out. I don't want you snooping."

"Now, Martin." She pushed past him, almost upsetting his walker. She grabbed his arm and steadied him.

"Damn you to hell! Get out!"

"Now, now." She went right on searching. "Aren't you a little old for tantrums?"

"Go to hell."

"And in front of Donna. It's right here, exactly where I said it was." She waved it in his face. "You should be ashamed of your language."

He snatched it. "Get out, you old busybody and let me work."

We retreated, and he slammed the door.

Mrs. Thorton smiled apologetically, "I guess he won't be joining us for tea."

"Does he often act like that?"

"More than he used to." She sat down, and with a trembling hand, poured my tea. Just sat there lining up the teaspoons and serviettes.

"It's his frustration, not him. He has such trouble getting published."
She sighed. "Oh, what's the matter with me? Here's your tea." She
handed me the cup.

"You're understandably upset. He has no right to talk to you like that."

"If he would just write what he knows," she said. "Fantasy can be
a dangerous thing—all that stuff about sex and aliens. People might
think he's going funny. You know he could write a history of Grenville."

"What?" That's the last thing on earth he'd want to write.

"There's lots to write about. Things people would want to read.
The Mennonites coming up from Pennsylvania, and there are families
here descended from Butlers' Rangers. He just won't listen. He has such
potential and is just throwing it away. I've told him many stories of
growing up on the chicken farm, how the chickens attacked each other
if one had a sore and how I hated the slaughter and gutting. But I've
also told him how I quoted poetry to the cows as I took them out to
pasture. When he chooses to base his writing on some family around
here, why choose the sad story of the O'Haras? I do like some of his
poetry, look at this one, Donna:

Preacher

Tom cat calling for his lady love.
Tom cat calling for his lady love.
Preacher praying to his god above.

Tom cat no use to call.
Tom cat no use to call.
She ain't comin out at all.

Preacher no use to pray.
Preacher no use to pray.
He won't hear what you've got to say.

She cat had kittens this fall.
She cat had kittens this fall.
And they drowned them, mama and all.

Preacher, ever since you come.
Preacher, ever since you come.
God been deaf and dumb.

"MAN'S CRUELTY TO animals and God's cruelty to man. Martin does have a way with words. Interesting, he writes of God; mind you, an unresponsive one."

She talked all the time I was reading. "I like it, too, Martin's always had a soft spot for cats."

"I worry. Lately his ideas are becoming pure fantasy."

"What do you mean?"

"He has this wild notion that someday, you'll go off with him to New York."

"That is crazy. He's depressed because he hasn't had more published."

"You're right. But he refuses to write more realistic stories. It's either science fiction or crime fiction. Some of the things he's written are what people around here would call smut."

I tried to change the subject. "What did you want to be when you were young?"

"That's a long time ago."

"Well?"

"I'll tell you a strange experience I had. One day in senior class I was bored and staring out the window. I saw a man with a briefcase walking up the hill. A stranger. I forgot the schoolroom and I was the adult with my briefcase. Perhaps I was a lawyer going to meet a client or an architect with plans for the new town hall or a writer, and the case held my first finished story. I felt faint and realized I was holding my breath. I didn't know where the man was going or what was in his case. Even though that hill led to Main Street, I knew Main led to the highway out of here. What is peculiar is that myriad possibilities were in one moment revealed to me and it was so wonderful to be alive I could scarcely breathe. I coughed and gasped, looked around the classroom and felt strange to still be — I don't know — a schoolgirl doing long division. What I miss now is that wonderful feeling of possibility. When I think of the future now, I'm scared. For what will become of Martin?"

"What did you plan to do when you finished school?"

"To be a foreign correspondent."

"Wow."

"Don't laugh. I was going to start university the year I met Brad. When you fall in love, you don't realize what you're giving up. Not fair to Brad. I did want to get married and have children. What did you want to be, Donna?"

"Nothing, just to have fun."

"Martin's drinking is such a worry."

"Why do you buy it for him?"

"I've always been against liquor. Seen it ruin too many lives. But I haven't the right to deny him. Other men have a drink when they want to. You told me Rick almost always has a beer or two in the evenings. That adds up to fourteen every week. Imagine the cost!"

"But it isn't the same."

"Why not? Isn't my son a man?"

"Of course, he is. And if Rick drank like Martin, I'd empty the bottles down the kitchen sink."

"Have you ever done that?"

"No, but when he overdoes it at the Legion, I make sure I vacuum early, really early, in the morning."

"Denying Martin a drink because he can't walk to the liquor store would be taking advantage of his condition. Besides, if I don't buy it, he calls a cab and has it delivered. At least this way, we save the cab fare."

"I should be getting home."

TUESDAY, WHEN GRETCHEN was over, I was reminiscing about how good her mother had been to me and my kids—all the Monopoly and card games. How often it'd made me think of when we were kids—all those evenings we sat around the old leather-topped card table.

"She didn't sit around playing cards when I visited with Owen. Always busy and so wrapped up in telling me her worries about Martin."

"Your mother worries about you too."

"That's an understatement. Dire warnings are her specialty. She predicted the demise of my marriage. 'You should've gotten married in the church.' Her reasoning was faulty but she was right that Kenneth would leave. Fortunately, Owen didn't choke on popcorn or a balloon, drown in his wading pool or get lockjaw from a rusty nail."

"That's her way of showing love."

"And buying liquor for Martin? Is that her showing love?"

"She can't say no to him."

"That's always been true and he's never accepted his drinking's a problem," Gretchen said. "Says stupid things like: 'Writers always drink, look at James Joyce, Kerouac, Dylan Thomas, Henry Miller, Hemingway.' I said sure. Kerouac and Dylan Thomas died young, and Hemingway shot himself. 'But they *lived*,' he said, 'so *smugly*.' He's the genius with all the answers. I better get home."

She rushed off as always. I'm scared of Martin, his demands. What would Rick and my kids think if they found out? That our family was a sham. They'd hate me, and I love them so much. Two years ago Rick and I celebrated our 25th with a party at the Legion — two hundred guests. Rick is the mainstay of my life.

I suppose I could deny everything. There's no proof except the letters and Rick can't read them. What if he showed them to Mrs. Thorton? They'd both be disgusted with me.

What should I have done? I'd get a letter like this one and go back.

> August 21, 1976
> *Dear Donna,*
>
> *Mother's again drawing my attention to birdsong. 'So lovely to hear the cardinal. He always brightens up a day.'*
>
> *I prefer traffic noises. Weekdays a motorcycle goes by at six a.m. and back again in the evening. Must be a guy going to work. His roar is better than the endless twittering birds that make me want to call 'here kitty-kitty, breakfast is waiting.'*
>
> *I went out for a walk. The shadows toyed with me. Their favourite game isn't "My Little Shadow" but "Trip Him Up."*
>
> *On a good day when the shadows move so slightly, like laundry on a line, I can almost see where I'm going. Today every shrub and tree was on the march. Their black leaves ate light's last particle.*

I sit here in the dark waiting for you. When you're here,
there is such warmth and light that I'm surprised the
neighbours aren't banging on the door demanding to know
how we stole the sun.
      Dear Donna, please excuse a lonely man his borrowings
and his metaphors.

READING THAT LETTER it's hard to believe he's become such a bitter person, so taken up with writing angry letters to the editors of those magazines you never see anywhere but at his house.

He writes book reviews—it seems only about books that aren't available in braille or on tape, because Mrs. Thorton's always having to read the books aloud and make recordings. He often says he only needs her to read the first couple of chapters to know what garbage it is. Sometimes, I'd read for him and start enjoying the story and suddenly he'd stop me. "That's enough. Utter crap, not worth a review."

When he isn't going on about his latest scrap with some editor, he's complaining about Grenville. He has such hate. I swear he remembers every taunting child and every head-patting old lady.

He calls everybody in Grenville squares and losers. Their puny little lives, he'd say, wouldn't know the difference between modernism and post-modernism if it was staring them in the face. I told him I didn't know the difference and he went into this long explanation that I didn't understand.

He likes to make fun of Rick being a salesman. He has no right to call Rick stupid. What does Martin know about running a business? Lots of businesses went bankrupt during the recession. Rick's didn't.

Sometimes I think Rick's too nice a guy to suspect anything. But when I danced with Steve Barkly at the Legion, Rick got quite nasty. He'd been drinking. "You got the hots for him?" He's not like that when he's sober. And I don't know why I shouldn't have danced with Steve. His wife was right there and she didn't mind.

Rick, who was such a great dancer in high school, won't get up on the floor. "It's the young'uns turn. I've been on my feet all day." All he wants to do is drink beer and shoot the breeze with his pals.

Even with all the letters and the amount of time I've spent with the Thortons, Rick hasn't a clue. He would say things like: "Poor bastard. Imagine, never able to get it up."

I've never figured out why Rick thought Martin impotent. Martin's blind and has problems with his legs—why would that make him impotent? Never thought it a good idea to enlighten Rick.

What good has all that literary stuff done Martin? There's a lot to be said for being ordinary. In my family and Rick's, no one has any artistic ambition, no would-be writers. I know it isn't easy for Martin but there are things he could do that would be appreciated.

The Beckwiths' boy is blind and in a wheelchair. Once, several years ago, his mom was telling me how little help there was for him. He was six, and both parents had to work. The babysitter just ignored him. I suggested to Martin that he volunteer to tutor him. He got really angry. "You think all I'm good for is babysitting?"

I felt like saying: "Actually you'd make a damn poor babysitter. You're too self-centred." What I did say was: "Don't be ridiculous, I thought with your handicap you could understand his and help him."

"Us crips belong together, is that it?"

THE LAST LETTER came just a few days after Gretchen came home.

> March 9, 1982
> *Dear Donna,*
>
> *As if my mother's mental deterioration wasn't making my life difficult enough, now I have Gretchen and her kid to deal with.*
>
> *Gretchen's taking our mother to the dentist Friday morning. Come over then. It's damn frustrating being with you when Mother's around, poking her nose in everything. She used to have the sense to give us some privacy.*
>
> *After 26 years, I've finally finished* Marsh Road. *This, my darling, is how it ends for them.*
>
> The cruiser's not far behind when Joe makes the next turn on three wheels. The car skids on the flooded road but comes out of it in time for Joe to look back and see the cruiser in the ditch.

He grips the wheel and floors the accelerator. Bye-bye, cops.

They'll just send more. Cathy's voice trembles. Just a matter of time. If you run, they'll think you're guilty.

They already do. Everything's a matter of time, but I have my plan.

Your plan is craziness.

Cathy, stop saying that. We're going toward the lake. Can't be more than a couple of miles from here.

So?

I'll get a boat.

There's no boat! she yells.

Darling, don't be scared. Everything'll be okay.

As Joe turns onto Cedar Point Road the headlights pick up the wooden signs leading to cottages.

He parks in a clump of trees, picks up his pack and they walk down to the beach. Cathy's silent. Sure enough, the cottages are deserted and Joe has his choice of canoe or row boat.

Lucky break they left the paddles, Joe says, flipping over the canoe.

You're not making sense, and I'm not going out in Lake Erie in November.

You don't have to. Listen to me. We're only about ten miles from the far end of Elgin Marsh. From there through the marsh our cabin is about another fifteen. I'll be there by midnight. You take the car and drive back to the highway.

The cops'll see me.

Right. And when they do, tell them I abducted you. Say I realized they'd find us, so I left. Just before you saw me get a ride with a truck driver, I told you I was going to Toronto. If the cops don't stop you, drive to the police station and tell the same story.

If the wind comes up, you'll drown.

No. I can do this. Cathy, as soon as you can get

away, take our canoe and come to the cabin. I'll be there before dawn at the latest.

If you get there.

Have faith in me. He hugs her.

Jesus, Joe. She hugs him back.

Listen, if you're there before me, light that big candle you brought last Christmas. Put it in the window and I'll know everything went as planned. He kisses her. I'm wearing the sweater you gave me, he whispers in her ear. It'll bring me luck.

You better get going then, says Cathy. He throws in his pack and shoves the canoe into the water. Get back to the car, you're shivering.

So are you.

I'm taking this tarp. I'll dry off. He wades into the water and climbs into the boat. Pulls the tarp over his shoulders, waves and blows kisses to her.

She waves and turns back to the car.

Paddling warms him up and the tarp keeps the worst of the rain off. An hour later the sun comes out. Joe strips off his wet shoes and socks and wiggles his aching toes. Soon he's perspiring. He dips a plastic cup into the lake and drinks. Should've thought about food. He hopes Cathy's safely home. The cops'll easily believe he abducted her. Never in a million years would they believes she loves him.

By late afternoon, he's reached the swamp and turns up the creek. He doesn't know the creek's name but in the long stretches between Cathy's visits, he'd explored every twist and turn of every creek throughout the thirty-mile wide marsh. It was the one place Bob couldn't find him.

Shivering at the image of Bob's bloody head, he paddles harder.

At least the rain has stopped. His feet rest on the folded-up tarp. The winding creeks make it hard, even with the compass, to stay in an easterly direction. The

creek is now so blocked with reeds he'll have to portage.
His shoes and socks, practically dry when he put them
back on, fill with muddy water. Not easy to carry the canoe
on his head and the pack on his back. His jagged gait
makes everything a challenge. On one especially rough
portage, he abandons the tarp, hoping the rain's over.

After sunset, the rain starts again — colder and
harder than before, making it almost impossible to keep
the canoe going forward, or is it just that he's exhausted?

He pictures the candle in the window. He can
almost smell cranberry-cinnamon. On Boxing Day —
she hadn't come on Christmas — they snow-shoed to the
cabin. They built up the fire and ate the cold turkey and
fresh rolls she brought. She gave him the Shetland
sweater and the candle. They lit the candle and as they
made love, the scent mixed with their own musk. After,
they opened the stove door and roasted marshmallows.

His corduroy jacket and wool sweater soak up the
rain like a sponge. If he paddled harder he would warm
up but he can't. With each lift of the paddle, he thinks of
Cathy. He'll make a fire, get warmed up and wait for her.

Well after midnight, he pulls the canoe up to the foot
of the hill leading to their shack. So stiff and tired he has
to crawl out of the canoe and into the reeds with the pack
still on his back. The stabbing pains in his legs are almost
unbearable. He's too tired to worry how wet the money
may be getting. Reaching the shack is all that matters.
Grabbing at shrubs and rocks, he drags himself up the hill.

Halfway, he stops, peers up through the rain. He
sees the weak light. The lit candle beckons him home.

He stands up and with a surge of strength, runs to
the door, slams his body against it.

The door opens to a whiff of cranberry-spice.
Sergeant Stevens stands there, gun drawn. Arms above
your head, fella.

Joe stands open-mouthed before he turns and staggers away.

Hold it right there, or I'll shoot.

Does he fall before he hears the shot, or after? He's rolling down the hill. Footsteps thundering behind him stop abruptly with a crash and enraged cursing. Stevens has fallen.

Joe rolls himself into the reeds and crawls on his hands and knees. As fate would have it, the rain has stopped, and the moon shines down. Stevens will see him. Joe touches his throbbing shoulder and his hand comes away wet with something thicker. No need to look, he knows it's blood. He drags himself to the canoe. Pushes it into the creek. Crawls into the boat. After a few yards of drifting, he slumps down, shaking violently.

For a long time, he crouches in the canoe. The wind has blown the clouds back and the rain starts up again. Blood has seeped down his arm to his hand. He struggles to unbuckle his packsack but keeps losing his grip. When he gets out the sheathed knife he brings the blade to his wrist. Watches, fascinated, as rain and blood slowly merge. Cathy, I still love you. He does the other wrist.

FINALLY, I HAD tea at the Thortons. Except for groceries and church, I haven't left the house in weeks. And a tense visit it was, what with Martin pushing me to go to his studio. "Get away from these hens," was how he put it. I was embarrassed and also scared he was going to spill the beans. His last letter really bugged me. He thinks I've betrayed him. I haven't. I've been his friend all these years. He's the betrayer — that stunt he pulled last summer.

In the old days he knew how to be subtle. When his mother got busy in the kitchen, he might say he wanted to show me a book and off we went.

"Get away from these hens," is hardly subtle. I gulp my tea and said I had to hurry back as Rick and I were going out for dinner. The fish sticks were thawing on the counter but it was the best I could come up with.

THE NEXT DAY Gretchen's over for coffee and I'm not surprised by what she tells me. Martin's drunk every night. She and her mother have to put him to bed and clean up.

"It's hell, plain and simple. He can't get it through his head that with cirrhosis he can't drink."

"Tell your mother to stop buying him liquor."

"Donna, you must know by now that *telling* them anything is pointless. How long has Martin been this bad?"

"At least a year."

"My mother shouldn't have tried to cope on her own."

"I think she finds it hard to admit how bad things are."

"True. She can't bear that her darling genius has turned into a drunk."

"Must be terrible for her."

"Yes but even now she makes allowances. Says he has more excuse than other people."

"Doesn't he?"

"Most people have plenty of reasons and for Martin living in Grenville would be reason enough. If I could just get him out of here. I've got the van and we could go away for a while. I suggested a writers' retreat in North Carolina. I enjoyed it, and he might find it stimulating."

I can't see that happening. Martin's too ill. Gretchen thinks it's simple. She'll get him to stop drinking and things'll be like they were long ago. She mentions the horses again.

After she leaves, all I can think about is maybe, when he's drunk he'll say something to Gretchen or Mrs. Thorton. I feel sorry for him but I'm scared, too.

His drinking was a real problem even last summer. Rick and I were barbequing on the back deck when Martin arrived. It was little Claire's birthday and the whole family was there. David and his girlfriend had driven down from Toronto and Katie, home from Europe, hadn't yet left for university.

Martin was so drunk I don't know how he managed to get here. He was using the walker but staggering so badly I was sure he was going to fall.

His greying curls hung down over his eyes. He hadn't shaved, his fly was undone. He slurred: "I've come for Donna." Katie's disgust was so evident I closed my eyes and willed her to stay silent.

"Martin, calm down," I said. "You've been drinking." Heaven knows what the other kids made of this. I went to take his arm and he grabbed my shoulder so hard I thought we'd both go down.

"Rick, you dumb bastard, I've come for Donna!"

"It's okay fella, you want a beer?" Rick went on turning the steaks.

"Beer's horse piss. Gimme a scotch."

"Sorry buddy, we don't keep the hard stuff. You'll have to settle for a beer."

"Settle for. Fuck you. I don't settle for."

"Watch your language. There's kiddies present."

"I'll walk him back to his place." I yanked his hand off my shoulder and placed it firmly on the walker. I gripped his arm and said: "C'mon."

"Can you manage?" Rick asked.

"Yeah. C'mon Martin."

"Bill, why don't you help your mother with Martin?"

I waved Bill away and steered Martin toward home. He stopped resisting when he realized I was going with him. When we got out of earshot, I hissed: "You idiot, what are you trying to do?"

"Come have a drinkie with me. I'm lonely."

"You've had quite enough."

Mrs. Thorton was looking out the screen door. She rushed down the steps to meet us. "I'm so embarrassed, so sorry, Donna." The pleading in her voice was the saddest thing I'd heard, maybe ever.

"Not your fault."

I steered Martin up the steps and into the house. Mrs. Thorton, who's always so controlled, whimpered as she followed us. I led him right into his room and gave him a push onto the bed-couch. The walker went flying and Mrs. Thorton hastily righted it. I was so mad, I shouted at Martin: "Don't you ever pull a stunt like that again!" And stormed out.

I didn't know what to do. I swore I'd never go back there. I still don't know what to do. If only Mrs. Thorton would visit me here. I feel sorry for her. Gretchen coming over regularly now reminds me how seldom Mrs. Thorton ever visited. Over the past twenty years I bet she's sat down in this house for a cup of tea fewer than a dozen times.

My invitations were frequent but she always had to get home to Martin and would suggest I come over there.

The first year I was married I had both Martin and his mother over for dinner. He spent the entire visit insulting Rick. Asked him what he thought of Plato's *Republic* and when Rick said he hadn't read it, Martin said: "Did you even finish high school?" Then he made cracks about used-car salesmen. Mrs. Thorton and I were both mortified. I never invited them back.

I admired Rick's restraint. All he said afterwards was: "That poor crip is pissed because he'll never have a job or a wife."

CLAIRE'S IN A dance recital. Doesn't seem possible it's my grandchild's turn. Of course, Billy married young and Claire's only four, but it does make me feel old. I'm too young to be a grandmother.

Why did I volunteer to sew all the butterfly costumes? Yards and yards of taffeta and tulle.

Worrying about Martin is grinding me down. Night and day he's all I think about. Wake up in the middle of the night, my heart pounding like heavy footsteps, an awful feeling of dread. Most nights I end up at the living room window, waiting for daylight. Waiting for something. An odd feeling, this constant waiting. Exhausting.

Get on with the sewing. Ten outfits to do in less than a week. Stop thinking about him. Think of Claire, a little doll with her sandy-coloured braids and big brown eyes.

The taffeta crackles like the crinolines we wore in high school. As the boys spun us, our skirts lifted to show our multi-coloured crinolines and maybe even our panties. How daring! How thrilling! I'd like to go back there. Live my life over. Do it right. Funny though, I have no idea what I'd do differently. Just stop time, maybe, stay there with our whirling crinolines.

Forget twirling crinolines and get the machine going. Said I'd have them ready for dress rehearsal on Friday.

I've got them all cut out in rainbows of colour. I'll sew Claire's first. She's the purple butterfly. I used to have a purple taffeta dress. Smooth over the hips with the skirt gathered at the hem and stuffed with tulle to make it puff out — called a harem skirt. Purple blooms swirling on a deep blue background.

I bought it for Rick's brother's wedding. His snobby dentist brother with his even snobbier wife. His brother's second wedding and this wife even more of an airhead than the first. I wasn't looking forward to it, though it was a big do at the Briar Hill Golf Club and I'd bought a pretty dress. There would be a dance afterwards.

I had told Mrs. Thorton about my dress and she wanted to see me in it. "Drop by before you go, if you have time."

We were leaving the kids on their own for the first time. Billy was fifteen and in charge. They were down in the rec room with a rented projector, a stack of movies and a generous supply of snacks. Rick and I were about to leave when he had to go and deal with a theft at the car lot. I ran over to show Mrs. Thorton my dress.

Martin said his mother was at the post office but she'd be back in a few minutes. She had to get some poems in the mail that day. He admired my dress. Loved how it rustled when I moved. He felt the tulle blousing out the skirt. We were in his room, not even in the studio. I started laughing. "Martin, I'm all dressed up and ready to go to a wedding!"

"I'll just touch the wedding present. See if I can guess what's inside."

"I'm not a present." But I laughed.

"A present for me. I've had no wedding presents."

"Martin stop, what if your mother comes in?"

Martin laughed and pushed up my skirt. I tingled all over as he pulled my pantyhose down to my knees.

It was like the old days when Rick and I would be making out on his parents' chesterfield. Every sound made us jump—were his folks awake? My crinolines, which I hadn't dared take off, crackled every time we moved. The more they crackled the more we sniggered and made even more noise shushing each other.

Astride Martin on the lounge chair, I took a deep breath and disentangled myself. I got in the door just before Rick drove in. Mrs. Thorton was with him. He'd given her a ride home. She wanted to be in time to see my dress.

"How lovely you look, Donna, just radiant. Isn't she beautiful, Rick?"

"Uh huh," Rick said. "Those damn Henderson twins took off with a car in broad daylight. Drunk out of their skulls. Lucky they weren't killed. The things teenagers get up to. Be ready in a minute. I'm just going to look in on the kids. Maybe we should've got a sitter."

The wedding was one of those dull affairs with prearranged seating and endless toasts. Rick and I were at a table with some of the bride's snobby relatives. Getting drunk is how Rick dealt with it.

By the time the dancing finally started he was too hammered to even try. At the Legion, he'd promised that it would never again be like that, spending the evening drinking and yakking with his pals.

I had to drive home. When I took off my dress, I saw that the lining was semen-stained, something Rick was in no condition to notice. A good thing it hadn't seeped through or I might have been caught. Mrs. Thorton would've noticed but would Rick? I sent the dress to the cleaners.

What kind of a grandmother am I? I sit here sewing costumes for little butterflies, while my head's in the gutter.

SUCH A LOVELY day, this June first Billy and I are out on the deck with coffee. The lilacs I've let grow wild since the kids were little a riot of blooms their little sisters, the phlox, is a cloud of pastels. So cold and wet all spring that we're all glorying in the welcome warmth. I shouldn't worry so much. Forget about the Thortons. Billy's a good son. He comes over himself to pick up the costumes instead of sending Ruth.

Rick comes out on the deck with the mail. "Hey, he's writing to me now."

"What?" I jump up. Martin's return address, in Mrs. Thorton's handwriting, is on the bulky envelope. Oh my, what's he done now?

"What's this son, a long coffee break?" Rick says."

"I better be getting back to the showroom, Dad. Just picking up the costumes Mom made. Bye, Mom, we'll see you at the recital on Saturday. You and Dad are coming for pizza first, eh?"

"For sure. Ask Ruth if there's anything I can bring," I say automatically, my eyes still glued to the envelope.

"Will do," Billy says. " See you back at the lot, Dad."

"You bet, Bill." Rick gives the envelope a little shake and tears it open. "What the hell is this? He sent me a tape?"

"Give me that." I reach for it. "Rick, it's meant for me."

"Why? It's addressed to me." Rick heads into the house.

I follow him over to the stereo. Surely he can hear my heart pounding at the walls of my chest. I've got to stop him.

"Let's see what your old boyfriend's been up to. Maybe he thinks he's a musician now." Rick puts the tape in the machine.

Dear Rick,

    It's time you knew the truth. Reality's a hard pill it's time you swallowed.

    Donna and I have been lovers for twenty-five years. To be blunt I've been fucking, shagging, humping your wife for twenty-five years. You poor dumb jock selling cars while I fucked your wife.

I'VE STOPPED BREATHING. Can't look at Rick. I gape at the window, at those moss green silk drapes I sewed a few months ago. They blur and sway. My whole life with Rick is in those curtains. Rick, honest good Rick. How could I have done this? I never meant to hurt him.

    Then he laughs.

    "Fucking my wife, eh? The poor, crazy crip. I shouldn't laugh. He's really gone over the edge. Hey, don't look like that. I know I shouldn't laugh but it's funny." He's laughing again and repeating: "Fucking, humping, shagging—at least the poor sod knows the words for it. God, what a life."

    I'm speechless. All I can think is, it's all right. I keep staring at my curtains. I don't look at or speak to Rick. There are no words.

    "After I have to go over there and pick him up off the floor, this is my thanks," Rick says. "Pathetic bugger. Pumpkin, honey, I know you're upset about him being so ill."

    The phone rings and Rick's needed back at the showroom. He switches off the tape player, gives me a quick hug and leaves.

    I snatch the tape out of the machine and stamp it to pieces. What if Billy had stayed, listened to it? He might not believe it. Find it hard to think such things of his mother. But Katie, who thinks herself hot stuff, would be ready to pounce.

    I don't think I slept at all that night.

    In the morning I find myself fuming at the clock. The clock, of all things! How dare it just keep ticking away as if nothing's happened? I don't know what to do with all this fury. I don't dare leave the house.

    What if Rick believed him? What's Martin trying to do to me? How could he? I've been his friend all these years. How could he betray me? What if he sends another tape—maybe giving details? Rick would catch on, or maybe he wouldn't. Of course he would. How could Martin do this? Mrs. Thorton addressed the envelope. Did she listen to the tape? No reason to think so. I couldn't bear for her to know. I'd be so ashamed. He could have sealed the tape in, and then told her to address it to Rick. I've got to get rid of the letters. They're evidence.

I haul the duffle bag from the closet. In the fireplace I light newspapers and kindling. One by one I add the letters. They burn but bits remain. I throw in more kindling. I've got a real blaze going. How will I explain why I made a fire in June? I'll say the house felt damp from all the rain we've had. I watch the last letter burn. Now just his word against mine. Rick already thinks Martin's delusional.

I have to talk to him but I'm afraid of a scene.

For days all I do is worry. What has Martin told his mother or Gretchen? Mrs. Thorton might think it's the alcohol talking, her son's wishful thinking. But Gretchen, she'd believe him. If they speak to Rick, he'll believe them. Why would Martin tell anybody? Revenge? Is that what he wants?

ALL MY CHICKENS coming home to roost. Can't get that dumb old saying out of my head. Last night I dreamed I was holding the silk drapes, but in a chicken yard, chicken dirt up to my ankles. I called out and the chickens with bloody combs and shit-encrusted feathers came cackling at me. I'm about to lose everything, including my drapes. Silly, how can curtains matter? Am I going crazy? Chickens and curtains mixed up in my head. I've never even kept chickens.

I want my ordinary life. How could I ever face any of them? They'd disown me, not want me around, certainly wouldn't want me around their innocent babies. Some grandma I turned out to be.

As the days go by, I get even angrier with Martin, if such a thing is possible, thinking about what might've happened and what still could happen if he does anything that stupid again.

I go over there, determined to talk to him. Difficult to have any private time with Mrs. Thorton hovering with the teapot. I go through the niceties and then ask: "Where's Martin?"

"In his room. He spends far too much time in there. He won't even have a cup of tea with us. He's been so down lately." As usual in that house Mrs. Thorton does most of the talking, while Gretchen sits like a stone.

"I'll talk to him." I sail past them, open Martin's door and close it firmly behind me.

He's stretched out in his lounge chair. When he senses it's me, he struggles to sit up and holds out his arms. "He kicked you out. It's okay. We'll go away. You're entitled to some money—you lived with him all those years. Come here."

Now, I'm ready to explode. "No, he didn't kick me out, you idiot. He thinks you've cracked, gone off your rocker. As a matter of fact, Rick laughed, thought the whole thing was a sick joke. Don't you ever pull anything so stupid again."

He stares at me. Doesn't say anything. Those sightless eyes in that gaunt face.

"C'mon, Martin, act normal. Get up and come out and have tea with us." I walk out of the room, leaving the door open.

"Come sit down, Donna. The tea's ready."

Martin doesn't join us. All I want to do is get out of here. How dare he say: "You're entitled to some money." He hasn't got hold of his mother's money so he's trying to get Rick's. Unbelievable!

A WEEK LATER, I'm cutting some peonies for the table when I hear the phone. I gather up the flowers and run in. It's Gretchen. "Donna, you better sit down ..."

I stand for a long time, my face buried in those creamy petals. Must've known how depressed he was. Maybe I could've helped, but I was so angry. Must've known something would have to happen. His desperation, how he was grasping at anything to escape that house and have me.

But I never thought of that. Cirrhosis takes a long time to kill you. I don't know how he managed it—getting up in the loft. That rope swing, where Gretchen and I so often played, still tied to the beam.

Usually, I look over at the house every morning after Rick leaves for work. Didn't this morning. If I had, I would've seen Dr. Purvis's car and then the hearse. I'd gone to the store to get stuff for Claire's birthday cake. They're all coming for dinner. They can't come. My creamy peonies were to be the centrepiece. I have to lie down. I crawl into bed. My first thought is: I'm safe. He can't tell anybody. God, I'm horrible. Oh Martin, why? Did you hate me?

When somebody commits suicide is it normal to feel rejected?

He had this crazy notion Rick would kick me out and then I would live with him. Would that have fixed everything? Of course not. He was an alcoholic. He wrecked his health. My living with him wouldn't make him the next Jack Kerouac. Did he think if only he had me, things would work out? Could he have been that deluded?

Or did he finally hate me? Did he think I played with his feelings all these years?

I never thought I was hurting anyone—even when I fooled Rick. Felt I was an okay wife and mother and a good friend to Martin. I was giving him what I could.

And wasn't that convenient? Little Miss Helpful. God, I hate myself. Why didn't I ever consider I might be a greedy woman who took what she could get from both men?

Did Martin think about who was going to find him hanging from the beam? Would he have cared it was Gretchen's boy, Owen? A shy awkward kid and now he has to deal with this. Do you care, Martin? Maybe you don't. How ugly life is.

I've always thought everything and everybody, including me, was basically good. My life with Martin had nothing to do with Rick. I told myself, this is the way the world works. You get pregnant, you get married and life is raising kids together, having barbeques and going to church.

But where did that leave Martin? He couldn't live like the rest of us. I loved him, wanted him in my life too. What was I supposed to do?

If only I'd handled it differently when he sent the tape to Rick. Not gone over and hissed at him, called him a jerk and told him Rick laughed at him.

I keep thinking about the way he stared at me. What could he see? My shadow? Maybe my nasty, selfish mind. I was too damn scared of my own little world tumbling down. Didn't I care Martin's life was falling apart? Not enough, that's obvious.

I'll phone Rick and go to bed.

THE DAY BEFORE the funeral I get up at dawn and start baking.

"You sure you're all right, Pumpkin? I could stay home."

"Please go, Rick. I've got a lot to do."

"Don't overdo the cooking. Lots of folks'll be bringing food."

"I know, now let me get to work."

He kisses me, and thank God, leaves.

I spent two days in bed. They had Claire's party at their house. Rick was going to stay home with me but I urged him to go. He told them I was sick. Dear kind Rick. Dear kind all of them. Claire made me a get-well card with red flowers and a big yellow sun.

I'm getting the mini-quiches out of the oven when I hear the mail fall through the slot. I'm shaking all over as I bend down to pick up the plain white envelope addressed in Mrs. Thorton's handwriting. He had a stack of those envelopes addressed to me. For a fleeting moment I think she could be writing me a note. But I know it's from him. I open his letter.

Dear Donna,
   With my last breath, I will still love you.
  Your lover, Martin

He planned it all. Could I have stopped him? With his letter jammed in my pocket, I turn off my electric mixer and rush downtown. Have to have something to wear to his funeral.

Rick, Billy, David and Owen are the pallbearers. The service is in the church. Your mother finally got you to church, Martin. See how stupid it was to die? Rick carried your casket. Oh, how would you have hated that.

I can't bear to look at Mrs. Thorton. In a daze, I pass around the sandwiches and squares—the church-goers voices are buzzing from some faraway place. Old Mrs. Steele: "Such a shame, he was a sweet boy." And Mrs. Titlow whispering to some old bat: "He drank, you know. My cousin drives a cab. He often made deliveries." The old bat replies: "Why did she allow it? She should've put him in a home." Mrs. Titlow —how we used to joke about that old gossip's name. Goddamn it, Martin, how could you let them win?

Now it's over. I'm in my own house and can lie down. I take off my itchy suit. Ugly grey tweed, hung in the window of Pearl's Ladies Wear all winter. Only in Grenville would there still be a Pearl's Ladies Wear. Why did I buy it? I wanted something ugly. Grey, all the grey days Martin knew. He said a sunny day looked different from a cloudy one. He said I brought the sun. I deserve to look ugly and to itch. My skin's broken out everywhere—can't be the suit. Hives, feel more like boils. Didn't God punish Job with boils? I pull on my nightgown.

I never want to talk to anyone ever again. Rick closed the drapes and left. Thank God. I was afraid I'd start to scream if he didn't shut up. "Can I get you anything, Pumpkin—a glass of water, maybe sherry would be better? Do you have a headache? Can I get you an aspirin?"

Rick wouldn't be so kind if he knew what a truly shitty wife I've been. Martin, you saw my rotten, stinking core and it killed you. Hives —I dig my fingernails into my belly. Rip the skin until it bleeds.

Martin, why? I can't ask you. I can never ask you anything ever again.

When you sent me that last chapter of *Marsh Road*, were you warning me? As you wrote of Cathy's betrayal, did you see me abandoning you? I'm so sorry. Sorry for that little boy who fell. And sorry for the whole big mess we made. What good is sorry?

I want to go to sleep and never wake up. The bed is soft. I hug the duvet. If I go to sleep, I'll be all right.

Who am I kidding? Nothing will ever be right again.

EARLY ON A Monday morning, I wake up still lost in my dream of wandering through a construction zone, bulldozers thundering all around. Then realize the racket's real. I nudge Rick. "What's going on?" I don't know why but I'm scared to get out of bed.

He goes to the window to investigate.

"What the hell," Rick says. "C'mere, Pumpkin, you gotta come see."

I pull on my bathrobe and go to the window. Can't believe this—a bulldozer, a backhoe, a large crane, even a wrecking ball, all roaring away across the road. They're tearing down the barn. The crane tweezes up the smashed boards and beams. Loads them into the waiting dump trucks.

"That's one way to deal with it," Rick says. "Still, must be costing them a fortune."

I burst into tears and Rick holds me. "Now, Pumpkin, I know you're still upset. So are his mother and Gretchen. At least with that old barn gone, they can sell off a building lot. Be worth quite a bit in today's market."

I push him away. "I'm going back to bed. I have a headache."

"You'll never sleep with that racket."

"Get me two aspirins, would you?"

"Sure, Pumpkin."

"And close the window, please."

After Rick leaves, I swallow the aspirins and bury my head under the pillow. Tearing down the barn, what good will that do?

ON WEDNESDAY, WHEN Gretchen comes over, she says: "For years my mother has been saying, 'The church is there patiently waiting for us.' Every morning since Martin's death I looked out my window at the barn and wondered if all our lives was the barn with its hulking frame, high beams and my old swing rope, waiting there for my brother? When the grass grows up, you'll never know there was a barn."

She's even thinner than when she first came home and she needs a haircut. She has her mother's eyes, eyes that have seen too much.

"Gretchen, I know you're upset and it's only been a month." I put my arms around her, give her a hug. "Think about our happy memories, all the fun we had in that barn."

She pulls away. "They're gone."

"You were the one that loved barns. You were going to get a horse and start riding again."

"Fantasy."

"Your mother would tell me how much pleasure it gave her to have your old pony in the barn. How she enjoyed looking after him. She was really sad when he died. Said she considered finding another one to take his place but decided that at her age that would be foolishness."

"And it would've been," Gretchen says.

"What did your mother think about tearing it down?"

"She was against it."

"And you did it anyway?"

"Yes. Think of Owen — somebody should. He found Martin."

"Tearing down the barn won't make him forget. That poor boy. Maybe you should think about counselling for him."

"At least we won't have to look at it. And Owen is going for counselling."

"How's your mother managing?"

"All she can talk about is poor Martin."

"It's only been a month."

"When I told her how worried I am about Owen, how he doesn't say two words from one day to the next, she said: 'Teenagers are often moody. He's always been a bit sulky.' How's that for sympathy?"

"She's in mourning."

"But what about Owen, my son, her only grandchild? Doesn't he count?"

"Of course he does." I try to hug her again, but she shrugs me off, stares out the window.

"All I hear from morning till night is 'poor Martin.' I took Owen and Mother out to the new Red Lobster and she spent the whole evening going on about how Martin never got to eat there."

"It'll get better with time."

"No, it won't. I was a fool to think there could be life after Martin for my mother. He used her all up. There never was anything left for me or even for Owen."

I STAND AT the living room window and watch the snow fall. Been over six months now. Maybe I'm safe. No one'll ever know.

I have tea with Mrs. Thorton the mornings Gretchen teaches. Poor woman is shrunken and sad and getting more confused. I know Gretchen's trying. She came home from school one day with a yellow Lab puppy for Owen. I guess Mrs. Thorton hit the roof—said the cats wouldn't like it. Owen loves the pup and has spent months training it. Funny thing is a couple of times when I've been over there, Mrs. Thorton has sat for half the visit stroking the dog while its head rests on her knee.

Rick's being extra nice, which makes me feel worse. I can never tell him. Sometimes, I wish I was Catholic and could go to confession. My need to confess becomes a pot about to boil over.

Gretchen often drops in for coffee on her way home from the high school. We talk about Owen or the school. We don't talk about Martin. What's there to say?

There's Gretchen coming down the hill.

I rush to the door. "Coffee's already on."

"Good, I need a pick-me-up after an afternoon of teaching *Merchant of Venice* to all three ninth grade classes."

"That's quite the storm out there. Can't believe you don't take the car."

"Good coffee. You make it nice and strong. I love walking in the snow. Last night after my mother and Owen went to bed, I was so restless I couldn't sleep. I put on my parka and walked downtown. Snow started, big soft flakes and I remembered Mother pulling Martin and me on the toboggan through a snowstorm. It was during the war, and we were going to the Christmas concert at the church. The scene was so vivid I felt I was reliving it. When I got back to the house, I started writing. Almost dawn before I finished."

"You still write? Years ago you gave me a magazine that had your poetry in it.'

"Do you remember when we were in high school, I used to go along with my dad on business trips?"

"Yeah." Where's she going with this?

"While he was at his meetings I'd wander around whatever town or city we were in and look at all the houses, wondering who lived there. I wanted to be all those people, the young woman hanging diapers on the line and the truck driver backing out his rig. As a writer you get to live in all the houses. Martin even got to live in other worlds. I've started writing a novel."

"About what?" Oh, God, if she writes about us.

"Growing up in Grenville."

"You're writing about Martin?"

"A novel, Donna, fictitious characters, but Martin's situation comes into it. What it was like for him, for me and my parents. Writing is a way of making sense of things."

She leaves. Damn, what'll she write about me and Martin?

MONDAY, GRETCHEN DROPS in after school.

" You tell me why, when my mother finally turns her attention to me, all she can do is criticize."

"What's there to criticize?"

"Oh, lots. For starters my being pregnant when I got married. Oops, I've never told you that." She gives an uncomfortable little laugh.

"Not the best way to start a marriage. I should know."

"I suppose not," she says. "But seventeen years ago I felt I'd finally caught up to you and the rest of Grenville High. I was such a little goody-goody. Even at university when other girls were sleeping with guys, I wouldn't. So uptight, scared stiff of sex." She sighs. "Stiff all right, detached from my body, the puppet master telling it what to do. And when I started teaching, it was even worse. Who was this mousy woman in her nylons and tweed skirts? She couldn't be me. I was the girl in blue jeans who galloped Misty along the beach."

"But what were you scared of?"

"I don't know. I met Kenneth and decided things would be different.

If I were the puppet master, I could make my body play a new role. It could read the script and learn."

"What script? What role? Gretchen, what are you talking about?"

"I wanted to be you, like you were in high school, wild and sexy."

"Oh shit, Gretchen, you didn't really know me."

"The puppet liked her new role." She went on as if she hadn't heard me. "The day I lost my virginity, I went for a long hike and lay on a riverbank. Listening to the rushing water and feeling the firm earth beneath me, I finally became part of the world."

Romantic nonsense, reminds me of Martin. "Did you love Kenneth?"

"Oh yes, he'd saved me, after all. And then I was pregnant and loved the whole world. Especially writing Mother and telling her I was three months along. We were getting married at City Hall and having a party afterward. Would she and Martin come?"

"They didn't, did they?"

"No, she said if I'd given her more notice, she might've been able to. As it was, Martin had a deadline for some book reviews and needed her help. Under the circumstances she understood I couldn't delay the wedding. 'I don't understand how you could be so foolish,' she said. 'It wasn't the way you were raised.'"

"Your mother's pretty straitlaced."

"I didn't care. It was my moment of triumph—that is, before real life began. I lost the baby at six months. Mother sent flowers but didn't visit. Suggested I come home for a rest. It was July, so I wasn't teaching. I did come home for a month."

"I remember that summer. Why didn't you tell me about the baby?"

"Mother didn't see any reason anyone in Grenville needed to know. 'Save everybody a little embarrassment' was how she put it."

"I wish you'd told me."

"I was pretty down for a long time. I suppose it was hard on Kenneth. I lived in a fog for the next couple of years. Then I got pregnant again. I was so happy after Owen was born and so loved being home with the baby, I quit teaching. Too focused on the baby. We split up when Owen was three. Kenneth had been cheating on me for the last couple of years."

"The bastard!"

"Not really." A dry little chuckle. "Though I thought so at the time. But I was a puppet going through the motions. Too uptight to ever enjoy being in bed with him. Funny, though, I could love the baby. Thank goodness, Owen didn't have a puppet master for a mother. I'd finally become the equal of the mother cat in the hay." Suddenly, Gretchen's crying; terrible gagging sounds.

I get up and hug her. Like her mother, she never cries.

"Life is nothing like I thought it could be," she says, sobbing. "You have everything, a husband, children, grandchildren."

"Oh Gretchen." And I tell her my whole shameful story. I stare at the floor and go on and on. About canning pears and me pregnant and going to his studio. About Rick buying me a new car and Martin and me driving back to the swamp.

Finally, manage to shut up. I can't bear to look at her.

I look up. How come she's smiling?

She says: "I knew years ago."

"What? Martin told you?"

"Mother told me."

"She knew? Oh, Gretchen, I can't bear it." I burst into tears.

She hugs me. "It's okay. Of course she knew."

"Oh hell, what must she have thought of me?"

"She was pleased with you. Anything for her genius."

"Shit, I don't believe this. Are you telling me the truth? All these years she knew?"

"Of course." She laughs. "Surely you didn't think you were fooling my mother. We figured Katie might be his. But we never let on to Martin about our suspicions."

I manage to pull myself together. "More coffee." My hand shakes as I refill our cups. "I know there's a resemblance. But it's not likely. Don't tell anybody. It'd just wreck ... everything." I can't go on.

Gretchen sits across from me and awkwardly holds my hand.

"Donna, it's all right. Nobody needs to know."

"Never be all right. Oh, your mother must think I'm a slut. She's so traditional."

"From the time you were fourteen, she was trying to give you to her darling son."

"That's crap. She must be disgusted with me." I stomp over to the window, stare out at nothing.

"Her main complaint all these years was you didn't visit him often enough."

I can't believe my ears. But why would she lie?

"You'd come see him in his studio," she says, "that's how Mother always put it. 'She was over to his studio and now he hasn't seen hide nor hair of her for two months. How can she not realize what that does to him?' Every visit home I had to listen to this. 'A man needs a woman. Women can get along doing without, but a man needs it. Doesn't she realize how hard her on-again, off-again behaviour is for him?'"

"I couldn't come more often. I have three children and a husband."

"Well, if you'd loved my brother ..."

"I did love him."

"Then why didn't you leave Rick?"

"Damn it, Gretchen, how could I have supported the children?" I glare at her.

"Could've left them with Rick. He would have gotten a house-keeper or remarried."

"I wouldn't let some stranger raise my kids. I love them."

"Well, there you have it. You didn't love my brother enough."

"I've always loved him."

"No." She isn't smiling now. "You teased him. Started when we were teenagers and you never stopped. On one of my visits home, he wouldn't come out of his studio. Mother told me he'd locked himself in there. 'He's weeping over Donna,' she said, 'in despair that she won't leave Rick.'"

"Oh, Gretchen, I never looked at it like that." I'm crying again. "I've made such stupid choices."

"Haven't we all?"

I choke back my sobs and tell her: "You haven't done anything terrible."

"That's what you think. I married the first man who paid me some attention. I was that desperate. Nobody else wanted me. Even in high school I couldn't get a boyfriend."

"You told me you loved Kenneth."

"I thought I did, but maybe I confused love with gratitude. I loved him before we were married. I couldn't wait to be with him. But after, sex was a routine carried on in the dark."

"Yeah, dating's a lot more fun. With your brother it was always a date, an adventure. Sneaking around, making sure nobody found out. We didn't take each other for granted like married couples do."

"Didn't you take him for granted? He was always there waiting for you. Months at a time."

"Oh, Gretchen, that makes me feel awful. I thought I was his friend."

"My mother said: 'It's good they have each other. He needs someone. Donna's his inspiration, his muse. How could anyone begrudge him?' I figured Rick might've begrudged him just a little."

"I felt so damn guilty, I used to just curse myself."

"But you kept coming back."

"He loved me. He needed me."

"Yes, poor Martin, anything for poor Martin."

She sounds so bitter. "He wasn't poor Martin. He was wonderful and I loved him."

"Then why didn't you divorce Rick?"

"Damn it, Gretchen, I just told you why."

"Hmmm." She gets up, looks out the window and sighs.

I study her knobby spine, her back rigid as steel.

"Weren't you ever tempted, I mean while you were married?" I ask her.

She turns and comes back to the table. "No." She smiles. "Maybe I wasn't married long enough."

"The stupid thing is I didn't figure I was hurting anybody. I've always felt my relationship with Martin had nothing to do with Rick, our marriage and our kids."

"You were set up. Even when we were children."

"What? That's crazy."

"When she knew you'd be coming over, she'd tell me beforehand: 'Don't you be going off with Donna after supper. You know your brother likes playing cards with her.' I felt like saying: 'Donna's my friend, leave her alone.'"

"I thought the three of us had fun together."

"Really?"

"Yes, really."

"Remember the time we went to the drive-in?" Gretchen asks.

"Yeah."

"My mother set that up."

"She, what?"

"Dad wanted Mother to go out for dinner and she said no, that Martin needed the car. He had a date. She told Dad I was going to drive them. He said: 'That doesn't sound like much fun for Gretchen.' I drove, though, if you remember. My mother was always the boss."

"Listen Gretchen, what happened after I was married was my fault, not your mother's and not Martin's. Nobody forced me to do anything. I loved getting his letters and his stories. But the time always came when the letters and stories weren't enough. I needed Martin like other people need a stiff drink. He was the 'something more.' I could go to his studio and I was sixteen again, and the world was in love with me and me with the world. With Martin the honeymoon didn't end for a long, long time. Damn it, I feel so guilty."

"You can quit saying that. Donna, it doesn't really matter, now. None of us helped him."

"I've often wondered what would've happened if I hadn't got pregnant and married Rick. All the important decisions in my life were made when I was a teenager who thought what was important was being the centre of a sock-hop."

"I would've given anything to have been the centre of something," Gretchen says.

"I wish your mother didn't know."

"Listen, Donna, if Mother could've, she would've offered you up, a virgin for her darling son."

After she leaves all I can think about is that it could've been different. Nothing meant what it was supposed to. My life is ripped in half. I can't go on like this. I pull on my coat and lock the door behind me. I walk till my legs ache and my hands are freezing. Back home all I want to do is lie down, but I can't sleep. I do know one thing, I can't live the rest of my life as Pumpkin.

AT DUSK ON a February day I sit on the bedroom floor with the leather duffle bag cuddled on my lap. I found it when I was clearing out my closet for the Salvation Army clothes drive. I'd forgotten I'd thrown it back in there that angry day when I burnt your letters. I opened the bag, sorry for what I'd done. You used to say, words on a page can speak even if the author is far away or dead. I wanted my letters. Is that why I searched an empty bag? But it wasn't empty, because under the ripped lining I found one I'd missed. It isn't dated, but I know it was written at least ten years ago.

Dear Donna,

Worked all night and most of the day on my novel. I'm going to send a chapter to True Romance, *that raunchy mag Gretchen used to bring home from the tourist camp. She told me a bit about it. They pay $200 for a story. The trouble is they don't want anything too adult or intelligent. Their readership has a five-minute attention span, same as about 99 percent of the population. Put Lady Macbeth in a story and you're likely to be asked what radio or television show she's on.*

All I need is one real break, and I'm out of here— New York where they've never heard of Grenville. You'd wow them in New York. You're wasted on this hick town.

I tried True Romance *mag once before. The editor said my work was too literary and this is a quote: 'Our audience wants a good romp that doesn't make them feel uneducated.'*

After supper now. I've been awake thirty-one hours. I listen to the pouring rain. Shall I flood all of Elginville—drown Ted and the police who come after Joe? Bring back Noah's flood, but without the ark? Let them all drown?

Now the rain's making such a racket I wonder if the gods resented me usurping their powers and will wash away my door and ignore my pleas for mercy.

I'm being silly. Must be lack of sleep. Sound and space have become distorted. Lack of sleep or lack of you, my darling.

I wonder if you're in your kitchen, washing dishes. Remember that day last fall when my mother was away, and you and I had lunch and did the dishes?

Your kitchen window faces north. You must hear the rain pelting the glass.

I like to think of you doing the dishes, and what it would be like to be standing at the counter, you handing me each plate, each cup. How slowly I would dry each one you'd touched. Draw out each moment to cherish.

OH MARTIN, YOU'RE the only person I'll ever know who could make romance out of a sink of dirty dishes. And make me believe it.

Acknowledgements

I WOULD LIKE to thank Guernica Editions' publishers Michael Mirolla and Connie McParland, and my editor Lindsay Brown. It was my great pleasure to work with Lindsay during the editing process.

I am indebted to Sylvia Andrychuk for editing this manuscript and for her technical support.

I would also like to thank the Ban Righ Writers' Group, especially Maureen Garvie, Bill Hutchinson, and Darryl Berger for their long time support and encouragement.

About the Author

KRISTIN ANDRYCHUK was raised in an area of stark contrasts between the conservative village of Ridgeway, Ontario, the vibrant summer resort of Crystal Beach, and just a few miles away from the bustling American city of Buffalo, New York. All three places majorly influence the stories she tells in her poetry, short stories and novels. She has been widely published in literary magazines and anthologies. *Mother's Genius* is her fourth novel. Her three previous novels are *Cadillac Road* (Guernica 2017), *Riding the Comet* (Oberon 2003) and *The Swing Tree* (Oberon 1996). She has three times been the recipient of scholarships to attend the Banff Centre's writers' studios. She resides in Kingston with her husband Don.